HUNTING THE SILENCE - THE YORKSHIRE MURDERS

DI HASKELL & QUINN CRIME FICTION SERIES
BOOK 4

BILINDA P. SHEEHAN

Copyright © 2021 by Bilinda P. Sheehan

All rights reserved.

No part of this book may be reproduced in any form or by any electronic or mechanical means, including information storage and retrieval systems, without written permission from the author, except for the use of brief quotations in a book review.

ALSO BY BILINDA P. SHEEHAN

Watch out for the next book coming soon from Bilinda P. Sheehan by joining her mailing list.

A Wicked Mercy: The Yorkshire Murders - DI Haskell & Quinn Crime Fiction Series

Death in Pieces: The Yorkshire Murders - DI Haskell & Quinn Crime Fiction Series

Splinter the Bone: The Yorkshire Murders - DI Haskell & Quinn Crime Fiction Series

Hunting the Silence: The Yorkshire Murders - DI Haskell & Quinn Crime Fiction Series

Hidden in Blood: The Yorkshire Murders - DI Haskell & Quinn Crime Fiction Series

All the Lost Girls-A Gripping Psychological Thriller

Wednesday's Child - A Gripping Psychological Thriller

PROLOGUE

LESS THAN A WEEK after he'd killed, he was back in the countryside. Sucking down a lungful of the fresh air, he hopped the fence and began his exploration of the garden. He'd watched her leave that morning, taking the small noisy dog with her; he could be grateful for small mercies, at least.

She'd set up a small floodlight in the back garden a couple of days after his failed attempt at getting into the house. Obviously, she'd listened to the advice of the police officers who'd paid her a visit. It wasn't such a problem for him, though. It was easy to loosen the wires so that the light failed to turn on when it was supposed to. He'd been more worried that she would get a CCTV camera, that would be much harder to avoid, but he'd been pleasantly surprised to discover she'd refused to invest in one. Clearly, she was a woman after his own heart.

He grabbed a couple of bricks from the broken barbeque area at the side of the garden. Carrying them over to the back wall of the house, he positioned them on top of the others he'd already added. It was easy to build a small pile over time, something she wouldn't notice because the progress of it was so gradual. Reaching up to the bathroom window, he tested the frame, and was pleased to discover she still hadn't realised just how damaged it was.

Hopping back down onto the path, he contemplated waiting around until she returned from work, and then changed his mind. It was almost time to pick up Lily from school, and he couldn't be late again or it would only lead to more grief from the, bitch.

With a backwards glance, he sighed, satisfied with the minor adjustments he'd made. It would soon be time to take action, but until then he would just have to relive the last one. He slipped back over the fence and jogged back to his car.

CHAPTER ONE

"I CAN'T BELIEVE you agreed to stay on call for the Christmas shift." DI Melissa Appleton slid into the vacant seat next to Drew's desk, and he glanced up at her in surprise.

"How do you know?"

She waggled her eyebrows at him. "I've got my sources," she said. "You're not the only one around here who can get their hands on info when it's needed."

"And my working the Christmas shift was 'needed' information?" Drew leaned back in his chair and stretched. Warmth spread down through his spine, as he rolled his shoulders and felt the stiff knots in his neck slowly unravel. His abdomen barely twinged, a sign that at least outwardly, he was more or less whole again.

"It is when it screws with our plans," she said, a

pout crossing her lips. Suddenly, the heat Drew felt wasn't just caused by the stretching out of his weary muscles.

"Excuse me?" He tried not to sound like a strangled cat, but failed. He coughed, straightening in the seat, as he swivelled around to face Melissa. "What plans?"

"The Christmas Party?" Exasperation tinged her voice, and she rolled her eyes in a typical display of histrionics. "Are you sure you haven't got some sort of early onset dementia? You'd forget your own name if it wasn't printed on the front of your mug," she said, jabbing a finger in the direction of the cup on his desk with his name printed on the front in large black letters. DC Green had thought it would be a nice gesture for the team. Monk had asked Green to join the team after the graft he'd put in on the trafficking case—and Drew couldn't deny that the young constable was an asset to the team—but the mugs had seemed a little too much.

"This wasn't my doing," Drew said, pushing the cup aside.

"Do you, or don't you remember our discussion about the Christmas party?"

He glanced back down at the reports scattered across the desk. "I remember."

"Good, so you haven't completely lost your marbles then." She sighed. "You working is going to make things right awkward."

"Maybe it's best if I steer clear then--"

"Stop trying to wriggle out of it," Melissa said indignantly. "You're coming to the party, and you're going to sing Karaoke whether you like it, or not. I've managed to pull some strings and rearrange everything for Saturday night. That way, everyone gets to go, you included."

"Or not..." Drew muttered beneath his breath and caught sight of Melissa's blistering stare. "Fine, I'll come, and do all the usual daft shit that happens on a night out, but I'm not singing no karaoke."

"Yes you are."

Drew opened his mouth to argue but noted the obstinate look on Melissa's face and changed his mind. "Fine." It was easier to capitulate now and keep things sweet. When Saturday came around he'd keep a low profile, if she didn't see him then she wouldn't remember the conversation.

"Good," she said, sounding more pleased with herself than she had any right to be. "That's settled, then. Saturday night, we're going to paint the town red."

"Can I get back to this report now," Drew said, with a long-suffering sigh. "Gregson wants it on his desk by close of day."

"You working on anything interesting?" she asked, leaning over his shoulder to peer down into the report he'd laid open on the desk. The scent of her Jo Malone perfume tickled his nose, and he fought the urge to sneeze. It seemed some things never changed, and Melissa's love of Lime, Basil, and Mandarin cologne was one of them.

Melissa caught him staring and glared at him. "Stop staring down my cleavage."

"I wasn't, I--" Drew cut off, grumbling beneath his breath as Melissa dropped back into her seat as she creased up with laughter.

"You should have seen your face," she said, gulping down a breath, she swiped a hand at the tears that had collected at the corners of her eyes. "Christ, Drew, I don't think I've ever seen you look so worried."

"Yeah, well, that kind of shit nowadays can get a person suspended," he said gruffly. "Or worse."

"It's nothing you haven't seen before," she said, with a shake of her head as she pushed onto her feet. "It's not like we haven't got changed in the same room when we were both in uniform many moons ago."

Drew kept his head down, his gaze trained on the reports in front of him. Not that the words were making any sense now. The words just blurred into each other, turning to gibberish before his eyes.

Laughing, Melissa patted his shoulder as though he were nothing more than an awkward child in need of reassurance. He kept his attention on the papers on his desk as she left him to his work.

What he needed now was something new to sink his teeth into. Something to help him move past the shit-show that had been Templeton's short-lived reign in charge of the task force. A palate cleanser, so to speak. Of course, getting that meant that some other poor misfortunate out there had to get served up a shit-sandwich. And no matter how he tried to spin that, there was just no good way around it.

Sighing, he glanced down at his watch. Just a couple of hours more, and he would finally be out of here, and free to once again roam the many listings on RightMove, in search of the perfect space to call his own. Why he'd ever thought it would be easy was beyond him.

Picking up his mug, he grimaced as the over-sized lettering with his name in bold, black print caught his attention. Drew pushed onto his feet and made a beeline for the coffee machine. That was the one truly glorious side to his promotion onto the task-force; no more shitty vending machine coffee. Templeton had been a man with many issues, but his choice in coffee was definitely not one of them, Drew thought, as he selected a pod from the basket and popped it into the machine.

CHAPTER TWO

"I DARE you to go into the woods, and spend the night there," Darren said, his brown eyes darted over toward the woodland that loomed over them.

"I can't do that," Oliver said, fear causing his voice to rise in pitch as he spoke. He gripped the handles of his bicycle tighter, as though that alone would be enough to ward off Darren's dare.

"I double-dog-dare you," Darren said, sounding somewhat braver the second time around. "If you don't do it, I'm going to tell everyone in school tomorrow what a loser you are."

Oliver shook his head and swallowed back the lump that formed in the back of his throat. "No, you won't."

"Yeah, I will!" Darren jammed a finger into Oliver's chest. "You're nothing but a scaredy-cat, loser, and I'm going to tell everyone."

"Mum won't let me stay in the woods for the night," Oliver said, seizing upon the very obvious solution.

"So tell her you're staying over at mine," Darren said.

"She won't let me on a school night."

Darren fell silent and chewed his lip thoughtfully as he glanced over at the forest. Oliver felt the tension slowly ease out of his shoulders. The fear-filled knot that tightened his gut began to unravel as the seconds ticked by. He'd outwitted Darren, and there was nothing he could do about it. He slipped his hand into his zippy-pocket and removed his blue inhaler. The plastic shell was warm in his hand as he lifted it to his mouth and took a puff. The medicated mist hit his throat and made him cough.

"Saturday night, then," Darren said triumphantly.

"What?" The inhaler very nearly tumbled from his hand, and he gripped it a little tighter. Mum would kill him if he lost another one.

"Saturday night, you tell your mum you're staying over at mine. And I'll tell mine, I'm staying at yours, but we'll come here instead."

Oliver shook his head. The fear that had just receded returned with a vengeance. "I can't--"

"We'll do it together," Darren said, excitedly. "We'll both go in there and spend the night. And then on Monday when we go into school we'll tell everyone what we did, and they'll think we're so cool!"

A bead of sweat formed in the middle of Oliver's spine and slowly tracked its way down over his clammy skin. "I suppose so," he said. "I mean, if we both did it, and he came for us, we could fight him off."

Darren nodded. "No way could he take us both. And if he grabbed you, then I could always go for help."

"Why would he grab me, and not you?" Oliver asked, indignantly. "He's just as likely to take you, as he is to grab me."

Darren shook his head. "I'm a faster runner than you, remember?"

He had a point, Oliver thought. He was a much faster runner...

"Okay," he said. "If we do it, then we do it together."

Darren's grin was wide and gap-toothed. "We're going to need supplies," he said. "Food, and sleeping bags, and torches--"

"And don't forget batteries," Oliver said. "You know in case the others run out."

Darren nodded. "Maybe we should bring some tins of dog-food, and ham with us."

"Why?"

"Because AJ from year nine said that you could stop him from taking you if you gave him dog food, and ham instead."

"I think maybe that's made up," Oliver said thoughtfully. "Why would dog food, and ham stop him from taking you?"

"Because isn't dog food made from like dead animals and stuff? And ham is made of pig so, to him, it tastes the same as people."

Oliver's face twisted up in disgust. "That's yuck!"

Darren nodded sagely. "I know. My older brother said cannibals call human meat, long-pig, because we taste like ham."

Oliver's eyes were wide, a mixture of horror and awe swept over his features before he finally nodded. "I can get us some dog food." Bixby wouldn't mind if he took a couple of cans.

"I'll get the ham," Darren said, before he glanced down at his watch. "I've got to get home. Mum said if I was late once more this week she'd take my X-box away, and I'm so close to completing this month's season pass on Fortnite." Darren kicked off on his own bike, and with one last wave over his shoulder disappeared down the hill towards home.

Oliver glanced up at the trees swaying overhead and shivered. The woods were the very last place he wanted to spend Friday night.

Zipping his jacket up to his chin, he kicked off on his bike, and followed Darren down the hill. Perhaps if he was lucky, Darren would have forgotten all about his hare-brained scheme by the morning, and moved onto something a little easier to tolerate.

Not that Oliver truly believed that. Once his friend got an idea in his head, he had a tendency to cling onto it like a dog with a bone. And in this case, the bone was one that might get them killed.

CHAPTER THREE

"IN THIS WEEK'S seminar we'll be examining the relationship between childhood trauma, and the development of aberrant personalities, and the consequences of that." Harriet smiled broadly. "We'll be taking a close look at serial offenders." Taking a moment to clear her throat, Harriet glanced down at the notes in front of her. There was a light shuffling of feet, as the small group of students gathered in the room with her got comfortable. This was what she enjoyed most about her work at the university. It was always much easier to deal with smaller groups, there was a higher level of engagement, and Harriet found in an environment such as this the students were far more receptive to what she had to say.

"Excuse me, Dr Quinn." A voice from the back of the group drew her attention away from the copious notes she'd brought with her. Harriet lifted her gaze from the papers and focused on the young man who had spoken. His sandy brown hair hung down into his brown eyes, and he swiped at it almost impatiently as he straightened up under her scrutiny.

"Yes, Craig, what is it?"

"Doesn't this kind of thing just excuse their behaviour?"

"How so?" Harriet asked, leaning back in her chair as the first frisson of excitement traced down her spine.

"Well, we're basically telling them they're not responsible for their actions because their mummy was mean to them." His statement caused the others in the room to laugh, and Harriet watched as the attention brought a broad smile to his lips. He puffed his chest out as he scanned the room, bathing in the appreciation of the joke he'd just made. The behaviour made Harriet smile inwardly. There was always one.

"And you think it's wrong to find the reasoning behind certain--" Harriet waved her hand in the air as she struggled to find the correct word--"undesirable behaviours?"

Craig shook his head. "That's not what I'm saying."

"Then what are you saying?"

"Well, I don't think we should give them a free pass."

"Who said we should?"

He shrugged. "Well, you did."

With a sigh, Harriet crossed her legs beneath the table. "I think you'll find that what we're doing here is examining the reasons for a behaviour. If this leads to a better understanding of offenders, and that breakthrough gives us the opportunity to rehabilitate certain individuals before they cross a line, then I cannot see where that is wrong. Are those who suffer not worthy of our help?"

Craig opened his mouth to answer, as a look of consternation crossed his face. "That makes me sound cruel," he said. "I just don't think we should give them an excuse for being evil."

This time Harriet was the one who laughed. "Religious constructs have no place here, Craig. No matter what your personal beliefs might be when it comes to science, religion will do nothing but muddy the water."

"Who mentioned religion?" He spluttered indignantly, colour mounting his cheeks. "I'm not sure I even believe all of that bullshit, anyway."

"The notion of good versus evil is a construct created by religions to explain behaviours we don't yet understand. It's simply a way of shirking responsibility. You cannot be held accountable for your actions if you're not responsible for them," Harriet said. "If you can claim something 'other' caused you to kill, then the blood of the victims are not really on your hands."

"But isn't that the same thing?" Craig insisted.

"If somebody who is supposed to love and nurture you abuses you, is that your fault?" Harriet asked.

Craig shook his head. "No, of course not."

"But if you then go out and kill another person because of the trauma and rage you developed during the time they abused you, is that your fault?"

Craig stared at her, and she could see the panic in his face as he struggled for an answer that wouldn't make him look foolish? "Well, it's complicated," he said finally.

"Exactly," Harriet said. "When it comes to the development of the mind and personality, nothing is black-and-white. We are complex beings. The development of aberrant personalities is equally complex."

Craig nodded and dropped back into his chair. From the other side of the room, Harriet found herself to be under intense scrutiny from Misha. She smiled at the young woman, who seemed to start as though Harriet's attention had pulled her from a deep reverie. It wasn't the first time Harriet had caught her staring at her, and she wondered just what could be so fascinating.

Returning her attention to the room, Harriet flipped open her notepad, and glanced down at the first sentence she had written. "Now, would anyone like to tell me about the ethical considerations we should have when examining an experiment such as the Bobo Doll experiment, and just what it reveals regarding children, and childhood aggression?"

LATER THAT DAY, Harriet sat in a different room, as far removed from her set-up in the university as was possible. She shivered as the air vent above her chair blasted cold air down onto her shoulders. Next time she would have to bring a jacket, or at the very least a second jumper.

The buzz of a door being opened in the corridor tugged her attention back to her surroundings. She chewed her lip nervously as the door to the interview room she sat in clicked open, and a guard directed Nolan Matthews inside. It seemed impossible, but Nolan appeared even more hunched over on himself than he had been during her last visit; he was practically skeletal as he shuffled across the hard floor to the chair opposite hers.

"You came back?" There was a curiosity in his voice that Harriet hadn't expected.

"I said I would."

Nolan shrugged. "Most people are liars."

"Has that been your experience in life?" Harriet asked. She fought the urge to lean her elbows on the table. A move like that would put her within striking distance of him, and Harriet was intimately familiar with the speed he could move at when he so chose.

"Hasn't it been yours?" He studied her beneath a hooded brow.

"I don't think so," Harriet said contemplatively. It would be too easy to give him a yes, or no answer. And anyway, while it hadn't been her experience that most people were liars, she'd come across her fair share of them down through the years.

"And what about Dr Connors?" Nolan asked, his dark eyes searched hers for something only he understood.

"I came here to discuss you, Nolan. Not Dr Connors."

He rolled his eyes, and dropped back in his chair, before he met her gaze with a contemptuous grimace. "You're all the same. You say you're coming here for my benefit, but that's not strictly true, is it, Dr Quinn?"

"I don't think I understand, Nolan. What benefit is it to me if I come here?"

"Because you're as lost in your own darkness as I've been," he sneered. "The only difference is that I accepted a long time ago what I am, and what I'm capable of. You still cling to the pretext of being good."

Harriet schooled her features into a bland expression. "If you'd rather I didn't come here, then I can always stop."

"You're not listening to me!" He exploded and slammed his fists down onto the table as his face contorted into a mask of rage. "None of you ever fucking listen to me." The guard who stood in the room behind Nolan took a step forward. The sound of his footsteps on the floor was enough to quieten Nolan, who shrank back in his chair. "I'm sorry. I shouldn't have done that." Nolan swiped at his greasy dark hair, pushing it away from his sweaty forehead as he gulped down air. The movement caused the neckline of his grey jumper to shift, exposing the dark ring of bruising around his throat.

"Nolan, what happened to your neck?" Harriet asked, pleased at least that her voice didn't betray the unease she felt.

"What does it matter?" He asked, his voice cracked as he spoke. "You don't care. I thought you did, but you don't."

"I'm here, aren't I?"

His laughter when it came echoed in the confines of the drab grey room. "You're only here because of the possibilities I offer your career. You're not here because you want to be."

From her side of the table, Harriet stilled. Nolan was playing a very different game to the one she'd thought they were engaged in. Admitting too much to him would only give him a false sense of their relationship, and that wasn't something she could allow. Of course, if she didn't give him some reason to trust her, then Harriet had the distinct impression that her visits would be ended in very short order by an act that could never be undone.

"They told me, you know," he said conversationally. "That by interviewing me, you'll get a big boost to your career when you write up a paper on it all."

"And that offends you?"

Nolan sighed and scrubbed his knuckle roughly into the corner of his eye. "You don't deny it then?"

"Why would I?" Harriet asked. "If I did that, then I would be just as bad as all the other liars in your life."

He paused and watched her for a moment. "Now, you're just playing with me."

Harriet shook her head. "Look, I won't deny that speaking to you won't be an asset to the work I do with the police." She sucked in a deep breath, before plunging headlong into the rest of her speech. "But I also come here because I meant it when I said I wanted to help you. But if you don't believe that I can do both things, then I respect that. At the end of the day, Nolan, the ball is in your court. You hold all the power here. If you want me to leave, then I will."

He studied her, and Harriet fought the urge to squirm beneath the intensity of his stare. For a moment she was convinced he was about to speak to her. Instead, he pushed to his feet. "I'm going to think about it, Harriet," he said, and the way in which he said her name caused the hairs to stand on the back of her neck. His voice dropped to a whisper. "I think of you often." Revulsion swelled in the centre of Harriet's chest. Of course, that was what he wanted from her. Nolan Matthews was a sadistic psychopath. Her discomfort would only serve as fuel for his fantasies.

Harriet met his gaze calmly. "Fine. I look forward to hearing your decision."

His smile when it came reminded Harriet of the Cheshire cat from Alice in Wonderland. "Be careful out there, Dr Quinn. There are others who wouldn't appreciate your worth the way I do..." The guard who had brought him into the room, guided him out.

As the door clicked shut, Harriet let go of the breath she'd been holding. Her shoulders slumped, and the tension keeping her rigid slowly ebbed away.

Perhaps Drew was correct in his theory regarding her sanity, or in this case lack of it. With a sigh, Harriet gathered up her belongings and left, as Nolan's last words played over in her mind on a loop. It was nothing more than an observation, a passing commentary on the work she did with the police. But if that were true, then why the hell did it feel so much like a threat?

Shaking her head, she tried to push her thoughts aside, and compartmentalise them. It was that ability that allowed her to get some sleep at night; because working with Drew had taught her one thing, it was never a good idea to bring such dark and destructive ideas home.

CHAPTER FOUR

SQUEEZING HER EYES SHUT, Olivia wished she'd remembered to pack the Migraleve tablets in her kit bag when she'd left the house. The telltale aura that usually preceded the debilitating migraine had slowly grown worse over the hours she'd spent sitting at her desk. Lifting the piping hot cup of coffee she'd managed to make, she sipped at the contents, mindful not to burn herself. Some people thought coffee made migraines worse, but Olivia had never subscribed to that particular school of thought. Coffee and chocolate were part of the major food groups that helped her to get through daily life. They could pry them from her cold dead fingers before she would ever willingly give them up, migraine be damned.

Closing her eyes against the harsh fluorescent overhead lights, she let the bitter warmth of her favourite blend melt away the tension that had gathered at the base of her skull.

A loud thud rocked the surface of her desk and Olivia jumped, slopping some coffee over the side of her mug. Grumpily, she cracked an eyelid in order to get a look at the fool who had chosen that moment to interrupt her quiet contemplation. Maz stood over her. A grin hovered at the corners of his mouth. It would be easy to wipe the smile off his face, but any kind of action like that would only bring the wrath of the monk down on her head, and the last thing she needed right now was a bollocking.

"What?" The gathering pain that tightened around her skull in a vice-grip brought a sharpness to her voice.

"What's got your knickers in a twist?" The DS dropped into the chair next to her desk, and the chance to rid herself of him slipped through her fingers.

"I'm on a break," she said acerbically, before she set down the coffee mug, careful to avoid the file he'd dropped next to her elbow. "What's that?" She didn't touch the file, instead eyeing it for the interloper it was. She had more than enough on her plate, she didn't need to add to her workload further.

"That is something I came across this morning," Maz said, the smile he'd worn earlier faded around the edges. "Something important."

Noting the change in his expression, Olivia

straightened up and took a second glance down at the unassuming file.

"Nobody thought to let us know…"

"So why do you have it?" Olivia asked, cutting him off. Her fingers itched with the urge to flip the file open and peer inside.

"I was following up on some loose ends for the paperwork," Maz said offhandedly. "Anyway, you remember that woman we paid a visit to during the trafficking case?"

"We did a lot of door to door," she said.

Maz nudged the file toward her. "You'll remember her."

Giving in, Olivia flipped open the file and peered at the contents. The top of the file contained a picture from booking of a drawn young woman with vivid red hair and smudged dark eye makeup. "Jessica Tamblyn, what has she got…" Olivia cut off as she flipped the top page in the file and caught sight of a crime scene photograph. The migraine intensified as she studied the image in front of her. "What is this?"

"Tamblyn is dead," Maz said. "One of her friends reported she hadn't been seen in a few days, and that they were concerned for her welfare considering the kind of work she's involved with. So a couple of PCs did a welfare check. One of them pushed open the letter box and by all accounts the smell was as foul as you'd imagine."

"What happened to her?" Realising the picture was upside down, Olivia twisted the photograph so that the bloody, wrapped mound in the bed became clearer.

"Murdered." There was no preamble in Maz's voice as he spoke. "They're going with the theory that she pissed off someone, probably a drug dealer, and they knocked her off."

Lifting a second picture free from the pile, Olivia twisted it around until the details came into focus. "They wouldn't do this," she said. The words slipped out before she could stop them. She glanced up at Maz, half expecting to see a look of ridicule on his face. Instead, he was nodding as he peered over the edge of the photograph she was holding.

"That's what I thought too," he said. "Not to mention it's bloody coincidental that we drop by for a chat, and then she winds up dead a short while later. I mean, we shouldn't just ignore that, should we?"

"I don't think so," Olivia said. Lifting her thumb to her lips, she chewed on the ragged edge of her bitten down nails. "I mean, we should take this to DI Haskell. He'll know what to do with it, if we're even supposed to do something with it."

Maz nodded, but there was no escaping the crestfallen expression on his face. "You thought I was going to say something else?" Olivia asked.

"No," he said. "You're right. We need to move this up the chain, it's just…"

"It's just you'd love to have a closer look at everything beforehand?"

"Well, yeah, don't you?"

Olivia glanced down at the images spread out on her desk before she shook her head. "As much as I'd love to play the maverick on this, it's above our pay-grade. We owe it to the DI that we give him a heads-up on this. He'll probably let us take a closer look anyway, and we'll have a little goodwill with him if we find anything."

The ghost of a smile hovered around Maz's lips as he nodded. "I suppose."

DI Haskell chose that moment to push in through the double doors of the office, Olivia took one look at the crabby expression he wore and made the executive decision that now was not the time to go bothering him.

"I wouldn't--" she said as Maz began to gather up the images.

"But you said--"

"I know what I said." Olivia inclined her head in Haskell's direction. "But I'm not sure it's the right time."

Twisting around to get a better look at their boss, Maz grinned. "Don't let the grumpy facade fool you. He looks like that every time he gets desperate for a cigarette."

"Wait, he's not still trying to convince himself that he quit, is he?" Olivia asked.

"Exactly," Maz said. "Hence the grumpy bastard routine. He'll soon get over it."

"Wouldn't like to bet on that," Olivia said, as Maz snatched the file from her desk and raced to catch up with the DI.

"SIR!" Drew turned in time to see his young DS barrelling towards him.

"Woah, what's the rush?"

Maz took a moment, gulping down air as he thrust an untidy and dog-eared file in Drew's direction. Suspicion curled in Drew's stomach as he noted the glint in the DS's eye, as though whatever lay inside the beige cover of the file was both exciting and terrifying in equal measure.

Folding his arms over his chest, Drew shook his head. "What is it?"

"Why is everybody so suspicious today?"

"You might not have realised this, but it's our job to be suspicious, mate."

Maz rolled his eyes, but the excitement Drew had sensed moments before only seemed to intensify. "When we were working the trafficking case..." The words practically tripped out of Maz's mouth faster than he could think to form them.

"Slow down, Arya."

"Sorry, guv, it's just something weird has come up since we wrapped up the trafficking case. And I was talking to DC Crandell about it, and she agrees that there's something fishy--"

"Oh, does she?" Drew raised an eyebrow, as he studied the file clutched in DS Arya's hands. He glanced over in Olivia's direction, but she was studying a blank piece of paper in front of her as though it contained the secrets to the universe.

"She does, sir. Well, we both do. Think there's something weird..."

"Maz, just spit it out."

Arya sighed, and flipped open the top of the file before he presented Drew with a booking photograph of a pretty, but exhausted young woman who stared down the camera as though everything that had ever happened in her life to bring her to that moment was somehow the fault of the person taking her picture.

"Jessica Tamblyn," Drew said, reading the name aloud. "Am I supposed to know her? Was she a witness in the case, or--"

"Well, sort of," Maz said. "DC Crandell and I were doing door to door when we met Ms Tamblyn. She was one of the local working girls pushed out by Dimitri Kolokoff and his crew when they started in on the area. I was going after some loose ends and I found this." Maz pushed another image toward him.

Drew stared down at the crime scene. The bloodied hand with its glittering finger-nails that seemed to be reaching out from beneath the mottled duvet pulled his attention more than anything else in the image. The hand hung over the edge of the dark mattress. Blood had dried to a rusty brown smear that was tracked down across the fingers. From the photograph he could tell that the blood on the hand had dripped onto the floor, forming a dark pool on the carpet.

"What happened to her?"

"Well, that's just it. They're assuming she was killed because of the work she was involved with. Or maybe it was connected to her drug habit..." Drew kept his mouth shut, sensing the DS wasn't quite finished, and his patience was quickly rewarded. "...But I'm not so sure, sir."

Drew glanced up at the DS. "Her lifestyle was high risk, what makes you think her death wasn't connected to that?"

"It just doesn't sit right, sir. According to the report, they found some items from the fridge had been disturbed, which suggests the person responsible spent time at the property. If you're cleaning up a mess, then you don't hang around after you've murdered someone, you get in and out as quickly as possible."

Drew nodded thoughtfully. Arya certainly had a point, but that didn't mean they could run roughshod over an investigation that belonged to someone else.

"Who has the case? I'll have a word and get the

lay of the land." Drew sighed and scrubbed his hand over his grizzled jawline. The feeling in the pit of his gut told him he was going to regret agreeing to this.

"It's a DS Perry." As soon as the words left Arya's mouth, Drew felt his heart drop into his stomach. "Is there something wrong, guv?"

Drew shook his head. "Nah, I'll have a look into this and get back to you on it." He turned away before Maz could ask him anything further. Making it back to his desk in record time, Drew flopped down into the swivel chair and closed his eyes, the memory of his last interaction with DS Perry replaying over in his mind. He'd been right to think this was going to be a shit-show. As soon as Perry knew he was poking his nose into this case, he'd lose his mind. Not that there was much to lose as far as Drew was concerned. But Arya was right, the coincidence, if that was what it was needed to be looked into. Opening his eyes, he straightened up in the chair and reached for the phone. If the shit was going to hit the fan, then he might as well get the ball rolling.

CHAPTER FIVE

PAUSING at the blue front door of the Victorian town house, Harriet contemplated turning on her heel and leaving. It had taken every ounce of courage she possessed just to make it this far. She couldn't turn away. Not now. And anyway, she was expected. From the corner of her eye, she caught sight of the twitching blinds on the bay-window. She pressed the doorbell. The buzzing sound echoed through the depths of the house beyond the door, and Harriet found herself holding her breath as she waited for someone to answer.

The woman who opened the door seemed somewhat familiar, and Harriet felt the air catch in the back of her throat. Blonde hair shot through with silver was cut into a delicate bob that framed the warm-toned skin of the woman in front of her.

"You're Dr Quinn?" Pippa Hopkins asked. Her

rich brown eyes were like two chips of granite, and Harriet fought the urge to shrink beneath the other woman's hardened gaze.

"I am," Harriet said. "Thank you so much for agreeing to this meeting."

"It's not as though I had a choice," Pippa said. She sighed and took a step back, her black pumps making only the slightest of noises on the black and white parquet flooring. "Gabriel wanted to see you. He's been quite excited about it, actually."

"I'm just sorry I couldn't come sooner," Harriet said, but her words sounded hollow and inadequate to her own ears. She knew the truth, she'd stayed away, deliberately. And from the expression in Pippa's eyes, Harriet could tell the other woman knew the truth too.

"You might be able to pull the wool over Gabriel's eyes," Pippa said. "But I'm not so easily fooled, Dr Quinn."

"Of course," Harriet said, opting for diplomacy. There was no point in trying to explain her position on the matter. The woman in front of her had already heard enough empty platitudes, she didn't need anymore.

"He's in the snug. He's most comfortable there. The light is..." Pippa trailed off, and Harriet was acutely aware of the softening in the other woman's gaze. "Well, let's just say he prefers the lighting in that room." Pippa closed the door as Harriet stepped into the large and immaculately decorated hall. "You're the first to visit," Pippa said, as though she could read the many questions Harriet had whirling in her mind. "At least the first from the university."

"I know Gabriel had a lot of friends--" Harriet trailed off as Pippa's derisive snort cut through her words.

"Friends." The word was spat out. "I told Gabriel with friends like those, who needs enemies?"

Harriet kept her thoughts to herself, but to her mind at least the sentiment seemed somewhat harsh, if not all out cruel. Gabriel needed people around him. He needed the company of his friends to help him deal with the trauma he had suffered. But Harriet knew better than to impose her opinion on another.

Pippa led her deeper into the house until finally she came to a halt at a pristine white panelled door. "If you upset him," Pippa said, her voice a low warning.

"I don't intend to do anything of the sort," Harriet said gently.

"If you hurt him, I won't be responsible for my actions." The underlying threat was clear and Harriet simply nodded in response. There was a table next to the door set up with hand sanitizer, masks, and plastic aprons. Pippa indicated that Harriet should utilise the materials. Pippa dragged on a pair of gloves and raised a mask to her face before she pushed the door open and stepped inside. Harriet followed as soon as she had donned an apron, gloves, and a mask of her own.

"Gabe, you've got a visitor." Gone was the harsh, cold tone Harriet had associated with the woman, replaced instead with a warmth that could only belong to a mother. "Dr Quinn is here to speak to you."

Harriet followed her inside, her eyes needing a moment to adjust to the gloom of the small room. In the corner Harriet spotted the small night light which had been plugged in. It was from there; the light was diffused about the space, leaving the side of the room where Gabriel sat to be bathed in shadow. There was a musty smell, as though it had been a long time since the windows, or even the door had been allowed to sit open. Pippa touched Harriet's arm and inclined her head in the direction of a small, comfortable looking chair in the corner of the room. "You can sit there."

"Mum, it's fine." Gabriel's familiar voice greeted Harriet. Despite knowing his voice, there was no mistaking the hoarseness that coated every word, and Harriet found herself wondering if that had something to do with the injuries he'd sustained at the hands of the infamous Star Killer, or if it was from simple disuse. "Sorry, Dr. Quinn, I'd stand up, but..." Gabriel's voice dissolved into a series of spluttering coughs that took a moment to clear.

"Do you need something to drink?" Pippa asked, taking a concerned step toward her son.

"I'm fine. You can go," Gabriel said, as soon as he caught his breath.

"Are you sure? I could--"

"Mum, please." Harriet could hear the pain in his voice as he made his plea to his mother. Pippa squared her shoulders, and with one last look over her shoulder she stepped out and closed the door behind her, leaving Harriet in the gloomy half light with her former Ph.D student.

"Please take a seat," Gabriel said. "It's weird having you standing over me."

Harriet smiled and sat in the seat Pippa had directed her to. The plastic apron crinkled noisily around her, and the mask made the already warm air much more cloying and thick.

"How long have you been out of hospital?" Harriet asked, struggling to figure out the shadow shrouded figure at the other side of the room.

"Two weeks," Gabriel said. "I'm sorry about the light. I..." Harriet could sense the hesitation in his voice as he cast about for the right words.

"You don't need to apologise to me, Gabriel. You do whatever makes you comfortable."

He sighed. "It's easier like this," he said. "That way I don't have to see the pity in everyone's eyes when they look at me."

"There are a lot of people who care about you," Harriet said.

Gabriel's bark of laughter sounded painful, and the noise grated on Harriet's ears. "You could have fooled me," he said. "Once word got out about how I looked, they all stopped calling."

"I find that hard to believe," Harriet said.

"Believe what you want," he said hotly. "It's the truth. Michael couldn't wait to get as far away from me as possible."

"I'm sorry to hear that," Harriet said.

"Don't be," Gabriel said. "You've done nothing wrong. You know he cried when he saw me. I was pretty out of it, but I can still remember it..." He choked up, and Harriet could make out the unmistakable sound of his own quiet sobbing. "He came back to see me once more after that, but he couldn't even look me in the eye. Even mum finds it hard to look at me. The nurses are the only ones who seem unperturbed by my altered appearance."

Harriet sighed. "Gabriel, I can't imagine the pain you've gone through, both emotional and physical, but is it possible that Michael's reaction—much like your mother's—was borne out of love and empathy?"

"I always wondered what he saw in me, you know?" Gabriel spoke as though he hadn't heard a word Harriet had said. "Was I just some kind of pity-fuck? Or did I just make him feel better about himself because I loved him so bloody much--"

Gabriel began to cough again, this time more violently than before.

"Gabriel, do you need me to get you anything?" Harriet couldn't make out any discerning details on the young man beyond his general shape at the other side of the room. The soft glow emitted by the night light plugged in at the corner of the room didn't allow for any more detail than that.

"I'm fine," he said finally. "He cheated on me before the Star Killer got his hands on me."

"I'm sorry to hear that," Harriet said.

Gabriel sighed. "You came here because you wanted something from me," he said.

"No." Harriet's voice was firm. "I came here because I wanted to speak with you. I wanted to know how you were."

"Well, I'm fine." His voice was flat, almost lifeless, and Harriet felt her chest constrict. She didn't want to sit at the other side of the room, away from him. She wanted to cross the space and sit next to him, the urge to comfort him, to give him back some of what Nolan had stolen from him was overwhelming, but deep down she knew she couldn't give him that. Nobody could.

"Have you seen him?" Gabriel asked. The question came out of nowhere and took Harriet by surprise.

"Who?"

"The Star Killer... Nolan Matthews. Have you seen him?"

She contemplated lying. It would be easier, but ultimately it wouldn't do either of them any favours. "Yes." Even in the gloomy light of the room Harriet could see the outline of Gabriel as he stiffened. "He asked to see me."

"And you just agreed to it?" There was none of the emotion that she expected to hear in his voice.

"I did."

"So you went to see him before you ever thought of coming to see me?"

Harriet sighed. "I wanted to come." She knew how pathetic it sounded, but it was the truth. He'd been through enough. She wouldn't lie to him now, even if that lie was meant in kindness. She'd spent enough of her life being lied to by others who thought they were doing her a kindness. She wouldn't make the same mistakes.

"But something stopped you?"

"Honestly, yes. I wanted to come, but I didn't think it was the right time."

"Is there ever a right time?"

Harriet smiled and dropped her gaze to her hands clasped in her lap. "Probably not, Gabriel."

"You're not very good at this, are you?"

"I never said I was." She sighed. "I'm struggling to read you. It's difficult when I can't see you."

"I don't want to be seen." There was a gruffness to his voice that Harriet could understand.

"That's not strictly true, is it?"

"Did you come here to berate me for my coping strategies?"

"You know me well enough, Gabriel, to know I will always be honest with you. I told you that the first time you came to me with your Ph.D topic. I won't lie to you, it wouldn't have served you then and it certainly won't serve you now."

Silence descended on the room, and Harriet half expected the young man sitting across from her to order her to leave. What she wasn't expecting was for a light to click on. It bathed the room in a warm golden glow, and it took Harriet a couple of seconds to grow accustomed to the sudden brightness.

"You said you wanted to see me," he said, his voice half bathed in bitterness. "Well, here you go. Eat it up, Dr Quinn. The only survivor of your pet project."

His face and neck were heavily bandaged in white gauze, which in places had taken on a pinkish tinge, and only one of his hazel eyes was visible above the bindings. One of his arms was bandaged from his hands all the way up to his shoulder, the other had bindings wrapped around only the upper portion of his bicep. She couldn't see the rest of his body, but judging by the bulkiness of his clothes, she assumed much of him was wrapped up in bandages too.

"He took one of my eyelids--" It was then Harriet realised Gabriel was still speaking to her. "Blinded me in my left eye completely. I've lost three of my fingers on my right hand due to infection. Many of the skin grafts initially failed, the most recent one put me back in the hospital because I developed a severe secondary infection."

"Gabriel--" Harriet said, but the young man across from her attempted to shake his head before he grimaced and gave up.

"Don't say you're sorry. If I hear one more person tell me how sorry they are, or how lucky I am to be alive." He sighed and closed his eye. "I don't feel lucky. Mostly, I just wish I was dead."

"And yet, here you are," Harriet said.

"Here I am," he said bitterly. "What did Nolan have to say?"

Harriet bit down on the inside of her lip, blurting the truth out would only hurt Gabriel further and he'd been through enough already. "He's not very talkative," she said tentatively.

"You said you wouldn't lie to me," Gabriel said. "A lie of omission is still a lie, or at least my mother would have me believe that." When Harriet said nothing, Gabriel sighed. "He doesn't speak of me at all, does he?"

"No." She kept her gaze steady despite the ache that had opened up in the centre of her chest. Even from across the room, Gabriel's pain was palpable.

"He's a psychopath," Gabriel said, and it wasn't a question.

"If it makes it easier for you to think of him like that."

He shook his head, and the movement must have cost him because he grimaced. "He's not a psychopath?"

Harriet shrugged. "I haven't done any kind of formal testing on him, so it's not as though I could give you a definitive answer."

"Nobody thought it would be a good idea to subject him to Hare's PCL-R? I would have thought you'd have done that first."

Harriet smiled, he clearly hadn't forgotten his training. The psychopathic checklist-revised, or PCL-R as it was so often known as was considered by most to be the ultimate in diagnostic tools. And Harriet had no doubt in her mind that Dr Chakrabarti would offer the PCL-R to Nolan, but it wasn't Harriet's place to participate in such things.

"It's not up to me," she said. "I'm merely there because he requested me, and his doctor thought it might be helpful. I'm sure they'll cover all those bases."

"Dr Quinn," Gabriel said, his voice low. He lowered his attention to the edge of one of the bandages on his arm as though it had suddenly become the most fascinating item in the room.

"Please, Gabriel, call me Harriet."

His smile was fleeting, there and gone in an instant. "Do you think he's sorry for what he did to me?" There was a quiver in his voice that hadn't been there before.

"I really can't say with any kind of certainty," she said.

"But professionally speaking, what do you think?"

It would be too easy to tell him what he wanted to hear, but she'd promised she would never lie. "Do you really want to know, Gabriel? It won't change what he has done, and it won't rid you of the pain."

"I know that," he said. "But I think I need to hear it from you. Everybody else has their opinions. Mum has tried to reassure me, but she doesn't know people like Nolan. She can't possibly hope to understand. Not the way you do."

Drawing in a deep breath, Harriet felt the weight of the responsibility Gabriel had laid on her. "Honestly, I don't think he's sorry. He's so wrapped up in his own traumas that I don't think he can see beyond that point, let alone empathise with the people he has hurt."

"But do you think he might one day be sorry?"

Harriet thought back over her meeting with Nolan before she answered. "I don't think he has it in him, Gabriel. I'm sorry."

He sighed, his shoulders drooping as though a great weight had been removed from them. "That's what I thought. I want to hate him, you know? He has stolen everything from me and left me with nothing but a lifetime of pain..." He trailed off and glanced over toward the window. "I've tried so hard to hate him, but I don't think I can. I won't forgive him, but I don't hate him either."

"You're entitled to feel whatever you need to feel, Gabriel."

"Nobody understands that."

"I do."

"Do you hate the man who attacked you?"

Harriet cast her mind back over the events that had led her to Robert Burton's door, and she shook her head. "No. I don't hate him."

"And have you forgiven him?"

"I don't think I'm quite there yet," she said. It was the most honest she had been since the attack, but as soon as she said the words aloud she knew it was the truth. She didn't hate Robert Burton, but forgiving him was still a long way away.

"At least I'm not alone," Gabriel said.

She stayed a little while longer, but as Gabriel tired, Harriet decided to leave him to rest.

BACK AT THE university and settling into the seat at her desk, Harriet glanced down at her fingers poised over the keyboard. Never had she thought she would find herself here. Dr Jonathan Connor had been such a large part of her life, a friend and a mentor. There had even been a time when she had seen in him the possibility of more, but those days were long past.

He couldn't be allowed to carry on. The risk he posed to others like Nolan Matthews was too great. How many lives could have been spared if he had just treated Matthews differently? How many of those who had suffered such brutal, tragic ends would be going about their everyday lives instead of lying in the cold ground? How different would Gabriel's life be if Jonathan had just done his job correctly? It wasn't fair; they deserved better. Even Nolan deserved more than he had got from Dr Connor. Closing her eyes, Harriet conjured the memory of Gabriel as he'd asked her if Nolan was sorry for what he'd done. When she opened them, her fingers began to move over the keys as she started to write the letter she hoped would see an end to the suffering Jonathan Connor had caused.

CHAPTER SIX

THE SOUND of the key in the front door caused the hairs on the back of Drew's neck to stand to attention. He'd long since given up wondering when the fear and panic would subside. Steeling himself, he remained seated and waited for the source of the noise to reveal itself.

He didn't have long to wait. Harriet appeared in the doorway. She flopped against the doorjamb, her shoulders drooping as she slipped out of her shoes, revealing a pair of bright pink, cat covered socks. She sighed pleasurably as she stepped onto the plush rug in the living room.

"You look how I feel," Drew said. At least his voice didn't betray the fear he'd felt just moments before. Progress was progress, and he wasn't so big-headed to turn his nose up at it.

"You really know how to make a woman feel

good." A small smile tugged at the corner's of Harriet's mouth as she let her laptop bag drop to the floor before she shrugged free of her jacket. "It's freezing in here," she said, the smile disappearing from her face.

"I didn't want to interfere," Drew said. "I'm already intruding enough as it is."

"So you thought sitting here in the freezing cold was a better idea?" She snorted and padded across the floor toward the kitchen. "Do you want a glass of wine?" Her voice drifted back in from the other room.

"I've got a beer," Drew answered, returning his attention to the brightly lit screen of the laptop propped up on his knees.

Harriet reappeared in the doorway a moment later. Drew kept his attention on the houses he'd flagged earlier as possibilities as she settled cross-legged onto the opposite end of the couch. He could feel her penetrating gaze and fought the urge to look up.

"How are you feeling?" She broke the companionable silence, giving Drew an excuse to look away from the computer. No matter how often she told him he wasn't intruding on her by staying in the spare room, he still felt utterly out of place. Of course, it didn't do anything to ease the guilt he felt over abandoning the house he'd shared with Freya. It seemed the more he got a grip on his fear after everything Nolan Matthews had put him through, the more space it created in his mind for the guilt to creep in. Harriet would probably tell him it was a good thing, a sign he was in recovery, but it certainly didn't feel like that to him.

"Pretty good," he lied, choosing to keep his gaze averted as he leaned over the edge of the couch and picked his bottle of beer up from its place on the floor. When he met Harriet's gaze, he could see that he hadn't been as convincing as he'd hoped.

"How are you finding the new dynamic of the team?" Harriet leaned into the pillow-back cushions on the couch, the picture of ease as she sipped the glass of red wine she'd poured for herself. But Drew could see the intensity that lurked beneath the surface of her blue eyes.

"We agreed on no psycho-analysis," Drew said tersely. For a moment he could see a flicker of pain as it flitted through her gaze, but it was gone so fast he instantly doubted himself.

"I wasn't trying to pry," Harriet said swiftly. "It's just..." She trailed off and turned her attention to the glass in her hand.

Huffing out a breath, Drew felt the tension in his shoulders slowly ebb away. "I'm sorry, it's not you, it's me. Every time I think I'm getting a handle on everything, I find myself spinning out all over again."

"You're still having the panic attacks?"

Drew shook his head. "Not so much. But for instance, when you came in the door, I could feel the panic rising. I controlled it, but..." He balled his hand into a fist, crushing his fingers into the flesh of his palm.

Her smile was sympathetic. "You've got to give yourself time, Drew. I know you hate to hear that, but it's the truth. You dived back into work, without giving yourself a little grace."

He rolled his eyes and drank down a deep mouthful of the bitter beer. "If I took anymore time off, I would have murdered someone myself."

"I get that," she said. "But it's still a shock to the system. And let's be honest, your job is not exactly stress free." She raised an eyebrow at him, and the speculative look on her face dragged a chuckle from him.

"Is that your not-so-subtle way of asking if there's anything going on at the minute that would benefit from your expertise?"

"Well, if there was, would that be so awful?" There was an eagerness in her voice that surprised Drew.

Closing the laptop lid, he slipped it back onto the couch. "There was something I wanted to ask you," he said.

"Go on." From the corner of his eye, he watched her take another sip of her drink.

"It's nothing more than a coincidence, but Maz brought it to my attention and before I go blundering in, I thought I'd mention it to you."

Harriet cocked her eyebrow at him speculatively,

letting him know instantly that she knew he was stalling. Drew sighed. "The last case we worked, Maz and Olivia—during their door-to-door inquiries—spoke to a witness, a Jessica Tamblyn. She's known to our lot, and the information she shared, well it led to us tying some threads together that we might not have otherwise." He sighed, running a hand down over his face. "This is ridiculous. I'm allowing Maz to get inside my head. Get me worked up over nothing but a coincidence."

"Drew, if it really is nothing, then why are you making such a big deal out of it? If it's nothing, then spit it out and let me make up my own mind."

"Fine, you're right." He let his hands drop uselessly back into his lap. "Jessica Tamblyn is dead. Maz found out today. I've requested the full case file, but I'm not expecting much to come of it."

"Why is that?" Despite the nonchalance in her voice, Drew knew Harriet well enough to know when she was intrigued. There was something in the way her body tightened, like a coiled spring that at any moment would erupt into action. And that was how she appeared to him now, every muscle in her body taut. The grip she had on the wine glass a little too tight, her eyes a little too wide, breathing a little faster than was usual.

"Our friend DS Perry is running the investigation." He let the words sink in, watching her for the moment when realisation struck. He wasn't disappointed. Harriet screwed up her nose in distaste as she lifted the wineglass to her lips and took a mouthful. "Yeah, him. The minute he knows I'm sticking my neb in where it definitely doesn't belong, he'll be only too happy to cut it off."

"I take it there's a good reason why both you and DS Arya believe there's more to Ms Tamblyn's death than meets the eye?" Harriet cocked an eyebrow in his direction as she leaned back into the pillows.

Rather than try to explain to her the gut feeling he had, Drew pulled out a copy of the file he'd obtained from Maz and slid it over to her. "You tell me."

He watched as she set the glass aside and took the file from him. He said nothing as she flipped it open, her attention riveted to the front page. When she turned the page, Harriet sucked in a sharp breath as she faltered. Her eyes widened momentarily as she took in the scene they'd found Jessica at the heart of, and Drew felt a modicum of guilt for not warning her of the grimness of the contents of the file.

"It says here DS Perry is treating this as retribution for your case, but he doesn't list any evidence, or witness statements to back the idea up."

Drew nodded. "Like I said, I've requested the full case-file but I've got a feeling that what we've got is pretty much the sum of it all. The investigation is a new one, but even so he should have something more substantial."

"And if he doesn't?" Harriet dragged her attention away from the scene and met Drew's gaze head on.

"Then Jessica's case will become another unsolved statistic."

Harriet nodded and returned her attention to the file. "On a cursory glance, I might be inclined to agree with your gut feeling, but I'd need a little more information. Initially, the scene presents as somewhat disorganised, but it says here there's no forensic evidence found at the scene which doesn't fit with a disorganised killer. Instead, that speaks to someone who came with a plan, pre-meditated enough to use forensic counter-measures."

Drew nodded. "I can't say how reliable that file is in regards to the forensic evidence. There's bound to be some trace DNA." Leaning forward he caught a whiff of the subtle perfume of her shampoo as a lock of her curls fell over her shoulder and into her face. A lump formed in the back of his throat. "It looks as though whoever killed her was out of control. Angry..." Drew swallowed hard, and shifted backwards on the couch, anything to put a little distance between him and the soft perfumed scent of her hair and skin. No sooner did the realisation hit him than he felt the familiar guilt over Freya rise unbidden in his mind. He'd run away from the home they'd built together, and now he was here with Harriet doing what exactly? It was a confusing concoction of guilt and discomfort, and by the time he dragged himself out of his own thoughts he realised Harriet had been speaking to him the entire time.

"If it's possible, I'd like to see the results of the post-mortem. Murders like this are always going to appear frenzied, but that doesn't necessarily mean it's true." She glanced over at Drew and the ghost of a smile hovered on her lips. "But you don't need me to tell you that." She closed the file, her hand pressing down on the cover as though that alone would be enough to keep the horror contained. "What do you need from me on this?"

Drew shrugged. "Honestly, I have no idea... Maybe I'm just grasping at straws, desperate for a distraction." There was a raw edge to his voice. He needed to move, to get away. To put as much distance between himself and the situation just so he could think clearly again.

"Only you can answer that."

He nodded and glanced down at his watch. "You're right. Look, if I find anything then I'll pass it along." He managed to sound half-strangled. Get a grip, Drew. The voice in the back of his head warned.

"Drew, I'm not dismissing you," Harriet said, and she sounded genuinely dismayed. She reached out toward him, but he shifted away.

Avoiding her penetrating gaze, Drew climbed to his feet and downed the last of his beer. "I know," he said. "I've got an early start, I should probably turn in."

"Is there something else you're not telling me?" From the corner of his eye, he caught her blue eyes searching his face for an answer.

"I'm just tired," he said. "And I've got a headache." He grabbed onto the first thought that popped into his head. It wasn't entirely a lie, ever since his run in with Templeton's shot-gun on the beach he'd suffered from a low-grade headache. He'd never realised just how painful a ruptured eardrum could be until he'd experienced one for himself.

"I'm sorry, I should have thought--"

"No, no, it's fine," Drew said, politely.

Harriet smiled awkwardly and bid him goodnight. He escaped out into the hall and took the stairs two at a time until he was back within the safety of her spare room. Every night ended the same, with them both politely side-stepping around one another. Inwardly cursing, Drew pressed his head against the door. If there was one thing he had learned, it was that physical injuries healed much faster than emotional ones; his eardrum would heal—was healed, just as the wounds Matthews had inflicted on him had done, but he'd allowed his emotional wounds to fester and they would not just go away. He'd heard time was the greatest healer, but for Drew patience had never been his friend.

CHAPTER SEVEN

OLIVER STOOD beneath the overhang of trees that Darren had chosen as their point of entry to the forest and waited for his friend. Glancing down at his watch, he pressed the little button on the side of the screen so that a small luminous yellow green light lit up the face. Six-forty-two; Darren was late. It wasn't anything unusual, Darren was always late, but today more than ever Oliver wished his friend could be on time.

Not that he was scared. Although if he allowed himself a moment to think about what he was doing out here in the darkness waiting for Darren, he knew it would be all the permission the terror needed to creep into his thoughts. Pulling his arms around his torso, he drew in a shaky breath, and tried to calm his frayed nerves. Just five more minutes. Five more minutes for Darren to get here, or he was out of here.

Oliver glanced down longingly at his bicycle in the long damp grass. If he went home now, he would get there in time to play a couple of games of Fortnite before his mum made him go to bed. When he closed his eyes, he could imagine the huge cup of cocoa she would make for him, with extra marshmallows, and—

Crack!

The sound jerked him from his thoughts, and he glanced down the road, but it remained eerily empty. Reaching into his pocket, he pulled his battered iPhone out, half expecting to see a direct message from Darren telling him he'd bottled it. But the screen was blank.

Oliver shivered, the December air chilling him to the bone, and he suddenly wished he'd added a couple of extra layers to his clothes before he'd left home. The tree branches overhead shifted and creaked as they swayed in the wind that had kicked up. There were no more leaves, but that didn't stop the bare branches from clicking and clacking together like the fingers of some giant beast that had crawled straight out of the Witcher video game.

Scrolling through the phone, he reached Darren's number and prepared to call his friend. Lifting the phone to his ear, there was another large crack from the tree line directly behind him. The noise could mean only one thing, and Oliver spun around, his eyes huge and saucer like scanning the darkness. The Owl Man had come for him. He backed up and stumbled over his discarded bicycle. A half strangled scream tore from his throat as he hit the ground with a jolt, and his phone fell into the grass. Turning away, he scrambled towards the road. Oliver's blood turned to ice, as a hand clamped down on his shoulder, and he lashed out with his fist, a last-ditch attempt at protecting himself from the creature who at that moment was hellbent on tearing him apart. His fist connected with something infinitely softer than he'd imagined, but Oliver didn't wait for the beast to regroup and raced up onto the empty road.

"You wanker!" Darren's voice drifted up from the grassy bank. "You broke my nose."

Oliver took a tentative step forward. He'd heard in school about the Owl Man's ability to mimic the voices of friends in order to lure you into the woods. Darren's head appeared over the long grass, his expression twisted into a grimace.

"What's wrong with you?" Darren demanded, pushing up onto his feet. Something dark and wet glittered on his face. Oliver watched as his friend swiped at the black blood beneath his nose with the back of his hand.

"What's wrong with me? What's wrong with you?" Oliver exploded. The nervousness he'd felt building in his chest needed somewhere to go, and lashing out at his best friend for trying to scare the shit out of him seemed like a sensible approach. "We said half six, and you don't show." His breath came in small wheezing gasps.

"Well, I'm here now," Darren said sulkily. "There was no need to kill me."

"I thought you were him!" Oliver's voice was husky with fear. "You're just lucky I didn't really try to knock your block off." Oliver pulled his inhaler from his pocket and pressed it to his lips. It would take a few moments for the medication to loosen the tight ball that sat in the centre of his chest. Tears sat at the corners of his eyes, and he did his best to remember his mother's calming words whenever she helped him through an attack. It seemed to work, and his breathing calmed.

Darren glanced up at his friend, scepticism alight in his dark eyes. "You can't even beat me on Fortnite, there's no chance you'd beat me in real life."

Oliver puffed his chest out, adrenaline bringing a surge of bravado that he hadn't been feeling just moments before. "I so could."

Darren scoffed and glanced down at the small pile of items Oliver had tied onto the back of his bike. "Is this all you brought with you?"

Heat rushed into Oliver's face, and he nodded. "I didn't want to raise suspicions with my mum."

Darren glanced nervously over at the pitiful pile he'd left near the tree line. "Neither did I..." He blew out a breath before he shrugged. "We'll be fine. It's warmer in the woods anyhow."

"We could just go back to my place," Oliver blurted. "We don't need to do this, we could just tell people we spent the night here."

Darren shook his head, but Oliver could tell his friend was wavering. "Nah, mate, they'll know we chickened out. And anyway, you're not really afraid of that urban legend, are you?"

Oliver swallowed hard. The fading adrenaline in his veins told him to brush off his fears. But the voice in the back of his mind tried to convince him to leave. "Those kids really went missing," he said, his voice dropping to a whisper. "They were camping, and they just vanished."

"It's all bullshit," Darren said, sounding infinitely more confident than he had earlier in the week. His friend's sudden courage made Oliver suspicious.

"What do you know?"

Darren's grin was secretive as he pulled a torch from the pocket of his jacket. "Follow me, and I'll tell you."

It would be so easy to say no, to grab his bike and return home. But Oliver never walked away from something that intrigued him, and Darren had known just what buttons to press to get him interested.

"Fine. But if you're just screwing around, I'm out of here," he said, resignation tinged his voice as he hopped back down into the long grass, and scooped up his bicycle.

Darren's grin widened. "Trust me, you won't regret this."

Oliver nodded, and followed Darren into the trees, but the knot in his stomach told him he was already regretting his decision.

OLIVER KEPT his gaze trained on each step he took, careful to avoid the half hidden tree roots and fallen logs that littered the path they'd chosen. It definitely wasn't one of the official paths in Dalby Forest. Before he'd heard of the legend of the Owl Man, Oliver had come to the woods with his parents and older sister. He'd been much younger then and The Go Ape section was particularly fun; not that he'd admit that now he was older. There was a part of him that wished he could back in time; life was simpler then. The rules regarding what he could, and could not do had changed, and now it just wasn't cool to admit to enjoying running and racing around in a forest like a little child.

They walked for what felt like forever, before Darren finally glanced up at the starry sky that peeked through the canopy. "I think we're nearly there," he said, studying their surroundings, before he glanced back down at a crudely hand drawn map in his hands. Darren turned and set off south through the undergrowth.

"Wait, what are you looking for?" Oliver asked,

scrambling after his friend. He raised his torch, and let it skim over the trees surrounding them, and his breath caught in the back of his throat as hundreds of eyes glinted back at them. "Holy fuck!" He breathed the words out as he caught Darren's arm.

"What is—" Darren cut off, and Oliver was only too aware of the sharp intake of breath from his friend. They came to a juddering halt, as Oliver trailed his light over the trees, and the eyes disappeared.

"What was that?" Oliver asked, his voice barely a whisper.

"I think that means we're close," Darren said, and this time there was no mistaking the underlying fear in his voice.

"Close to what, Darren? What have you dragged me into?"

Darren tried to shake free of Oliver's grip, his wide eyes scanning the surrounding woods. "They said if we found his lair and spent the night there—"

"Found who?" Fear caused Oliver's voice to rise an octave. Ice trickled down his spine, and his legs felt wooden.

"The Owl Man," Darren said. In the pale light of the torch, his skin was ashen. "They said if we found the eyes, then we were close..."

"Whose eyes were they?" The ground felt incredibly uneven beneath Oliver's feet, and he struggled to stay upright.

"The ones he took," Darren said solemnly. "AJ said they're all still here, waiting, and watching..." Something rustled in the undergrowth nearby, causing Darren to cut off. "Fuck..."

"We need to leave," Oliver said, his words tumbling over one another as he tried to speak in hushed tones.

"No," Darren said. Despite the fear in his voice, he seemed strangely adamant. "We can't leave until we get it."

"Get what?" Cold, hard fury knotted in the centre of Oliver's chest as he realised his friend's betrayal. "We're here because AJ said he'd give you something, aren't we?"

Darren had the good grace to look ashamed. "He said he could get me a brand new PS5 before anyone else, if I got him something."

"You asshole," Oliver said. "You know he has no intention of getting you a PS5, right? Those things are impossible to get."

"His dad works for a GameStop supplier, so he can definitely get his hands on one."

"Even if that's true, it doesn't mean he's going to give it to you," Oliver hissed. A tree branch cracked on the path behind them, causing both boys to move closer together.

"We just get in, and out," Darren said stubbornly. "We've gone this far."

Oliver shook his head. "You can get it, but I'm not

moving from here." As though to emphasise his point, he stamped his foot on the ground, and the dirt shifted beneath him, causing him to pitch sideways. He went over the edge of the embankment in the darkness, his torchlight extinguishing as his hand smashed against a rock, sending pain ricocheting up through his wrist and into his arm. Oliver rolled down the slope, bumping and slapping into the tree branches, and other debris that he couldn't fathom in the darkness until finally he came to a halt at the bottom.

He noticed the musty smell first, because it reminded him of the time their bath had leaked, causing mould to flourish beneath the tiles. It had cost his parents a bomb to get it all ripped out and replaced, but the smell had lingered for a while after. Mum had said it had permeated everything in the room and had replaced all the towels and bath mats with new ones.

"Are you all right, down there?" Darren shouted, his voice bouncing off the trees, making it sound as though it was coming from everywhere and nowhere at once.

"I think so," Oliver said, wincing as he tried to move his arm. Pain shot up to his elbow, and it brought scalding tears to his eyes. "I think I broke my arm."

"Shit!" Darren said, his disembodied voice made Oliver feel disorientated. Or maybe that was the fall?

He shifted into an upright position and felt something hard and sharp poke him in the leg. Oliver tugged it free of the dirt, but it was too dark to make out anything beyond the fact that it was long, and had a jagged end that had almost broken the skin of his thigh. He placed his good hand down on the ground, and felt around for the torch, but it was nowhere to be found.

"Can you shine your light down here?" He called up to Darren. "My torch is bust." Delicately, he cradled his injured arm against his chest, and swallowed back the pain that threatened to overwhelm his senses. The cold was quickly seeping in through the thin layers of his clothing, numbing the rest of his limbs.

Bright white light appeared overhead, almost blinding Oliver. Raising his good hand, he tried to block the worst of the light. "What's that next to your foot," Darren said.

"You need to call my mum," Oliver said, ignoring his friend. "Tell her to come and get us." There was a wobble in Oliver's voice as he spoke, and instinctively he knew it would be only a matter of time before fear reduced him to the same blubbering mess Darren's little sister often was.

"Yeah, but that thing there beside you," Darren said. "It's weird."

Oliver spotted his own torch on the ground a

couple of feet away. "Call my mum, please," he whimpered.

Darren must have finally registered the pain in his voice. "I'll have to go back to the road, there's no coverage here," he said.

The thought of being left on his own out here was almost enough to make Oliver change his mind, but the sound of his friend moving away told him it was already too late.

Tears blurred his vision and spilled over his face.

He fumbled around in the darkness until his hand closed over the torch that had fallen from his grip during his rapid descent. He flicked on the switch, but was unsurprised when nothing happened.

"Please, just work," he whispered, his voice hoarse with pain and fear. The tears came thick and fast as he fumbled one handedly with the torch, trying to get it to work. His chest was beginning to constrict with panic, his breathing growing shallow. He jiggled the torch back and forth until something within the hard plastic body clicked. Without a second to waste, Oliver flipped the switch a second time, and was rewarded with a small puddle of yellow light that threatened to fade out at any moment. Sucking down a breath, he felt in his pocket for his inhaler and was relieved to find it still safe and sound.

A couple of puffs later and with the limited

amount of light from his torch, Oliver felt marginally more in control, and some of his fear receded. He swept the light back and forth as the pain continued to build in his arm.

He'd broken his other wrist when he was seven by falling off a roundabout that Darren and a couple of other boys had been playing together on. They'd spent their time trying to make it spin as fast as they could, and those who were on the roundabout had to hold on for as long as possible. When Oliver's grip had slipped, he'd gone flying, and had crashed into the ground at a sickening speed. He could still remember the moment of impact, and the crunch of bone that accompanied it. That break had been far more grisly, and when he closed his eyes, he could still remember the way the bone had protruded out through the skin of his arm.

Mum had looked faint, as she'd sat with him until the ambulance came, but she'd helped to distract him from the pain, and it was her Oliver thought of as he sat in the semi-darkness of the woods. She was going to kill him...

Taking his scarf off, he wrapped it around his arm the way they'd taught him in the basic first-aid training he'd received as part of Cub Scouts. Tightening the scarf made him nauseous, but as soon as it secured his arm against his chest, he felt a little better.

There were no sounds to betray Darren's return,

so Oliver let the pitiful beam of light from the torch skim over the leaf covered ground. He scanned the dirt until he came to rest on the place Darren had been so interested in. Whatever he'd seen sat just above the surface of the dirt, the dome shape a creamy colour in the light from the stars, and the torch he held in his hand.

It reminded him of some large mushrooms he'd found out in the back garden. His dad had called them white puffballs, but to Oliver they had looked like footballs sprouting directly from the ground. Staggering onto his feet, he crossed the leaf covered ground until he came to a halt above it. Crouching down next to the object, he tentatively reached a hand out, and let his fingers trace down over the rough lines that marred the otherwise smooth surface.

His fingers found a hole in the object's top, and he hooked his fingers into it, before he tugged it from the dirt. It lifted easily enough. Dirt had compacted up inside the hollow centre, and some larger clods dropped away as he hoisted it into the air. Swinging the torch light over it, Oliver noted the two round sockets, and a triangle section that looked suspiciously like something on a skull.

Horror dawned slowly, the pain in his arm dulling his senses. He let it drop back into the dirt, the torch beam following it down as it smacked into the damp leaf strewn earth with a dull thud. The impact knocked some dirt free, and the skull rolled until it lay with its empty eye sockets facing the sky. There was one tooth left in the front of the upper jawbone, but with the lower jaw missing, it took Oliver's mind a couple of sluggish seconds to fill in the pieces of the puzzle he was looking at.

And when it finally clicked into place in his mind, a scream bubbled in the back of his throat for a moment before he flung himself toward the embankment and the scream finally ripped free.

CHAPTER EIGHT

DS AMBROSE SCOFIELD shovelled chips into his mouth, as fast as his hand could get them there. The younger DC sitting on the other side of the desk rolled her eyes in disgust as he belched loudly and then grinned.

"You want one?" He asked, leaning over the desk toward DC Martina Nicoll. She shook her head and glanced back down at the report she'd been skim reading. "What, you don't eat now?" Ambrose asked, scooping up another fistful of chips, and heaving them into his mouth without bothering to take a breath.

"Didn't your mother ever tell you not to talk with your mouth full?" Martina said, keeping her gaze downcast. Ambrose wasn't the worst. In fact, if she were rating the sergeants she'd had the misfortune of working with over the years she'd been on the force, she might even have said he was somewhere up near the top. But his eating habits definitely left a lot to be desired.

"Don't go bringing my mum into this," Ambrose said indignantly. Martina glanced up in time to see him jabbing a chip in her direction. "She didn't have the best of manners, but she was an absolute angel on this earth."

Shaking her head, Martina turned her attention back to the file, before she surreptitiously glanced at her watch. Just another fifteen minutes, and then she could leave.

"You two are up!" The DI's voice carried across the small cramped space of the office, and Martina felt her heart sink. Why was her luck always so shit?

"What we got, guv?" Ambrose scrubbed his hand across his mouth, smearing the grease into the fine hairs that dotted the back of his hand.

"Some kid found a body out in Dalby Forest, I want you two up there to coordinate everything until we've got a grip on the situation."

"Sir, with all due respect, do we have to go?" Martina asked, trying to keep her voice even. DI Brooks glared across at her.

"You might be used to getting your way elsewhere, Nicoll. But you'll learn pretty sharpish that I don't let my detectives skate by."

"Sir, I--"

"You got a hot date or something?" Ambrose

asked, a teasing smile playing on his lips. Martina shot him a dirty look as the DI stalked away, leaving them alone.

"What did you say that for?"

"What? I was just asking if you had yourself a date. I didn't think that was a crime." Ambrose actually sounded somewhat injured, and Martina regretted the sharpness in her voice.

She sighed and shook her head. "Forget about it," she said. "It's nothing."

Ambrose kept his mouth shut, and for that she was grateful. That he knew when to stay quiet was definitely a tick in the plus box for Ambrose. She slipped her phone from her bag as he pushed onto his feet. "You go on ahead. I'll be there in a second."

He studied her for a moment before he nodded. "See you in the car."

Martina waited until he was out of sight, before she dialled the number, and listened as it rang on the other end. Drumming her fingers against the desktop, she held her breath until finally when it appeared the call would go unanswered, a voice picked up on the other end.

CHAPTER NINE

PAUSING outside the Brew York Tap Room and Beer Hall—the bar the team had chosen for their Christmas party—Harriet felt the tension in her shoulders slowly ratchet up. She'd spent much of the day thinking over and over about the invite she'd received from the monk. When she'd received the email from the DCI, she'd genuinely believed he'd done so by mistake. Of course a quick phone call had cleared it up, and she'd been left in no doubt that there was no mistake in his invitation.

However, there was a part of her—as much as she hated to admit it—that felt wounded by the fact that Drew hadn't thought to invite her himself. Sure, things were a little odd between them. He was definitely dwelling on something, and she wasn't one to pry. Instead, she'd been secure in the knowledge that when Drew was ready to speak about whatever issues he was struggling with, he would do just that.

"Hey, Doc, didn't expect to see you here!" The shout went up behind Harriet, and she jumped as DC Olivia Crandell slammed her hand down on her shoulder. "Really didn't think this would be your scene."

Harriet smiled tentatively as she took in the young DC's casual attire. She'd grown so accustomed to seeing Olivia in dark slacks and baggy suit jackets, that to see her out in a blush pink jumper and tight blue jeans was a complete novelty. "I'm still not sure that it is, but the mo--" Harriet cut herself off before the nickname Drew had christened his superior officer with slipped out. "DCI Gregson seemed to insinuate this was mandatory; a team building endeavour I think were the exact words he used."

Olivia rolled her eyes. "Of course he did. Trust the monk to make everything hard-work." Olivia's smile brightened. "You coming in, or are you planning on freezing to death out here?" Olivia shivered as though to emphasise her words.

"I'm definitely coming in," Harriet said, squaring her shoulders as the DC steered her toward the doors.

A couple of moments later, surrounded by the press of bodies inside the crowded beer hall, Harriet felt herself swept along by the jubilant emotions of those who were determined to enjoy themselves; if they could get drunk at the same time, all the better.

She followed Olivia through the press until they found the rest of the team grouped together at a long wooden bench style table. Harriet scanned the area, but was surprised to find there was no sign of Drew. DI Appleton's face lit up as soon as she laid eyes on Olivia, and she beckoned to them both.

"Come on in and join us!" Her voice carried surprisingly easily over the noise of the surrounding conversations.

"Budge up, Maz," Olivia said good-naturedly as she squeezed onto the bench next to him, leaving a gap barely wide enough for Harriet to fit onto.

"Where's the big man himself?" Melissa asked the moment Harriet had settled onto the bench.

"You mean Drew?"

Melissa's eyes were a little glazed, and her face was flushed—either through the heat of the space or the beer she was working her way through. Not that Harriet could tell. "I haven't seen him today," she said, leaning toward Melissa. "I thought he'd be here already."

"So did I," Melissa said thoughtfully as she settled back on the bench and downed the last of the amber liquid in her glass in one gulp. "We need another round!"

Harriet satisfied herself by settling back on the bench to observe the behaviour of the other officers.

The chatter flowed as easily as the beer, and Harriet found herself swept along by the jubilant atmosphere created by those around her. Breaking away from the group, she made her way through the crowd to the bar. As she neared the counter, her gaze snagged on the sight of Drew as he made his way in through the main doors. Unobserved, she stood back and watched as he brushed the droplets of rain from his hair and swept his hooded gaze over the rowdy crowd.

He caught sight of her almost immediately, and something in his body language relaxed as he made a beeline toward her.

"I didn't think this was your kind of thing?"

"You know, you're not the first person to say that tonight. I think you must all have a very poor impression of me," Harriet said, only half teasing.

Drew shrugged. "I wouldn't worry about it. This isn't my scene either."

Harriet smiled. "That doesn't surprise me. I was just going to get a drink. Do you want something?"

A furrow appeared in the middle of his brow. "I know how to have fun," he said.

"I never said you couldn't."

His gaze probed at her until finally his expression closed and became unreadable. "I'll get these," Drew said. "It's the least I could do considering you're letting me crash at your place." Something had shifted between them, she could feel it but he was shutting her out and she couldn't get a handle on his mood.

Before she could answer, Melissa bounded up behind them. "Finally!" Her voice carried over the din, drawing the attention of the others gathered at the table. "I thought you'd chickened out." She jabbed her finger against Drew's chest, emphasising each one of her words as she spoke. Harriet took a step back as Melissa manoeuvred her body so that she blocked Drew's body with her own. If she didn't know any better, she might have thought it was a possessive move designed to isolate her from Drew.

From her vantage point, Harriet studied the other woman, watching on as she placed her hand on Drew's arm, her fingers stroking against the fabric of his wool coat. Melissa tipped her chin upwards, angling her gaze up at Drew. And through it all, Drew seemed utterly oblivious to his colleague's flirty behaviour. That knowledge brought a small smile to Harriet's face.

"I'm a man of my word," Drew said. From where she stood, Harriet couldn't help but think that Drew looked like a man completely out of his depth.

"Put your wallet away," Melissa said. "The first round is on me."

Drew shook his head. "Nah, I'll get this. I was going to buy Harriet a drink, anyway. I owe her--" He trailed off before he finished the sentence and caught

Harriet's eye from over the top of Melissa's blonde head.

Melissa's attention momentarily swept over Harriet, leaving her with the distinct impression that if Melissa could have wished her a million miles away in that moment, she would have done it. "I'll get something for you both," she said grudgingly. "What'll it be Doc?"

Harriet started to answer, but Melissa raised her hand. "Actually, don't. I know something that's perfect for you." She turned on her heel and began to push through the crush before Harriet could utter a reply.

"I was going to say I'm not really a beer person," Harriet said, more to herself than anyone else.

"When in Rome," Drew said with an easy smile. "I wouldn't worry about it, Melissa's just as likely to come back with a glass of wine as she is to bring you a beer. She's a little unpredictable."

"I wouldn't have said unpredictable," Harriet said, watching Drew carefully. There was a look of consternation on his face, as though he couldn't quite make up his mind about Melissa and her behaviour. She realised then and there that she could put him out of his misery, let him know what Melissa was thinking. But she couldn't shake the feeling that doing so would be too much like overstepping, and after the rocky start their friendship had got off to, it was the very last thing she wanted to do. Suddenly aware of the silence that stretched between them, Harriet cleared her throat awkwardly. "Perhaps we should join the others?"

Drew nodded and followed her lead back to the bench table.

"Good to see you, Guv!" Maz said, pushing up onto unsteady feet. There was a flush in his cheeks and his eyes were rapidly developing the glazed look of someone who had indulged a little too much. He raised his pint and some of the amber coloured liquid slopped over the side.

"Watch it!" Olivia warned as some of the liquid dripped down onto her bare arm. "God, you're such a light-weight," Olivia said, nudging him into the thigh with her elbow, causing Maz to wobble a little more.

"I am not." Maz glared down at her, and Harriet felt a smile tug at the corners of her lips as she watched the playful argument break out between the two detectives.

"This is for you," Melissa said triumphantly as she returned with a glass in each hand. She passed one to Drew and then turned to face Harriet and presented her with the second. "Go on," she urged. "Try it."

Harriet stared down at the drink. Some of the bubbles popped, causing the familiar scent of hops to waft up and tickle her nose. With Melissa's gaze trained on her, Harriet felt as though she had no choice but to acquiesce or risk appearing rude. She took a sip, the bitter taste washing over her tongue, and she fought the urge to pull a face. It wasn't unpleasant, far from it, but it didn't change the fact that she would never be a connoisseur of such things.

"Well, what do you think?" Melissa probed.

"It's great," Harriet said. "What's it called?"

"Cereal Killa," Melissa said, before she creased up with laughter. "Get it? Cereal Killa. Because you hang out with nut-jobs like Matthews. This stuff was made for you."

The others at the table laughed raucously, but Harriet was acutely aware of the tension that radiated from the man next to her.

"That's not exactly appropriate," Drew said gruffly, drawing a speculative look from Melissa.

"Shit, I'm sorry, Drew. I shouldn't have mentioned that lunatic. It's just when I heard what the good doctor gets up to in her spare time, I couldn't resist."

"I'm not sure I understand?" Harriet said. Her grip tightened on the glass in her hands as heat crawled up the side of her neck.

"I don't know how you do it, Doc," Melissa said. "I just couldn't do what you do. I couldn't feel sorry for bastards like Matthews, not even if my life depended on it. They're a waste of good air if you ask me."

"Nobody asked you," Drew said sourly. "Change the subject, Melissa." The tension in the group rocketed, and Harriet felt the eyes of the rest of the team on them as silence descended.

"It was just a joke," Melissa retorted.

"It's fine," Harriet said, struggling to smooth the situation over. "If we were all the same, life would be very boring."

"See, the Doc gets it, Haskell. No need to get your knickers in a wad." There was an unkind edge to Melissa's voice, and Harriet noted the darkening in Drew's expression as her words hit home.

"Time for food!" DC Green said, pushing onto his feet with an overly enthusiastic smile on his face. "I think we need food, and this place is legendary for its grub." The others paused, their attention locked on Harriet, Drew, and Melissa.

"You're right," Olivia said. "I could definitely eat. What about you, Guv?" She pushed up onto her feet and caught Drew's attention.

There was a beat where Harriet knew the situation would swing in one of two ways, but the moment passed and Drew's shoulders relaxed as he released a breath. "I'm starving," he said.

"That explains the grumpy bastard routine," Melissa said, and despite the smile on her face Harriet could hear the edge beneath her teasing tone.

The others on the task force joined in the chorus, and within seconds the tension dropped. Harriet took a seat on the end of the bench and let go of the breath she'd been holding onto. She set her drink down on the table and watched the condensation drift down the side of the glass.

"That was a close-call," Olivia said as she dropped onto the seat next to Harriet. "It's never boring with you around, is it?"

Harriet gave the other woman a lop-sided smile. "I try to keep things interesting."

"That you do," Olivia said, sidling closer. "There was something I wanted to ask you."

"You want to know whether I've had a chance to look over the files?"

"Yeah, how did you know?" Olivia seemed genuinely surprised, causing Harriet to chuckle.

"I get the sense you're a workaholic. You want to succeed, so it makes sense that no matter the situation you're always 'on'."

Colour mounted Olivia's cheeks. "I suppose that's a fair assessment. I didn't know I was so transparent."

"Sorry," Harriet said. "It's a professional hazard. I make my living trying to figure out those around me, I find it difficult to switch off."

"What do you make of those two then?" Olivia asked, inclining her head subtly in the direction of Drew and Melissa, who were, at that moment, locked in a heated debate.

"I'd say they have history," Harriet said diplomatically.

"That's not an answer," Olivia said with a smile.

"But I'm not going to push you. Did you get a chance to look at the files?"

Harriet took a mouthful of her drink. "I did."

"And?" Olivia needled. "You're killing me here. What did you think?"

"I don't have the complete file, and I really would need that before I could give a full and informed opinion."

Olivia's shoulders drooped. "So you don't think it's anything more than somebody cleaning up?"

"If I was to hazard a guess, and bear in mind this is just a guess, at least until I can have all the facts; I'd be leery to call it just a run-of-the-mill retaliation. Initially, the scene suggests a level of disorganisation and heightened emotion that I wouldn't expect to see in a murder that's motivated by retribution. The way Jessica Tamblyn was attacked feels quite personal. In her bed, still wrapped in her blankets... There are elements of a blitz attack, but after the initial frenzy the wound patterns suggest something more akin to experimentation."

The colour drained from Olivia's face. "You got all of that just from the file Maz gave to DI Haskell?"

"Drew managed to pull the post-mortem, but I don't think he has anything beyond that."

Olivia blew out a breath. "If she wasn't murdered out of retribution, then what are we looking at?"

Harriet's stomach clenched uncomfortably. "Jessica's line of work is one that could be considered high-risk. Those working in the sex-industry already face a much higher risk of violence, not to mention that they are less likely to report crimes committed against them. Public perception has been less than favourable towards them for far too long, and it has made them wary of asking for help. However, the person responsible for her murder didn't attack Jessica in public, he broke into her home and attacked her while she slept. There's a personal element at play, and the level of violence and the fact that this person appears to have been comfortable enough to stop to have a snack is extremely concerning."

"You think they'll strike again, don't you?"

Drawing in a deep breath, Harriet glanced around at the members of the team who laughed and joked with their colleagues. "I do," she said quietly. "There will be others, if there hasn't been already. My biggest concern is that what we're looking at here is the potential for a massive escalation."

"A serial killer?"

Harriet nodded. "Yes." The moment she spoke the words aloud, she knew it was true. There would be other deaths, other innocents murdered. How many would have to die before the true pattern emerged? How many lives would be snuffed out by a perpetrator driven by such a desire for pain and violence. She didn't have the answers, and that bothered her most of all.

CHAPTER TEN

HOURS LATER, thanks to taking a wrong turn despite the SatNav in the car, Martina followed Ambrose through the forest. They'd left the trail twenty minutes previously and were now beating a fresh path through the undergrowth in the direction of the scene.

Martina lifted her torch and let the light play across the surrounding trees. Something flashed in the corner of her vision, and she paused, bringing her torch up so it illuminated the small round discs on the tree trunks. "What are they?"

Ambrose paused as she called after him and followed the direction of her gaze to the trees surrounding them. "No clue," he said half beneath his breath as he took a tentative step forward. She reached the tree at the same time as he did and watched as he seized the small object from the trunk.

A chunk of bark came away with the small disc, and Martina could see the nail still embedded in the tree.

"Is that a reflector from a bike?" Martina asked, eyeing the hard plastic circle cupped in the meaty palm of Ambrose's hand.

"Looks like it," he mumbled, before he glanced up at their surroundings. "Give me that a minute, would you?"

Before Martina could protest, he grabbed the torch and let it drift over the trees. Within seconds, other reflectors gave up their position, shining in the light. It gave the scene an eerie atmosphere, making Martina think of hundreds of eyes watching her from the darkness.

"That is just fucked up," Ambrose said. Martina was glad to find she wasn't the only one feeling unnerved by the odd situation.

"You're telling me," she whispered. Who would have done such a thing? And why go to so much effort? "We should get somebody to take a closer look at this," she said, mostly to herself.

"Why bother? It was probably just kids, anyway."

"Because it's weird, that's why." There was a firmness to her voice that brooked no argument. Ambrose gave her a once over, before he shook his head. A wry smile played around his lips. "Not to mention they're placed conspicuously close to the place where a body was dumped?" She cocked an eyebrow at him but Ambrose continued to smirk. "What?"

"Just you can tell you grew up in the city, and not out in the country," he said patronisingly, and Martina half expected him to pat her on the head indulgently.

Before he could say another thing, she snatched her torch back from his hand, and started down the path again. A couple of moments later, and Martina emerged onto an embankment made of dirt. She glanced down at the forensics team who worked around in the small hollow. They'd set up several enormous lights that threatened to blind anyone who glanced at them head on. And among the leaf mould, Martina could see the glint of the metal plates they'd set up; like stepping stones across a pool of orange and brown leaf litter. In the centre lay the body they'd begun to excavate.

Despite the distance, Martina could tell there was something not quite right about the positioning of the bones.

"Oi." She called out to the nearest man in a white paper suit. He glanced up at her. Only his eyes were visible above the white mask he wore, and Martina fought down the urge to take a step back. It was unnerving to see so little of a person, and it didn't matter how many crime scenes she visited, she knew she would never get used to the impersonal nature of it all. "Who moved the body?"

The man glanced back down in the direction of the hollow, and shrugged. "No clue."

Martina sighed with frustration, as Ambrose joined her on the lip of the hollow. "What is it?" He sounded vaguely out of breath, and Martina wondered when he'd last visited the gym. Not that it was any of her business. If he wanted to resemble a human jelly-baby, then that was his business.

"Does the body look right to you?" she asked, tilting her head to the side.

"Well, it's a skeleton," Ambrose said. "It's not going to look right, is it?"

"That's not what I mean," Martina said, agitation colouring her words. "Look at it. The placement of the bones..." She trailed off as realisation overtook her mind. "The head is in the wrong place. That's not my imagination, is it?" She glanced up at Ambrose, who shrugged.

"I suppose not," he said somewhat unsatisfactorily. "But they said the kid who found the body moved the head."

"Right," she said, scrutinising the scene further. "I suppose animal predation could account for some of the distance between the bones."

"Bound to be a few foxes out here," Ambrose said.

With a sigh, Martina turned from her position on the hill when another shout went up from somewhere a little further into the woods. Following Ambrose through the undergrowth, they pushed out through the tangle of brambles and branches in time to see a forensics officer setting a perimeter around what looked suspiciously like nothing at all to Martina.

"What is it?" She asked, turning to the nearest SOCO who had tried to scuttle by her. "Are there more bones over here?"

The woman shook her head and then glanced back over her shoulder in the direction of the scene they'd begun cordoning off. "We don't think we've got another body," she said. "But until we take a better look, we won't know what we've got."

Martina felt her patience fraying. "Just spit it out. What is it?"

The woman heaved a sigh and glared at Martina over the rim of her mask as though she'd just been asked to lay her profession on the line. "Toys."

"Toys?" Ambrose parroted the word back, but when he said it, it sounded more like a question than a statement. Martina glanced over at him and noted the sudden pallor of his skin.

"Yeah, the kind children play with." The woman huffed out a breath behind the mask. "Now if you'll excuse me, I've got to go."

"Wait, why would toys be so interesting?" Martina asked, but the woman they'd stopped wasn't listening, and had melted back into the growing melee among the trees.

"We should get out of here, before we muck it all up," Ambrose said, indicating that Martina should go back the way she'd come.

"Why would toys be so interesting?" she asked, as they both tracked through the woods to the higher vantage point that overlooked the position of the body.

Ambrose shrugged. "Your guess is as good as mine."

"I saw your face back there," Martina said. "You've thought of something that you're just not sharing with me."

He glanced down at the scene unfolding beneath them. "It's probably nothing."

"Your face says otherwise," she pressed.

Ambrose glanced over at her and pulled a face. "It's just when she mentioned toys, it made me think of the three kids who went missing from these parts several years ago."

"You think this could be them?"

Ambrose shrugged. "I've got no clue, Nicoll, but if it is, then we're going to have a hell of a job finding the person responsible after all this time. Not to mention it's going to rip all those old wounds right back open."

"But if it is, then it'll help the families who have lived with that pain all these years. They'll get some closure from it..."

Ambrose shook his head and stared down at his boots. "Yeah, maybe... And then again, maybe it'll just bring them more pain." He sighed. "I'm going to head back to the car and let the DI know what we've got here."

Martina nodded, barely registering what he'd just said. As far as she was concerned, this could be the case that brought her the attention she was after. And maybe she would move up in the ranks. With everything going on at home, a pay rise wouldn't go amiss.

She glanced down at the people moving carefully back and forth. Perhaps the night wasn't a complete loss after all.

CHAPTER ELEVEN

DC MARTINA NICOLL slipped her arms into the navy suit jacket she'd left out the night before. Silently, she tiptoed around the room, and picked up her black boots from their position next to the cream wooden chair by her bed. By the time she made it out onto the landing of the small council terrace house she shared with her parents, the grey morning light had crept in through the window at the top of the stairs.

The house was blissfully silent, and she contemplated stopping long enough to make a quick cuppa before she was due in on shift. With her mind made up, she slipped downstairs. Pausing outside the kitchen, she reached up and took the key from the ledge above the entryway. Careful to keep noise to a minimum, she unlocked the door, and slipped inside. Setting her boots on the floor by the back door, she moved confidently around the space. Grabbing her travel mug from the cupboard, she dropped in two tea bags from the box of Yorkshire tea in the cupboard. Filling the kettle, she set it back on its base and flicked it on, momentarily dazzled by the brilliant blue light that lit up the small kitchen.

Thankfully, they'd replaced the whistling kettle two weeks previously, and things were better now.

"You're off out early, love." Her father's whispered voice took her by surprise, and Martina whirled around to face him. He stood framed in the doorway, the same grey cardigan he'd worn the night before, hung off his gaunt frame. Martina was certain it wasn't her imagination that told her his cheeks were hollow, and the dark circles beneath his eyes were blacker than usual.

"Sorry." Guilt rose in her throat like thick tar that threatened to choke her. "We caught a new case late Saturday night, and if I do well, I might get the chance to move up."

Her father's smile was worn around the edges, and the tension in the centre of Martina's gut increased. "It would have been nice if you could have stayed around for breakfast," he said. "But it's fine. I know you've got work."

Martina sighed. "Once this case is done, I'll be around more."

He shook his head. His blue eyes glistened in the half light that peeked through the blinds on the windows. "It's fine, Marty. I know you're doing your best."

"Do you want a cuppa?"

He nodded, his smile broadening. "That'd be lovely."

Martina set about taking down her father's favourite mug. She prepared the tea silently, aware of his presence in the room. When she turned around, she found him sitting at the table with his head in his hands. His greying hair was thinning on top, and as she set his cup on the table next to him Martina couldn't help but notice the purple bruise that had blossomed across his pate. "When did that happen?" Despite wanting to hit the road early, she felt compelled to drop into a chair opposite him.

"She didn't mean it," he said, his gentle voice tugged at her heart.

"She's getting worse. We both know--"

"I don't want to talk about it right now," he said. There was a firmness to his voice that belied the weariness in his face, and it took her by surprise.

"Well, then when are we going to talk about it?" She didn't mean to sound so harsh, but the words came out that way just the same. It was always this way.

"Marty, not now. Please."

If she pressed him, it would only end in an argument. That was all they did lately. There had been a time when she'd known her father to only raise his voice in merriment, but those days were long gone. It was strange; her mother's illness was whittling away at her memory, robbing her of the years they'd shared. And yet, that wasn't all it was slowly stealing from her. The more of her mum she lost, Martina was forced to witness the slow disintegration of the man she'd called dad. The weight of it all draining him of the life he'd once enjoyed; leaving this husk of a man in his place. Emotion, hot, and raw burned in the back of her throat, but she'd cried all the tears she had in her when they'd first received the diagnosis of mum's illness, and now there was nothing left.

"I'll try to get off early, come home for dinner," she said. She reached over to brush her fingers against the back of his work-roughened hands. They were cold to the touch, and she fought the urge to take his chilly hands in hers, and chafe some warmth back into his hands the way he'd once done with hers when she was a child.

"That'd be good," he said wistfully. "Your mum would love to see you. She misses you, you know?"

A sharp retort hovered on the tip of her tongue, but Martina bit it back. Her mother hardly remembered her, instead she called out for a Martina that had long since grown up. There were moments, brief sparks of happiness, where she remembered who she was supposed to be, but they were growing scarce, replaced by a suffocating darkness that swamped the house.

"I know you don't believe me," he said sadly, curling his hands around the belly of the mug. "But I see the moments more than you, because I'm here."

"And I'm not," Martina finished for him. The sting of his unspoken words caused her to press up onto her feet.

"That's not what I meant," he said hoarsely. "Marty, that's not what I meant."

"I know, dad. I need to go."

"Of course, love. Have a good day." There was an emptiness to his words that dug a hole in the centre of Martina's chest, as she gathered up her travel mug, and slipped her boots on at the back door.

"Do you need me to bring you home anything?"

He shook his head. "I'll be fine. Dorothea will be in later. I can always pop to the shops then."

"Right." Martina paused awkwardly in the door. "I really will try to get off early."

"Of course you will."

She left him sitting at the table, his gaze almost as vacant as she knew her mother's to be. By the time she made it to the car, she'd bottled her emotions up and pressed them down into a rapidly hardening ball in her chest. It was easier that way, easier to compartmentalise so that nobody knew just what she went home to every evening. If they knew the truth, Martina wasn't sure she could live with the pitying looks they would throw her way, like she was some kind of stray dog in need of affection.

Ambrose greeted her with a barely audible grunt as she slipped into the passenger seat, and Martina slipped her seat belt on, before she settled back against the faux leather slip covers. She sipped her tea and stared out the window.

"Have a good night?" Ambrose asked, finally breaking the silence.

"It was fine," she said curtly. "What about you?" That was all the encouragement Ambrose needed, and he launched into a full report on his pregnant wife's latest cravings. It was what Martina needed, and she fixed a smile on her face as she pretended to have an interest in his half-hearted morning moan.

Martina nodded and gave him the obligatory responses necessary to keep the conversation flowing. Keeping him at arm's length was best for everybody involved. Martina sighed and sipped more tea. Easy was good. Easy was right.

THERE WAS ALWAYS a distinctive smell that accompanied a trip to the mortuary. It was the kind of smell that, once it was in your hair and clothes, you stood relatively little chance of ever getting rid of it. Martina had learned early on that formalin was the potent chemical that crept up inside her nose and lodged in the back of her throat.

"You'll get used to it," Ambrose said, a smile curling his wide mouth as he leaned back against the wall. How he could be the picture of ease considering the scene that awaited them on the other side of the door was something Martina had never sorted out in her mind. There was a time when she'd wondered if his nonchalance was because of a lack of care, but she'd worked with him for long enough to know that wasn't true.

Even if he didn't show it, Ambrose cared. She'd asked him once why he did the job, and he'd told her it was because of his kids. She wasn't convinced that was the truth. After all, he hadn't actually been a father when he'd first joined. But when she'd pointed that out to him, he'd told her not to be such a pedantic prick.

"I couldn't ever get used to this smell," she said, wrinkling her nose in disgust. "If I worked here, I'd use an entire tub of Vicks every day. In fact, I know I'd use it so much I'd end up buying shares in the company who makes it." As she spoke she slipped the tub of Vicks Vapo Rub from her jacket pocket and smeared a thin film of the potent mixture beneath her nostrils. The scent instantly transported her back to her childhood when mum used to rub it on her chest anytime she had a cold.

Martina pushed the memory away; now was not the time to get caught up in such a sticky web. Dr Jackson stepped out of the examination room, his nose buried in a blue plastic folder. As he approached them, Martina coughed, causing him to lift his gaze.

"Oh, it's you," he said, making the statement sound like an insult. "I didn't know I was expecting you down here this morning." He frowned at them both, before he turned his hand over and glanced down at his watch. There was a momentary flicker of consternation on his face as he noted the time, but it was gone as quickly as it had arrived.

"You told us yesterday to come down on Monday. It's Monday now," Ambrose said amicably. From the corner of her eye, Martina watched the DS straighten up from his position against the wall, so that he towered over the forensic pathologist. If the doctor noticed the subtle shift in the energy in the room, he gave no indication of it.

"The forensic anthropologist isn't finished with her examination of the remains," he said dismissively. "So you've wasted your morning coming down her."

"Is there anything you can tell us?" Martina asked. Frustration made her voice a little sharper than she'd intended, but it caught the attention of the forensic pathologist.

"This isn't really my area," he said. "The flesh, and organs is where I specialise." He snapped the folder shut. Martina felt her shoulders drop. "However, from a cursory examination along with Dr Grieves when the body arrived here, we're both in agreement that the victim was male, mid to late twenties. There's evidence of a severe curvature of the spine which would have been consistent with a diagnosis of scoliosis. Dr Grieves noted some oddities along the larger joints."

"Could he have been dismembered?" Martina asked, unable to keep the excitement from her voice.

"I really couldn't say," Dr Jackson said exasperatedly.

"Could you give us an approximation of the time the body spent out there?" Martina asked. The more information they could glean from the doctor, the better their chances of getting an identification of the victim.

"Rough estimate the body has been there at least twenty years," Dr Jackson said. "We'll know more once the forensics team have finished collecting their evidence, and of course, you'll have to look into the details yourself, but from the evidence we have found on the body, I'd reckon it has been about that long."

Martina caught sight of Ambrose as he stiffened, and she glanced over at him. His face was pale, and Martina had the sudden urge to drag him away from the forensic pathologist and ask him just what he was thinking.

"Now, if that's all. I've really got to get some things sent off to the labs…"

"Of course," Ambrose said. He didn't wait for

Martina, and she had to practically run down the hall just to keep up with his long stride.

"What is it?" The question burst out of her mouth as soon as they stepped outside.

"That's roughly when those kids went missing," Ambrose said. "I mean they went missing twenty-one years ago from Dalby Forest, and Dr Jeckell in there reckons our guy has been out there for at least twenty years. That's too much of a coincidence."

"So how do you think it's connected? I mean, it's obviously not the body of one of those children. They were, what, ten when they disappeared?"

Ambrose nodded and scrubbed his hand up over his face. "I know it's not them, but this is too much to be a completely separate matter," he said. "We can't ignore what's obviously staring us in the face."

Martina raised a hand and chewed a fingernail as she pondered Ambrose's statement. He was right about one thing; it was definitely too coincidental to just be ignored.

"Where exactly did the children disappear?"

Ambrose screwed up his face in concentration. "I'm not sure exactly. They went camping, I think, and didn't come back..."

"Come on, Ambrose, we need a bit more than that. Dalby Forest is huge."

"It's not that big," he said.

"It's eight thousand acres," Martina said confidently. When they'd found the remains in the woods,

Martina had gone home that night and familiarised herself with the location. It had surprised her to learn there was such an extensive area of woodland practically on her doorstep, and she'd never bothered to go and investigate it. Not that she'd ever been the outdoorsy type. The idea of spending a night in the woods in a tent, sleeping in a bag, and the subsequent insect activity you would inevitably end up with didn't fill her with joy, and her mother's illness had taught her that life was far too short to do things you didn't enjoy.

Ambrose blew a low whistle out between his teeth, his eyes widening at the prospect of such a large area to cover. "So it's bigger than I remember it being as a kid."

"Just a tad," Martina said with a smile. "If we're going to look at a connection between this body, and the disappearance of those children, then we need a little more information to go on. Agreed?"

The DS nodded. "Fine. You're right. But if I'm right, you owe me a pint."

Martina shrugged. "Whatever."

"That's not a yes," Ambrose pressed.

"Fine. If you're right, I owe you a pint. I didn't think this was a competition."

"Ambrose's smile was broad. "Isn't everything?"

Martina shook her head as she followed him back toward the car. "We should start with MISPERS from that time, focusing in on young males who disappeared at the same time."

Ambrose cast a speculative glance back over his shoulder. "Are you fishing for my job?"

Martina shrugged. "Hey, you said everything was a competition; I'm merely following your example."

Ambrose's laughter warmed her to the core, and Martina couldn't help but smile. It felt good to be out here, finally, with something worthy to sink her teeth into. As she slipped into the car, she felt lighter than she had in a long time. This was what it meant to be alive, and at least out here she could forget the pain that awaited her at home. Out here, she could be free.

And that, she realised with a start, was all she'd ever wanted in life.

CHAPTER TWELVE

HARRIET PAUSED NEXT to Drew's empty desk. She tried not to review the case files he had spread out all over the wooden surface, but her curiosity got the better of her, and Harriet found it impossible to avoid scrutinising his impossible handwriting.

"I wasn't expecting to see you here today," he said, his voice making her jump. Harriet took a step back from the desk and plastered a smile on her face.

"I thought if you were free we could pop around to your place so you could pick up some more of your stuff."

A cloud momentarily passed over Drew's face, but then it cleared, and he was an impassive, blank slate again. "I've got a lot of work to get through here," he said. It was clear from his tone of voice that he was avoiding the inevitable.

"How about tomorrow, then?"

He pulled a face, and Harriet sighed. "I understand you don't want to go back there, but it's only temporary. Just as soon as you have what you need, you can leave again. But constantly putting this off isn't going to do you, or your wallet any favours."

His eyebrows disappeared up towards his hairline. "What does that mean?"

Harriet indicated the shirt he wore. "That's another brand new shirt, isn't it?"

Colour crept up Drew's neck above the line of his collar. "I don't know what you're talking about. I've had this old thing for years."

"I can see the creases from where the shirt was folded in its plastic packet, not to mention the plastic collar liner is still in place," Harriet said, not unkindly as she gestured to the edge that peeped out from beneath the white material.

Drew's hands shot to his neck; he caught the edge of the clear plastic collar stiffener and tugged it free. Screwing his face up, he pulled at his tie half-heartedly. "I was wondering why it felt so bloody tight," he grumbled. "Why do they put these bloody things in, anyway?" He caught Harriet's eye and sighed. "Fine, maybe I am avoiding it."

"You're building this up in your head, Drew. The more you do that, the harder this is going to be for you."

He bunched the collar liner up in his hands and closed his eyes. "Don't you think I don't know that?"

"But?"

He sucked a low breath in through his teeth. The whistling sound hurt Harriet's ears, but she didn't say anything to him. "Because when I go back there, then it's really over."

"This is about Freya?"

He shrugged. "I don't know anymore, but she's wrapped up in it, yeah."

"Do you want me to give you my professional opinion, or do you want my friendly advice?"

Drew cocked an eyebrow at her. "They're different?"

Harriet shrugged. "Sometimes."

Glancing around at the office, Drew nodded. "I'd like your advice as my friend," he said softly.

"As your friend, my advice is that you get your coat so we can go over there right now."

Drew glanced up at her in surprise. "I wasn't expecting that."

"Personally, I'm a fan of tough love," Harriet said. "And as your friend, I'm afraid it's time I told you to face up to your fears."

Drew glanced down at his hands, and without thinking about the repercussions, Harriet reached out to touch her fingers to his shoulder. He glanced up at her, a question lurking in the depths of his gaze. Withdrawing her touch, Harriet let her hand drop back to her sides.

"Anyway, I'll be right there with you."

"Fine, I suppose you're right." He glanced back down at the paperwork.

"I promise it'll be there tomorrow," she said gently.

Drew clambered to his feet and tugged his jacket off the back of the chair. "You know if this goes tits up then I'm going to have to reconsider our friendship," he said.

"That's not fair," Harriet said stiffly. "I gave you the choice."

Drew's laughter was tinged with tension. "It's a joke, Harriet." He sighed and glanced at her sideways. "Thanks for doing this."

"Wait until this is over to thank me," she said.

"I'm saying it now in case I forget to say it later," he said. "I know I can be a grumpy bastard, and I don't say it often enough."

Embarrassment caused heat to crawl up into Harriet's face. "You don't need to thank me. I know you'd do the same for me."

His grin brought an unfamiliar warm glow to the centre of Harriet's chest. "Anytime you need me to force you to do something you'd rather not, just give me a shout."

Harriet returned his smile with one of her own. "I might just have to hold you to that."

CHAPTER THIRTEEN

IT WAS dark by the time Drew parked his car outside his house. It felt like a lifetime ago since he'd last been here, but in reality, it was just a couple of weeks. He hadn't been brave enough to cross the threshold then either. Harriet's car came to a stop next to his, and Drew sighed. This time he wouldn't have that same luxury. If there was anyone on this earth who could force him to go inside and face up to the mounting fear he felt over everything that had taken place there, it was Harriet.

Why she cared was beyond him. There was nothing in it for her, which meant the only reason she was here was because she cared. It felt strange to admit that. The last person who had cared about him like that had been Freya. Not that she'd cared enough to stick around. The thought was loaded with bitterness, and no sooner had it popped into his head, Drew regretted it. Freya had been ill.

Even now, after all the time that had passed since her death, it was still strange to think of her in the past tense. She wasn't an 'is' anymore. All that remained of everything she had been, every possibility that had come together to form her into the person he had loved, was now nothing more than a memory tinged with sadness and regret.

Drew sighed and pressed his face into his hands.

A rap on the window next to his head made him jump, and he glanced up to see Harriet shivering outside the car door. It was now or never.

Pushing open the car door, he stepped out, acutely aware of the icy wind that slapped him in the face as he tried to suck in a lungful of clean air. Harriet chaffed her gloved hands together, and despite just getting out of her own car; Drew's gaze was drawn to the rosy tip of her nose.

"I didn't think the temperature was supposed to drop," she said, shivering inside the red coat she wore, which looked as though it was made more for fashion purposes than to provide any actual protection against the elements.

"Aye," Drew said, fishing his keys from his pocket; his own fingers stiff and unyielding, the reason for which had nothing at all to do with the inclement weather. "They're putting bets on whether we'll have a white Christmas."

Harriet rolled her eyes. "They do that every year, but I don't think we'd ever be that lucky."

Surprise caused Drew to halt and glance over at the woman next to him. "I definitely did not have you pegged for someone who liked snow."

Harriet shrugged. "You don't know everything about me."

She was right, and if he was honest with himself, there were a lot of things he didn't know about Dr Quinn. "What do you like about it?"

Her expression softened, and there was a wistfulness in her eyes as she glanced up at the sky overhead. "I have this memory of a Christmas when it snowed," she said. "I think I must have been very young, because it's so hazy. Kyle helped me to build a snowman in the front garden, and I remember thinking it was the happiest I'd ever been in my life." She sighed, and cleared her throat, glancing down at the ground underfoot, but not before Drew caught sight of the tears that glistened in her eyes.

"That's a beautiful memory," he said gently. Harriet nodded and sniffed loudly before she lifted her gaze.

"Well, are we going to stand out here, or are we going to bite the bullet and go inside?"

Drew swallowed past the panic that threatened to crawl up and out of his throat. He'd never thought himself a coward, but now he wasn't so sure. They paused on the doorstep of his house, and he turned the keys over in his hands. Talking to her had made it easier to get this far, but now it was down to him to take that next step.

"I can open the door if you'd prefer?" Harriet asked, her voice gentle, but insistent; letting him know that she'd got him this far, and she had no intention of letting him off the hook now.

"No, I can do this." He wasn't sure why it was so important for him to say it aloud, but it felt right. His hands shook as he raised the key and pushed it into the lock. His mouth was dry, as he leaned against the door, and turned the key so fast for a split second he wondered if a higher power would save him from having to go through with it all by causing the key to snap off in the lock. Not that he'd ever been so lucky.

The door popped open, a musty smell flooded out to greet them as he let the door swing inwards revealing a large stack of mail on the doormat. Drew glanced down at Harriet, half expecting her to shove him through the door, and when she didn't, he fought down the disappointment. As ridiculous as it would have been, having her physically manhandle him over the threshold would have been easier.

He lifted his leg, his foot a lead weight on the other end. "Maybe--"

Harriet shook her head as he glanced down at her. "You can do this, Drew. I know you can."

"I realise that," he said harshly. His heartbeat galloped in his chest, and sweat drifted down his spine. He could do this, couldn't he? His foot touched down on the carpet inside the door, but to him it didn't feel like the rough coir fibre he'd stepped onto a million times in the past. His eyes slid shut as the sound of crinkling plastic filled his ears.

He'd been so stupid to not see the trap Nolan had laid for him. Arrogant, even.

"Drew!" There was a sharpness to Harriet's voice that reminded him of that night. Christ, when she'd walked into the middle of it all had been the moment he'd lost hope. And it wasn't because he didn't think she wasn't capable. Just five minutes in Dr Quinn's presence was enough to inform anyone that she was capable of anything that came her way. No, for him it had been the knowledge that his own failure had brought her there to die, and there was nothing he could do to stop it.

It was that realisation that tipped him over the edge. "I can't--" he said, half falling, half lunging backwards out the door. Harriet stepped out of his way, shock marring her features as he rushed back towards the car. He didn't pause his headlong escape until his palms slammed into the still warm bonnet of the car. His mind reeled, and he was only vaguely aware of the ear-splitting sound of the alarm. He fumbled with the car keys, desperate to silence the panic.

Harriet's soft hands closed over his, stilling his frantic movements. She pressed a button, and silence swept in around them so insidiously Drew wondered if he'd lost his hearing altogether. Moving around to the driver's door, he turned and leaned against the solid hulking shape of his vehicle, before his knees gave out and he slipped down into a crouch.

"Drew, talk to me," Harriet said, kneeling in front of him. She peered up at him, concern etched into her features as she studied him.

"I suppose you think I'm a fool?" He couldn't hide the shame and scorn from his voice.

"That would be ridiculous," she admonished. "You're not a fool. You've been through something seriously traumatic. If I thought anything else, then I would be the fool."

He laughed, the sound a strangled bark that hurt the back of his throat. "You might not think I'm a fool, but I do. What kind of idiot can't even bring himself to go into his own fucking house?"

"The kind of man who almost died there," she whispered. Drew flinched, as though her words had the power to wound him as easily as Nolan's craft knife had.

"I've had other close shaves," he said. "But this..."

"I know," Harriet said. "This one was different."

"Do you really?"

"Do I really what?" She leaned forward, the cold pinking up her cheeks.

"Do you really understand?" He peered up into her blue eyes. It didn't seem possible that she could understand, not when he could barely wrap his own brain around it.

She cocked her head to the side, reminding him of a small bird watching a juicy worm in the dirt. "I can't entirely know how you feel," she said carefully choosing her words. "But I have been through my own traumas. I understand how painful they can be, how destructive they are."

"When Robert Burton tried to kill you, I don't remember you behaving like a complete knob the way I am."

Harriet's laughter was bitter, and she dropped her gaze so that her dark curls fell forward, hiding her face from him. He realized then just how much the extra length suited her.

"Don't you worry, I was just as much of a 'knob' as you think you are," she said. Harriet kept her gaze fixed on the ground, and Drew longed to ask her exactly what was going through that strange head of hers. "I actually had a meltdown in front a full lecture hall."

"I'm not sure I believe that," Drew said. Some tension he'd been feeling released slowly, like the unfurling of a tight fist in the centre of his chest. "At least, I'm certain nobody noticed."

Harriet's laughter was pure and unfettered; hearing it brought a smile to Drew's lips. "What's so funny?"

"You're talking about me as though I've somehow

processed my trauma far more deftly than you. When the reality of it all couldn't be further from the truth." Harriet cut off abruptly. Her expression shifted and Drew knew she'd locked him out.

"I suppose I've taken up enough of your time," he said, stiffly.

Harriet glanced up at him, her eyes quizzical, which made him think that she struggled to read him at least half as often as he struggled with reading her. "If you're sure you don't want to try again," she said.

Drew sighed and lifted his gaze to the house before he shook his head firmly. "No. I've had my arse kicked enough tonight." A lump formed in the back of Drew's throat.

"Well, if you're certain?"

He nodded. "I'm sure. You go on ahead."

"I don't like leaving you here like this."

He smiled. "I'm fine. Honestly, Harriet. I'll probably just head back to the office anyway. The paperwork won't do itself. You don't need to wait up for me."

"You need to give yourself a break sometime, and rest. You'll wear yourself out."

Drew rolled his neck and grinned up at her. "I get plenty of rest. I'm getting far too old for that kind of macho all nighter-shit that Maz pulls. And anyway, if I'm going to prove myself where this task force is concerned, then I need to at least get a couple of hours' kip at night."

Pushing onto her feet, Harriet extended her hand towards him. When his fingers closed around hers, the warmth he discovered there gratified him. Drew climbed awkwardly to his feet and regretted the moment he had to let her go. He dusted himself down as he noticed the silence that stretched between them.

"You know where I am if you need my help," Harriet said, her voice somewhat stilted.

"Sure." Clearing his throat, Drew closed his fist around his car keys as he tugged open the car door with his other hand. He studied her as she started back towards her own car and then paused. When she glanced over her shoulder, he could practically see the cogs turning inside her mind, but whatever she was thinking was lost on him. She opened her mouth, and then seemingly, she changed her mind and shook her head.

"Goodnight."

"Night then!" Drew slipped in behind the wheel of his car, as Harriet did the same. Her engine revved to life, and she carefully reversed out of her space. She kept below the speed limit, he noted as she pulled onto the road. Drew waited until the red flare of her rear lights disappeared left at the junction at the end of the road, before he blew out a long breath.

What the fuck was wrong with him? Had the trauma of everything that had happened between him and Nolan scrambled his brains more than he'd first believed? It was about the only explanation he could think of for his odd behaviour. Or perhaps it had more to do with the fact that he knew Harriet was seeing Matthews now. He squeezed the well-worn leather of his steering wheel, as a variety of images danced through his head. The idea of Dr Quinn spending even a second on that complete waste of oxygen killed him; not that he would ever tell Harriet that. There were some things she shouldn't be privy to, and that was definitely one of them. She wouldn't understand his disgust and knowing her, she would only take it personally. Drew couldn't let that happen.

Closing his eyes, he pushed the thoughts aside and brought his breathing under control. The tremor was gone from his fingers as he pushed the keys into the ignition. The car rumbled to life beneath him, and the headlights illuminated the front of the house he'd shared with Freya. Even now, despite the time that had passed, he found it difficult to accept that she was truly gone. There would probably always be a part of him who expected her to bounce into a room, her smile enough to thaw the ice that had taken hold in his chest.

Reversing out of his space, he swung the car around on the road. The squeal of rubber tyres on the tarmac seemed loud in the silence of the still night air. He would go back to work and finish the seemingly never-ending pile of paperwork on his desk. Sighing, Drew pulled away from the house without a backwards glance. The further he drove from the place where Nolan had nearly cost him his life, the easier it was to breathe.

Perhaps he would never again cross the threshold of that place. The idea was enough to create a bubble of laughter in the centre of his chest.

CHAPTER FOURTEEN

PUSHING the key into the front door lock, Harriet slipped into the dark hallway. She didn't bother flipping on a light; she knew her way around her own house to know the obstacles she needed to avoid. Slipping her coat off her shoulders, she popped her shoes off and set her keys on the small table in the entryway. The image of Drew's pale and drawn face hovered in her mind. How could she have been so stupid? Stupid and selfish, pushing him so hard. Some psychologist she'd turned out to be, especially when she couldn't even accurately read the level of trauma Drew was clearly suffering under.

Why hadn't he just spoken to her? Would it really be so terrible to share the burden of his pain with her? She'd thought they were finally getting somewhere. Ever since he'd agreed to stay with her, he'd seemed less troubled, lighter even. Had it all been a facade? If that were true, then Drew was a much better actor than she'd ever given him credit for.

Pressing her hand over her eyes, she leaned back against the wall and sucked in a deep, steadying breath. She couldn't make him talk, not if he didn't want to. It didn't matter that she knew it would help him; he needed to understand it too, and that was something that couldn't be forced.

"Stupid, Harriet, so stupid." She clenched her hands into fists and opened her eyes. He'd told her not to wait up for him, but despite how late it was getting, she was far too wired to sleep. Making her way through the house into the dark kitchen, Harriet flicked on a light and made a beeline for the fridge; the contents of which were more than pathetic. One of these days she would remember to go to Sainsbury's and pick up some essentials. Her hand hovered over the open bottle of wine, but she changed her mind at the last second and pushed the fridge door shut. She had far too much work to catch up on, and she'd promised herself that she would make some more notes based on the case notes that Drew had copied for her from the Jessica Tamblyn case.

"Coffee it is," she said, crossing to the kettle. It took her brain a couple of seconds to realise that the faint tapping at the kitchen window wasn't in her imagination. Fear crawled into her throat like a rabid animal that refused to be tamed. Her throat closed as the pressure built in her chest. She scanned the opaque window that overlooked the small patch of scraggly grass that made up her back garden, but it was impossible to penetrate the darkness that shrouded the glass. Sidling towards the door that led into the hall, Harriet's hand slid up the wall as she fumbled for the light switch. The second she flipped it, the room was plunged into darkness. The tapping —which up until that moment had been insistent— ceased instantly, sending Harriet's mind into overdrive.

Precious seconds ticked by as she stood with her back pressed to the wall and waited for her eyes to grow accustomed to the darkness. Slowly the world beyond the dark glass came into focus, but Harriet couldn't see anything past the swaying of the shadow cloaked trees of her neighbour's yard.

She hadn't imagined the noise; she was certain of that. Slowly, peeling herself away from the wall, Harriet crossed to the window and studied the small garden. There was nothing, at least nothing, that could have accounted for the noise she'd heard. There was a part of her that wanted to open the door to the outside and investigate any possible culprits, but good sense told her not to be so stupid. Instead, she checked the door was still locked before she turned on her heel and left the kitchen. Before she made it to the stairs, she checked the locks were still secure on the front door too. Only when she was fully satisfied did she feel some of the tension that had gathered between her shoulders slowly begin to dissipate.

Perhaps she had imagined it? She'd certainly had a lot on her mind. But the extra mental load wouldn't be enough to make her so jumpy she was imagining things that weren't really there. It wasn't until she was safely ensconced in her bedroom that Harriet truly let her guard down. Slumping onto the end of the bed, she contemplated calling Drew but changed her mind at the last second. She'd been alone for most of her life and had learned to look after herself. She didn't need anyone to ride to her rescue. Not to mention, it would only worry him and he had more than enough on his plate to juggle without her adding to his stress. She would tell him some other time. And anyway, in the cold light of day, things would look very different. Satisfied at last, she felt the last of her concern melt away. Tomorrow would come and it would bring with it some much needed clarity.

CHAPTER FIFTEEN

"OLIVER, do you think you could tell us exactly what you were doing out in the woods that night?" DC Martina Nicoll leaned forward, her expression sympathetic as she took in the pitiful-looking boy on the couch. His right arm was in a purple cast, held up on his chest with a white sling. His skin was pale, almost luminous in the lamplight.

"We were just messing around," he said sheepishly, letting his gaze fall towards his lap. With his unbroken hand he picked at invisible fluff on his jeans. Martina had seen her fair share of teenage boys when she was growing up, and her instincts said he wasn't likely to tell her a lot with his mum keeping watch over him.

"It was pretty late to be just out 'messing' around." Ambrose interjected. "Something drew you out there."

Oliver shook his head vehemently. "No. I'm telling you, it was nothing."

"That's not strictly true though, is it?" Martina probed. "We spoke to Darren, and he told us what was really going on." It wasn't strictly a lie. They had spoken to Darren, but his sullen silence, and his mother's insistence that he had nothing to tell them had hampered any chances of getting to the bottom of the situation.

"He did?" Oliver lifted his gaze, surprise causing his eyebrows to disappear beneath the mop of blond hair that had fallen across his brow. His face was rounded with youth, cherubic, Martina thought to herself as she studied him. Right now it gave him an innocent look, one that he probably used to his advantage. But that would change as he grew older, and she had a feeling that by the time he reached eighteen his youthful good looks would no longer be an asset. "I don't think Darren would talk to you," he said decisively. Oliver forgot himself, and tried to fold his arms over his chest, but the cast brought him up short, and he let his hand drop back into his lap.

"You know what we found out there, right?" Martina asked, deciding a different approach was needed.

"I don't think that's an appropriate line of questioning for my son," Mrs Poole said, interrupting the conversation. She sat stiff backed next to her son, her expression twisted into one of distaste. "My son had nothing to do with that."

"With all due respect, Mrs Poole, your son was the person responsible for discovering the body in the woods. We need as much information from him, as he is willing to give to us."

"You can't possibly think he had anything to do with it? He's far too young." Mrs Poole shook her head and glanced away. "It's ridiculous. Why on earth would you come back here? You should be out there searching for the person responsible." There was something in the other woman's demeanour that caused Martina to pause and take a second look at Mrs Poole.

"What makes you say that?"

"Excuse me?" Mrs Poole's attention shifted back to Martina. "What makes me say what?"

"You said Oliver was far too young. What makes you say that?"

"Well, it's obvious, isn't it? It was a skeleton the boys found in the woods..." Mrs Poole shifted a little closer to her son. "It must have been there for quite some time."

Martina's smile never touched her eyes, and she glanced down at the limited notes she'd taken from the meeting so far.

"Oliver, if you're not being honest with us, it's important you tell us now. We're going to find out the truth. It would be better if it came from you."

"That's quite enough," Mrs Poole said, making a move to stand. Oliver caught her arm with his free one.

"Mum, it's all right."

"No, this isn't right. If your father was here now, he wouldn't be happy to hear the turn this conversation has taken."

"They're right," Oliver said miserably. "I'm not being honest. I didn't mean to lie, but Darren said we should…"

"Why would Darren want you to lie?" Martina asked, shifting forward in her chair. From the corner of her eye, she caught sight of Mrs Poole's shocked expression, and couldn't help but feel somewhat gratified by it. "He said we'd get in trouble with AJ if we told."

"Who is AJ?" Ambrose asked.

"He's a couple of years above us. Darren has been hanging around with him. He said AJ promised him a new games console if we spent the night in the woods. I didn't want to do it because of the Owl Man, but Darren said if we did, we'd go back to school as legends."

"When you say Owl Man, who exactly are you talking about?" Martina tried to keep the interest from her voice.

Oliver shrugged. "I've never seen him myself, but we all know about him. If you go into the woods at night, he watches you and waits until he can grab you."

"That's nothing but a fairytale," Mrs Poole said somewhat harshly. "The police don't need you wasting their time with stories."

"It's not a story. We saw his eyes that night in the woods. They were everywhere, and they glowed in the light from our torches." Oliver sucked down a harsh breath, his eyes wide and serious. "And he's taken other kids," Oliver said firmly. "Everybody knows the story, mum."

"Please, excuse my son. Sometimes his imagination runs away from him."

"These other children," Ambrose spoke over Mrs Poole, completely ignoring her plea. "Do you know anything else about them? Like maybe where Owl Man might have taken them to?"

Oliver shook his head. "Darren thinks maybe he ate them."

Martina glanced over at DS Scofield as his eyebrows shot up towards his hairline. "And where did Darren hear that?" Ambrose's voice was devoid of emotion.

"I think maybe that's enough for today," Mrs Poole said, and this time she didn't hide her irritation.

"Mrs Poole, if there's something your son can tell us then--"

"He's just a young boy. There's nothing he can tell you about this whole thing." She wafted her hand in the air, as though the fact that her son had discovered a dead body while out in the woods at night was nothing more than a minor inconvenience. "And as for encouraging his imagination, I think we can all agree that it's a bad idea."

Martina nodded and pushed onto her feet. "You're right, we've taken up enough of your time."

Ambrose stubbornly remained where he was, and Martina fought the urge to reach down and pull him onto his feet. Instead, she pasted a smile onto her face. "If you remember anything else, no matter how innocuous it might seem; you know where to find us."

Mrs Poole nodded and darted a concerned look in Ambrose's direction at his lack of action. "We'll be getting out of your way." This time Martina didn't hold back, and nudged her superior with the toe of her black boot, causing him to grunt a response. Wearily he clambered to his feet, but Martina could tell from the expression he wore that he was lost in thought.

She followed Mrs Poole to the front door, and bid a farewell from the both of them, as Ambrose ambled out to the car parked in the driveway.

"What was all of that about?" Martina asked as soon as she made it over to the car.

"What?" Ambrose glanced up at her, his brow creased.

"That, in there," Martina said, gesturing subtly in

the direction of the house they'd just left. "The minute that kid mentioned missing children, you went all Rain Man on me."

Ambrose pursed his lips. Martina knew him well enough to know the look on his face meant he was debating telling her something he knew. Of course, she also knew pressing him wouldn't get the truth out of him any faster. If he didn't want to tell her something, then he wouldn't. No amount of cajoling on her behalf would change that.

"How does a kid that age know anything about a bunch of missing children from twenty something years ago?"

"You know how these things go," Martina said, climbing behind the wheel. "Kids tell each other stories to freak each other out. This whole Owl Man thing, it's probably become some kind of Urban Legend around these parts."

"You mean like The Hermit of Falling Foss?" Ambrose asked, as he folded his large frame into the passenger seat. He tucked his anorak around his body, blowing warm air down inside his scarf as Martina set about getting the engine and the heaters running.

"Never heard of him," she said, as she fiddled with the dials until finally warm air blasted from the vents.

"There's a cave carved out of a boulder down near Falling Foss," Ambrose said. "Locals call it The

Hermitage, dates back to the 18th century. Apparently some bloke lived there a long time ago, they called him the Hermit, he lived off the forest; foraging for food, and fuel."

"I was thinking of an urban legend more like Slender Man," Martina said with a grimace.

"Who's that?"

"Some kid dreamt him up on the internet, a veritable ghost story. Anyway, a couple of girls a few years ago in America tried to murder their best-friend in the woods near their home and told police that Slender Man made them do it."

Ambrose whistled low under his breath as he tucked his chin down into his scarf. "I swear this world is getting weirder, and weirder."

"You're telling me," Martina said. She sighed and put the car into reverse.

"We're not going to get anything useful from either of the kids, are we?" Ambrose said thoughtfully.

"Standard really," Martina said, as she navigated the busy cul-de-sac deftly. "They found the body by accident. They know nothing."

"You could be onto something though with that urban legend thing," Ambrose said, taking her by surprise. "You remember all of those reflectors we found nailed to the trees."

"You think that's a part of it?"

"Well, Oliver said they saw eyes in the forest.

When we were up there, they kind of looked like eyes watching us in the trees."

As Martina took them back towards the station, she had to admit he had a point. It was a possibility, but she was beginning to understand that the entire case was built on possibilities. She glanced over and caught Ambrose checking his messages. "Any news from the forensic anthropologist yet?"

He shook his head, and Martina's shoulders slumped. What they needed was a positive ID, something to build the case on. And until they had that, they would continue to stumble around in the dark.

"When we get back to the station, I'm going to go through the MISPERS list again," she said. "Something is bound to come up." She sighed. "At the very least it should narrow our list."

CHAPTER SIXTEEN

CREEPING along the edge of the house, he paused at the French doors, and peered in through the glass to the gloom beyond. Anticipation thrummed in his veins as he slipped away from the door and over toward the small downstairs toilet window. He pressed his gloved hands against the frame, sliding his fingers over the rough wooden surface until he felt the place where the timber had rotted. As he tugged gently, pieces of the frame came away in his hands before the window gave with a muffled thud.

He paused, listening to the silence that filtered back in around him. Despite being certain she was out, there was still a part of him that feared discovery. Fear was the wrong word; it was so much more than that. The idea of her returning to find him here, waiting for her, it caused his heartbeat to quicken, as his breathing came in short shallow pants.

The last one hadn't been as satisfying as he'd believed it would be. It had been wonderful, but over far too soon. This one he would savour. He would take his time, enjoy their time spent together before the end.

Pulling the window open, he climbed the bricks he'd painstakingly stacked against the exterior wall, and hauled himself through the downstairs window. She was always later to return these days, as though there was an instinctual part of her that knew about him, knew what he had planned and persuaded her to stay away.

Using the toilet seat as a step down, he landed lightly on the balls of his feet, before he let the window swing shut behind him. The air was still, the house quiet, but not as quiet as it would be once he was done here.

Confidence swelled in his chest as he moved over to the door that led to the rest of the house. Moving unseen through the house, he made his way to the stairs. From there it was just a few quick strides to her bedroom. He'd imagined it in his mind, visualising every aspect based on his observations of her behaviour over the months since he'd first laid eyes on her. Of course, after their last encounter, he'd backed off; tried to give her the time she needed to relax her guard. He climbed onto the bed, feeling the mattress sink beneath his weight. He could almost imagine she was beneath him, terror-stricken as he moved over her.

Killing the last girl had been a release of sorts, but now he was done playing games. There would be no more reprieve. Pressing his face into the pillow, he drew in her sweet scent, and closed his eyes against the flood of desire that thrummed in his veins. She wouldn't refuse him; that he was certain of, and not just because he wouldn't give her the chance to reject him. She was different. She would welcome him.

It was a lie, one he told himself to make the daydreams more pleasant. She wasn't strictly his type, a little too old for his taste if he was honest; but in the dark he learned that every hole was the same.

He lay on the bed, as the shadows stretched across the ceiling. The heating clicked on; the timer jarring him from his pleasant reverie. Pushing up onto his feet, he slipped open the dresser drawer and rummaged through the items. Pulling a pair of silk briefs from the depths of the drawer, he examined them in the dusky light that filtered in through the windows. They'd seen better days, but they would serve their purpose. He slipped them into his pocket before he reluctantly left the bedroom and returned down the stairs.

Pausing in the kitchen, he eyed the fruit bowl on the table before he gave into temptation and dropped onto a chair. Pulling an orange free, he peeled it quickly, discarding the skin on the tabletop. He popped the segments into his mouth, savouring the juicy pop of the flesh as he contemplated the peel. Leaving it out and exposed like this was a bold move. She would know somebody had been in here, wouldn't she? But hadn't he decided that this was it, didn't he want her to know her time was ending?

He left the peel behind as the sound of a car entering the drive pulled his attention back to the front of the house. Raised voices caused the hairs on the back of his neck to stand to attention. She wasn't alone. Fear gripped him, as he crammed the last of the orange into his mouth, and raced for the bathroom door. He made it inside as the key in the lock of the front door sent a shudder racing down his spine. The triumphant yip of her dog brought him out in a cold sweat as he climbed onto the toilet. Pushing open the window, he swung his leg out onto the ledge as the voices filtered through from the kitchen.

The whine of the dog at the door told him that at least one member of the house knew he was here. Heart hammering in his chest, he clambered out through the window and let it drop shut. The glass rocked in its frame, and for a moment he half expected it to drop out onto the ground, and give him away entirely. If that happened, it would be all over.

Closing his eyes, he waited for the smash of the glass, but it never came. Instead, he was greeted by the whining bark of the dog as it realised its prey was escaping.

Sweat dripped down his forehead as he ran for the side of the house, and the new gap he'd found in her fence line.

"Freddy, stop scratching. If you want out, then here--" The words were accompanied by the sound of the back door opening and the familiar sound of the little shit's nails tic-tacking over the patio.

He hopped the fence, and watched from his position of safety, as the dog sniffed around the bricks. It raised its hind leg and urinated against them, and he felt rage swell in his chest. She never brought people home with her. She was always alone. It was the reason he'd chosen her. She was safe. The epitome of a low-risk victim, and everything he'd ever needed. He'd picked her because he'd known when they finally met there would be nobody riding to her rescue. No accidental drop-by from a boyfriend. They would have as much time as they needed together. And he would finally have the chance to indulge in all the acts he'd seen in the videos from the internet.

And now, it was all crumbling around him. She was no longer as alone as he'd first thought. No longer the safe play thing he'd imagined she was.

Freddy the dog had burrowed through the shrubs that lined the fence line and peered up at him in the darkness. The dog stripped its muzzle back, exposing white canines in the twilight as a low growl slipped between its teeth. He stared past the dog as she appeared in the doorway.

"Freddy! Come on, boy!"

A man appeared behind her, and nausea slipped up the back of his throat as he watched her expression soften as she leaned back into his arms.

"Fuck!" He swore beneath his breath. As he spoke, Freddy gave up his pretext of growling and started to bark in earnest.

By the time Caroline Dunsly made it to the fence line, he was long gone.

CHAPTER SEVENTEEN

AFTER SCHOOL THE NEXT DAY, Oliver stood at the end of road a couple of yards from the town pond. Dalby woods stretched away behind him, the cycle path winding off into the trees. It was their meeting place—his and Darren's—the place they always met. He kicked the dirt with the toe of his trainers, knocking over a muddy clod of dirt. He lifted his hand to glance down at his watch, but sighed as he realised he'd swapped wrists because of the cast. The break wasn't as cool as the last time. Mum had been so much nicer then, but this time she was really pissed at him for lying.

Not that he could really blame her. If he was honest, he still felt bad about lying to her. She'd always done her best by him. When she'd arrived at the hospital and found him there on a bed in the A&E department, he'd seen the disappointment in her eyes and it had cut him to the quick. Not that he would admit that to her. That wasn't the sort of thing you told your mum, no matter how much you cared about her.

He sighed again. Darren had said he would be here.

Glancing over his shoulder towards the woods, he contemplated cutting through them to get to Darren's house. He'd probably forgotten his promise, being too busy with Fortnite to remember their plan. The trees loomed overhead, and Oliver swallowed down the fear. It was the forest that had got him into this mess in the first place. It wasn't strictly true, the path he would take to Darren's house was nowhere near where they'd gone in when they'd been searching for Owl Man. The other kids at school treated him differently now. He wasn't timid little Oliver Poole anymore. Now he was the kid who'd found a dead body and broken his arm in the process. The accident had given him a level of respect he hadn't been counting on. And of course Darren had been off with him ever since.

Darren was like that. When the limelight wasn't shining down on him, he got sulky. Oliver contemplated returning home and quickly changed his mind. Mum would only have more questions, and that wasn't something he wanted to face right now.

Sucking in a breath, he turned toward the woods, and the path that wound back through the tall trees.

He'd done this journey so many times before. This time would be no different.

Oliver adjusted his sling and started down the path. Just a short ten minutes and he would be at Darren's. It was simple... And there was absolutely nothing for him to fear.

CHAPTER EIGHTEEN

MELISSA CAUGHT up to Drew in the hallway as he tried to slip away without the others noticing him. "Where are you off to?"

"I've got stuff to do," he said evasively. Ignoring the curiosity in Melissa's eyes.

"No, you don't," she said confidently.

"And you would know this how?" Drew said dryly, pausing in the hall as he slipped his coat on.

"Because I know you, Haskell. You haven't changed a bit in all the years I was away. You're still the same old boring bastard you always were." There was a teasing note in her voice intended to take the sting out of her words, but there was still a part of Drew that felt the implied barb in her words.

"I didn't think anybody cared what I did in my personal time," he said. He cringed at the unintended harshness in his voice and watched as Melissa's expression shifted to something more contemplative.

"You know I didn't mean anything by that," she said. Melissa sighed, and pushed her hand back through her blonde hair, causing it to fall over her face. "Sorry, I know I can be pretty full on. I sometimes forget that my tongue is sharper than a razor blade." She smiled ruefully up at him, and Drew felt his irritation melt.

"It's fine. I'm just tired."

"You're still not sleeping properly, are you?"

"How did you know?"

Melissa's cocked an eyebrow at him. "You're not the first officer to get his bell rung by an offender, Drew. I've had my fair share of traumas through the years." For a split second her expression darkened, but the clouds that had momentarily passed behind her eyes were gone in an instant. "We should grab a drink, share war stories. You know, for old times' sake."

A rejection hovered on the tip of Drew's tongue. It would be easier to turn her down flat, but doing that would mean another evening searching for a place to live.

"All right then," he said, surprising himself and Melissa. "Just so we're clear, you're getting the first round in."

"Really?" Her brow arched, and a hint of a smile hovered around her mouth. "I'm fine with that. Let me grab my coat, and I'm all yours." She was gone before he could answer, and Drew wondered if he'd done the right thing. Perhaps it was nothing more than a mistake...

Melissa reappeared before he could change his mind completely. She took one look at his face and shook her head. "No chance, Haskell."

"What?"

"You're not worming out of this now. You're coming, and I'm getting the pints in. Now get a move on." Playfully, she shoved his shoulder, and Drew smiled despite himself.

"I'm going. I'm going," he said, laughing, as she continued to shepherd him down the corridor and out of the station.

A short while later, Drew sat at a booth in the Wetherspoons pub at the Angel Hotel in Whitby. Christmas decorations gave the place a festive air, and Drew found the tension in his body slowly unwinding as he leaned back against the dark leather seats. When Melissa had asked him where he wanted to go, this place had stuck out in his mind after his visit to Whitby the weekend before. His search for a new spot to call home had taken him all over, but he'd found himself drawn back to Whitby over and over. Freya would have said it was a sign; he thought it had more to do with liking the fish and chips.

Melissa carried two glasses over to the table and set them down on the dark wooden surface. She pushed the pint of Sharp's Doom Bar towards Drew, before she slipped into her seat opposite him.

"So, is this your local?" She glanced around, taking in their surroundings with a keen eye as she shrugged out of her dark jacket.

"Not exactly," he said, eyeing the drink. He could already imagine how it would taste. The cold, lightly roasted malt flavour would drift over his tongue, and quench his thirst easily. "What is that?" He asked, raising an eyebrow at Melisa's pale yellow pint.

"Cordial," she said. "Lime, actually." Noting the incredulous expression he wore, she shrugged. "I'm on-call."

"Fair enough." Clearly something had changed since he'd last known Melissa. When they'd been younger, she hadn't exactly been the most responsible, and the number of times he'd had to confiscate her keys, and call a taxi just to stop her driving drunk had been too numerous to count. In the intervening years she'd spent in Southampton, something had obviously changed to break her of that nasty habit. But Drew knew better than to press her on it. If she wanted to tell him what had happened, she would do it in her own time.

"You still having nightmares?" Drew almost choked as she blurted out her question.

"Nightmares, what makes you think that?" He coughed to cover his surprise at her insightful questioning.

"Like I said back at the station, you're not the only one who has run afoul of a bastard who wants to wear your guts for garters." There was a raw edge to her voice that Drew couldn't ignore.

"What happened to you?"

Melissa shook her head and glanced down at the roughly scarred surface of the table. "I've put it behind me now. It was a long time ago. I even went and had some counselling."

Drew felt his eyebrows creep up his forehead in surprise. "You really have grown, haven't you?"

Melissa screwed her face up and stuck her tongue out before she took a sip of her drink. "This stuff really is disgusting."

Drew laughed, the sound rumbling up through his chest and out through his mouth before he could stop it. It had been so long since he'd laughed so heartily, and he felt a little rusty at it. He choked off self-consciously.

Lifting his gaze, he met Melissa's contemplative expression. "It feels like an age since I heard you laugh so freely," she said.

"It feels the same for me," he said honestly. It didn't exactly surprise him that he was being so honest with Melissa, she'd always had that effect on him. The ability to slip beneath his barriers and needle her way through to the heart of his problems. It was a skill, and one he wasn't always pleased she'd mastered. "God, listen to me. I sound like some sort of old fool."

"Nah," she said abruptly. "Tell me how you got working with the head shrinker?"

Drew shrugged, awkwardness made it difficult for him to form the words. It felt wrong somehow to sit here and talk about Harriet behind her back. "She helped me with a case."

"And what, she was just so good you kept going back for more?"

If it had been anyone else, Drew might have thought there was an inappropriate undertone to the question, but because it was Melissa, he shrugged. "Something like that."

She shook her head, her blonde hair falling forward onto her face, concealing her from view as she studied the tabletop. "I've never understood that, you know," she said. "The fascination with psychologists. I mean, yeah, they're fine. And I'm not saying your psychologist isn't smart, but what we do... well, it doesn't need outside interference. We've always managed just fine without others sticking their nose in where it didn't belong."

Drew shifted in his chair defensively; just what was Melissa getting at? "You just don't know Harriet, that's all. If you knew her the way I did, you'd see she was an asset to the team."

Melissa raised her hands in surrender. "I'm not arguing with you, Drew."

"Then what are you saying?"

She shrugged with one shoulder. "I'm just telling you to be careful is all. These things have a tendency to go tits up fast. The team is too new to handle any kind of bad press."

Drew gripped his pint tightly. He could see her point, but he couldn't bring himself to agree with her. Harriet was different, he was convinced of that. He needed to convince the rest of them of the same thing.

"I'm sure I just need to get to know her," Melissa said abruptly. "Pay no mind to me, Drew. You remember what I'm like, always diving in where angels fear to tread." She smiled winningly at him and raised her pint of lime towards his. "Here's to working together again."

They clinked glasses, and Drew studied her surreptitiously as she set the glass down and tucked her hair behind both ears. She seemed uneasy, as though something had changed between them. When she glanced up at him, Drew smiled to set her at ease.

"Do you remember how we left things?" the question came out so abruptly that Drew found himself suddenly in the spotlight.

"Well, yeah—I mean, I guess so."

She nodded. "I wish we hadn't just let it all go like that."

His tongue felt thick in his mouth making it difficult to form words. Melissa smiled sadly. "You like her don't you?"

"Who?"

"The head-shrinker..."

Drew's phone vibrated, and he jarred his pint, causing the liquid to slop over the sides onto his fingers. "Shit," he said gruffly, as he reached inside his jacket with his free hand.

"Saved by the bell," Melissa said. Her brow crinkled as she pulled her own phone from her pocket and glanced down at the screen.

"It's a message from the DCI," she mouthed at him, as he lifted the phone out.

"The Monk is ringing me," Drew said, answering the call before he pressed the phone to his ear.

"Something has come up," the DCI said. "I know you're off for the evening, but this isn't something I can give to just anyone."

Drew pushed his untouched pint away. "What do you need from me?"

"I want you and DI Appleton to head over to Darkby, it's a small village near Thornton Dale. A woman has just reported her son missing. I've sent all the pertinent information to DI Appleton, and you should have the same once you get off the line."

"How old is he?" Drew felt a hollow pit open in his stomach. Kids were never easy, especially missing kids. Emotions ran high, and when the shit hit the fan things tended to spiral out of control far too quickly.

Gregson sighed. "Just gone eleven."

Drew watched the colour drain from Melissa's face as she scanned the message she'd received. He pushed onto his feet, and she followed suit. "We're not far away, sir," Drew said.

"We?" the monk asked. "Is Dr Quinn there with you?"

"No, DI Appleton is," Drew said, keeping the irritation from his voice. The way everybody else behaved, you'd swear he and Harriet were joined at the hip. "Should I call in Dr Quinn, sir?"

"I'll do that," Gregson said. "You just concentrate on getting to the house ASAP." The line went dead before Drew could say another word.

"The preliminary report suggests the kid has been missing for four hours," Melissa said, as she tugged her car keys from her pocket. "You want to come in my car?"

Drew nodded. "Fine by me," he said. "That way I can get us up to speed on the details."

Melissa's expression was businesslike, as she led the way out of the Angel pub and across the road to where she'd left the car in the Sainsbury's car park. "I hate when it's kids," she said through gritted teeth as she tugged the car door open.

It had started to rain since they'd gone inside, and Drew could feel the rain as it trickled down the inside collar of his jacket. He waited until they were both in the car before he answered her. "He's probably just stayed out too late, and forgot to call his mum," Drew said. It was a simple answer, but there was a part of him that just didn't believe it. He glanced down at the email he'd just received with the details of the case so far. There was no doubt in his mind that Oliver Poole's mother had exhausted every avenue before calling the police. After all, a missing child was every parent's worst nightmare, and most parents that Drew knew would have moved heaven and earth before admitting their child had become a devastating statistic.

"I hope so," Melissa said, as she gunned the engine. The tyres squealed on the wet tarmac before they caught traction. "But when are we ever that lucky?"

Drew didn't answer her, because the answer was far too depressing to admit out loud. Instead, he pulled his seatbelt across his chest and scrolled through the email as they drove through the darkness.

CHAPTER NINETEEN

HARRIET PERCHED in the chair opposite DCI Gregson's desk. He'd been oddly cordial to her, and it had set her senses on high alert.

"Why I really invited you here, well it's a delicate matter," he sighed and puffed out his doughy cheeks, seemingly incapable of meeting her direct gaze. He kept his eyes trained on the open set of files laid out before him.

"We haven't had the easiest of beginnings," Harriet said. "But I think the track record of my working with DI Haskell speaks for itself." Harriet fought the urge to fold her arms over her chest. The DCI didn't need to know just how defensive she felt. "I know the previous DCI wasn't my biggest fan."

Gregson's laugh was mirthless, and he glanced up from the files. "I think you and I know that's an understatement. He might have agreed to take you on because of the pressure coming down from on high, but he was happy when you turned him down." Gregson shook his head. "Why do you think he left Haskell high and dry?"

Harriet hid her surprise behind a bland smile. She'd known the DCI didn't like her, but she hadn't known that he'd deliberately left Drew out of the loop in order to guarantee she wouldn't agree to working with the team. It was beyond petty, but Harriet could also understand—at least on some level—why he'd wanted nothing to do with her.

"It was safer for him to keep you out of the loop, that way nobody knew his business, or exactly what he was up to." Gregson sighed and shook his head. "Damn waste if you ask me."

"You don't agree with his actions?" Harriet quirked an eyebrow as she leaned back in the chair.

"He was off his bloody rocker. We're not in the business of taking the law into our own hands here, Dr Quinn. If we were, there'd be a lot fewer scumbags taking up precious space in our prisons." He cut off, and the tension he was carrying seemed to melt away. "And while I know my team are more than capable of handling anything that gets sent our way, I'm not so narrow-minded so as not to realise we're better with you on board." Colour spread up through his face, and Harriet had a feeling that his admission had cost him something.

"I appreciate that," she said, a lump forming the

back of her throat. Praise from somebody as hard-headed as DCI Gregson was praise indeed, and that fact was not lost on Harriet.

"Don't thank me yet," he said gruffly. "If you try to damage this team--"

"I wouldn't dream of it," Harriet said archly.

"If you bring us unnecessary scrutiny from the press, and it interferes with our ability to do our job, I will consider that damaging to the team."

"I have no interest in the press," Harriet said, an uneasy knot forming in the pit of her stomach.

He studied her for a moment, his gaze searching her face. Whatever he saw there must have satisfied him, because he shrugged, and glanced down at the desk. "Then let's try to keep it that way," Gregson said.

"I think I've got a right to know what has brought this on," she said, tightening her grip on the arms of the chair.

"Suffice to say, not everybody is a fan of yours, Dr Quinn. And while that should be your business, I've got a feeling it will not play well for this team. So long as I know you're serious about your position here, and that you won't intentionally endanger the team, or the work we do, then I'm willing to stand behind you."

Harriet narrowed her eyes. "There's something you're not telling me," she said.

"Your friend Dr Connors is not your biggest fan, is he?"

Harriet felt her mouth go dry, and her throat constricted. "What has Jonathan got to do with my working with the task force?"

"I've got a contact in the press, and she has informed me that your mentor plans to write a tell all story about you, and the work you do with the police." Gregson's gaze was hard and penetrating, and Harriet tried not to wilt beneath the weight of the accusation in his voice.

"Why would he do that?" Her voice was strangled, and she coughed to clear her throat. Gregson was a man of action, he wouldn't take too kindly to seeing her flaunt any kind of weakness in front of him.

"You know him best, only you have the answer to that," Gregson said, not unkindly. "But I want you to think long and hard about this; have you shared any kind of operational information with him?"

Harriet blinked rapidly. "I would never share sensitive information with him."

Gregson glanced down at the desk. "Not even when you thought he was your ally?"

Harriet's stomach lurched uncomfortably. There was a time when she'd believed Jonathan was a friend, when she'd confided professionally in him. He'd quickly shown his true colours, but had she told him enough to endanger any of the cases she'd worked on? Harriet pressed her hand against her head, as a headache formed behind her eyes.

"Are you all right, Dr Quinn?"

"I'm fine," she said curtly. "I appreciate your warning regarding Dr Connors, but as far as I'm concerned I haven't told him anything he could use to disrupt any of the cases we have worked together on."

"Nothing about Robert Burton, or perhaps Nolan Matthews?" Gregson asked, cocking an eyebrow at her.

"Nothing he couldn't have read from a newspaper," Harriet said. If she was honest with herself, she couldn't fully remember everything she'd said to Jonathan, but she was certain it wouldn't have been anything he could use against them. There was a part of her that wanted to refuse to believe Gregson, but she knew better now. Jonathan was capable of anything, and his jealousy was the kind of destructive emotion that would make him want to destroy anybody who he perceived to be more successful than he was. "If that's all?"

"Not quite," Gregson said. "I wanted to make sure we were all on the same page here before I involved you."

"Involved me in what?"

"We've got a missing eleven year old. I've sent Drew and DI Appleton over to the scene already."

"But you wanted to test my loyalty before telling

me anything?" She arched an eyebrow at the other man, but if he was bothered by her words he never let it slip.

"I had to be certain."

Harriet nodded. She could understand Gregson's motivations and on some level she admired him for it. But it left her in no doubt that her position on the team was tenuous at best and that the least little incident would see her kicked to the curb. "I understand."

"Good. The team is over in Darkby, I'll send the exact location to your phone." Gregson nodded, and Harriet pushed onto her feet. She reached the door before he spoke again.

"If you get into any kind of difficulty with Dr Connors, I would prefer you come and speak to me about it," Gregson said.

"I'm sure I can manage anything Dr Connors might attempt," she said sternly.

"That's the beauty of being on a team, Dr Quinn, you don't have to do anything on your own. I get the sense it's something you're a little unfamiliar with; but it's important that you understand it because anything that he tries to do to you, will inevitably reflect on the rest of us." He sighed. "We all make mistakes regarding the people we think are our friends at some time or other. Live long enough, and you might even find yourself married to one or two of them."

Harriet didn't know whether to take his statement as a kindness, or if he'd intended it to sound like a threat. Judging by the lack of censure in his voice, she took it as a kind warning for her to watch her back. Not that she'd needed him to tell her that Jonathan's behaviour had taken her by surprise, but she'd learned her lesson, and she'd sworn she would never allow herself to be so vulnerable around another person.

"Thank you," she said stiffly. "I'll bear that in mind."

"That's all I ask," Gregson said, before he nodded for her to leave. Stepping out into the hall, Harriet paused and leaned back against the wall with her eyes closed. She'd only just got here, and already she was making a giant cock up of the whole situation. Of course, if Jonathan knew what she was doing, he would be pleased. She would just have to ensure that he never found himself in a position to have the upper hand against her ever again. She contemplated the letter of concern she'd sent to the directors of the hospital where he worked. She hadn't heard anything new and the lack of information made her a little nervous. Despite all of that, Harriet couldn't bring herself to feel bad about her actions. The letter was a damning one, and if she was correct in her thinking then it would as good as destroy his career. But deep down she knew it had been the right choice. But what would his response be? Was this threat to pen a tell-all piece in the paper part of his revenge? He'd already proven himself to be somewhat unpredictable in his behaviour.

Discomfited, Harriet pulled her bag in against her chest. She wasn't the frightened little girl he'd once known. Her phone bleeped in her bag and Harriet pulled it from the dark depths and scanned the address. There would be time to contemplate her actions later, but for now she would have to put all thoughts of Dr Connors and the repercussions of her letter aside and focus on the task at hand.

CHAPTER TWENTY

THEY PARKED up outside the semi-detached house on the edge of the picturesque village of Darkby. Drew climbed out of the car first, painfully aware of the twitching curtains from the neighbouring houses. He caught sight of the marked police car parked haphazardly across the front drive and made a beeline for it.

One of the uniformed officers stood in the open car door, and Drew caught fragments of the conversation he was having with the control room.

"DI Drew Haskell, and this is my colleague DI Melissa Appleton," Drew said. He didn't have to look over his shoulder to check that Melissa was with him. They'd worked together enough times in the past that they instinctively knew each other's moves. And having her at his back made him feel comfortable, like returning home after a hard shift. "Please tell me you've got good news about the boy."

The PC looked to Drew to be a man in his mid-forties, broad, and stocky. His features were nondescript—no doubt allowing him to blend in seamlessly with his surroundings—his bald head glistened in the mist that fell around them. Drew felt the other man's blue eyes rake over him from head to toe. It was a hazard of the job, and something Drew had been guilty of on more than one occasion.

"You lot got here fast," the other man said with a broad Yorkshire accent. "Unfortunately, we've got nothing on the boy yet. Control room is going to check CCTV in the area."

Drew nodded. "Who's inside?"

"We've asked control for a FLO, and PC Grey is inside with the mother. We've been trying to get in contact with the boy's father, but he's a long-haul trucker and we're having a few difficulties getting a hold of him."

"We need to get some more uniforms down here. Start going over the boy's last known footsteps," Melissa interjected, her voice heavily laced with authority. "And can we start door to door enquires. I'd rather we didn't wait on something like that. If the boy turns up in the meantime then no harm no foul, but if he doesn't..." She left the last of her sentence unspoken. It wasn't something that needed to be said. They were all painfully aware of the statistics in a situation like this. If he'd just run off, then getting him home safe and sound was a priority, but if he'd been taken. Drew pushed the thought away. It was far too soon to think so negatively.

"I'm going to head inside," Drew said, addressing Melissa. "Do you want to coordinate with the uniforms?"

There was an almost imperceptible tightening around her mouth, but Drew knew her well enough to notice it. "That's fine," she said. "I'll see what I can do with getting more uniforms out here."

Drew said nothing, and instead started up toward the red front door, which stood ajar. From the hall, he could hear the panicked voice of what he assumed was Oliver Poole's mother. He followed the sound into the open plan living room.

"My name is DI Drew Haskell," he said, as he moved in through the living room door. The woman he assumed was Oliver's mother sat opposite the door, her face buried in her hands. She raised her panic-stricken face as he spoke.

"Did you find him?"

Drew shook his head. "I'm sorry. We don't have anything new about your son. If it's all right with you, I'd like to ask you some questions."

"Why, what good will that do?"

"We need as much information as we can possibly get. That way we stand the best chance of getting him home, as quickly, and as safely as possible."

"He wouldn't stay away like this," she said, sounding more distraught as the seconds ticked by. "He knows not to stay out like this."

"You said he'd been out at the weekend," PC Grey interrupted. "That he'd stayed in the woods with a friend of his where he broke his arm, is that correct?" Drew wasn't keen on the bored tone in the uniformed officer's voice, but he remained quiet. It wouldn't do them any favours to muddy the water right now.

"With Darren Makston, yes, that's correct. But I don't see what that has to do with anything?"

"Is it possible Oliver went over to his friend's house, and they've lost track of time?" Drew asked.

"Don't you think I already thought of all that," Mrs Poole said, her voice rising. "Darren was the first person I called, but he hasn't seen Oliver this afternoon. He said they'd agreed to meet after school, but he was late getting to their meeting spot, and there was no sign of Oliver." She groaned and shoved her hands into her hair where she tugged at it violently as though trying to rip it out by the roots. "I should be out there, looking for him." She pushed onto her feet, and made a lurch toward the door, but Drew blocked her escape with his body.

"I don't think that's a good idea, Mrs Poole." He held his hands out and herded her gently back towards the couch. "Is there anyone else Oliver would go to see? Or has anything particularly upsetting happened lately that might cause Oliver to want to run away from home?"

"He wouldn't just leave," she said weakly.

Drew waited patiently for her to pull herself together. "If you'd give me a couple of moments with my colleague here, Mrs Poole, I'll be right back." Drew indicated with his head for the uniformed officer to step out into the hall, leaving Mrs Poole to sob silently into her hands.

"Did you get a description of the boy?" Drew asked. He kept his voice low so the woman in the other room wouldn't hear everything he said.

"We've got one," PC Grey said with a kind of confidence that grated on Drew's nerves. "I took down the details of his friend Darren Makston too, we could go around there and have a word with him?"

Drew nodded. "The mother mentioned he broke his arm over the weekend. Do we know what actually happened there?"

PC Grey shrugged nonchalantly. "You know what young lads are like, sir. They were probably rough housing in the woods, and he broke his hand."

It was a possibility, but Drew preferred to deal in certainties. "I'll ask the mother," he said, taking a step back toward the living room.

"Sir, we're not really thinking anything has happened to him, are we?"

Drew cocked an eyebrow in the direction of the gangly PC in the hallway. "I hope not, PC Grey. But until we know exactly what has happened here, we have to take this seriously. If the boy has just run off, fine, we'll bring him home safe. But if somebody is stopping him from coming home..."

PC Grey nodded. "Got it, sir, I'll go and drop by the friend's house."

Drew said nothing as he pushed open the living room door and found Mrs Poole rummaging through photographs in an album. "I've got some other recent pictures," she said frantically, holding a pile of pictures out to Drew for his perusal.

"This is very helpful," he said, as he took a seat next to her on the couch. Carefully, he gathered the bundle of pictures she'd given him, and flipped through them. "You said Oliver broke his hand at the weekend. Can you tell me how that happened?"

Mrs Poole paused, and while Drew didn't think it was possible, her face seemed to whiten. "He fell. Hit his hand on a rock and broke his wrist."

"And Darren was with him at the time?"

She nodded. "It was a dare..." The words were whispered, and Drew straightened up, as the tone of her voice set off alarm bells in his head.

"A dare? Darren dared Oliver to do something, and he broke his wrist?"

She shook her head. "There was an older boy at school—I think Oliver said his name was AJ—he dared Darren to spend the night in the woods."

"And Darren brought Oliver along?"

She nodded and swiped at the side of her eye almost absentmindedly. There was a knock on the door, and Drew glanced up, somewhat irritated by the interruption. Clearly there was something Mrs Poole wasn't telling him about her son. Either he was involved in something he shouldn't be, or Darren was, but Drew knew if he got to the bottom of it, he would be one step closer to finding the missing boy.

Harriet stepped into the room, her expression sympathetic as she took in the scene. Drew pushed onto his feet and indicated toward Harriet as he spoke. "Mrs Poole, this is my colleague Dr Quinn."

"I don't need a doctor," Mrs Poole said. "I need my son." There was a strength in her voice that hadn't been there a moment before.

"I'm not that kind of doctor," Harriet said. "I'm a forensic psychologist. I work with the police on some of their cases."

The last remaining colour drained from Mrs Poole's face. "Oh God, you think he's dead, don't you?"

"Right now, we don't have enough information to lead us to that conclusion," Drew said. "We're treating your son as a vulnerable missing person, and we will conduct our enquires based on the assumption that he is alive, and that we will bring him home to you." Making the statement aloud, left Drew with an uncomfortable knot in the pit of his stomach. It wasn't a lie, but it felt a little too close to him, making a promise he wasn't entirely sure he could keep.

"I'd just like to learn about Oliver," Harriet said gently. "Can I sit with you?"

Mrs Poole nodded and cleared a space on the sofa for Harriet. Drew watched as Dr Quinn settled in next to the woman. He hadn't realised until she'd walked in the door that he'd felt tense without her, but now that she was here he felt somewhat relieved. As though her presence alone would guarantee a positive outcome. It was ridiculous, of course, and he knew it, but he couldn't shake that feeling.

"DI Appleton was looking for you when I came in," Harriet said. "Some kind of crossed wires."

Drew smiled tightly. "I'll come back in a few minutes," he said.

"Would you like to show me a picture of Oliver?" Harriet asked, all of her attention focused on the woman next to her.

It seemed to be just what Mrs Poole needed to hear, and Drew left the two women alone in the living room, as he retreated out into the cold air.

DREW MET Melissa in the entryway as he escaped from the living room. "What's going on?"

"Two coppers have just turned up here," she said. "A DS, and DC who seem to think this case belongs to them." There was no escaping the irritation in Melissa's voice, as she folded her arms over chest.

"Why would they think that?" He kept moving, forcing her to step out onto the doorstep, or be left behind.

"How would I know? They didn't get the call on this, we did. What's that in your hands?"

Drew glanced down at the pictures he clutched in his fingers. "Mrs Poole thought these might be helpful," he said raising the images so that the top smiling photograph of the young missing boy caught the porch light.

"I can get these into circulation," Melissa said, scooping them up.

Drew spotted the two detectives the moment he stepped outside, and without waiting for Melissa to say anything, he started toward them. "DI Haskell," Drew said cordially. "My colleague, DI Appleton, said there was an issue?"

The male detective was tall, his shoulders so broad Drew was surprised he'd managed to find a suit jacket to fit him. In contrast, the woman next to him was petite, her face gaunt, and as Drew came level with them he noted the dark circles beneath her eyes.

"DS Ambrose Scofield," the man said, as he thrust

his hand out towards Drew. "And this is my partner, DC Martina Nicoll. We've come up from York."

"What brought you out this far?"

"There was an incident at the weekend, and we happened to be on call," the DC said, her voice clipped with barely restrained anger.

"This incident wouldn't by chance have had anything to do with Oliver Poole, would it?"

Ambrose nodded. "He broke his arm. Was out with his mate Darren Makston and fell into a hollow in Dalby forest. We called by here yesterday afternoon for a quick chat."

"Why would you do that?" Melissa asked, derision coating her words. "Don't you have anything better for doing? Is that why you've come down here? You've got nothing up there, so you're down here sniffing around our patch?"

From the corner of his eye, Drew caught the subtle shift in the DS as he stiffened beneath Melissa's insult. "It's not like that--" Ambrose started to speak, but it was the young DC next to him who beat him to the punch.

"For your information, we were down here investigating a murder. While you were all off living it up at the weekend, the rest of us were doing real policing." Drew took a step forward and held his hand up before Melissa could get another word out.

"We don't need to be at each other's throats," he said amicably. "We're all on the same side here."

"Tell that to her," DC Nicoll said, pointing at Melissa.

"That's ma'am to you," Melissa said, visibly bristling.

Blowing out his cheeks, Drew moved so that he was blocking the young DC from Melissa's view. "You said you were investigating a murder." He directed his question to the detective sergeant, who stood with his hands jammed into his pockets. "I'm not sure I understand what that has to do with Oliver Poole. He broke his arm, but he wasn't murdered."

Ambrose grinned. "Aye, that he wasn't. When he took a spill, he landed on a body. Well, a skeleton really."

"Excuse me?" Drew couldn't keep the incredulity from his voice. "You're telling me that our missing boy literally tripped over a body at the weekend, and nobody thought to inform us?"

"We're informing you now, aren't we? Although why we've even bothered, I don't know," DC Nicoll said bitterly. "You lot with your task force will pounce on our case, and sweep it all under the same bloody rug."

"Do you have an ID on the body yet?" Melissa asked, and all traces of her earlier anger had disappeared. It was her ability to blow hot and cold on him that Drew had forgotten about, but he certainly hadn't missed it. The memories came back to him, and he remembered thinking that her constant mood swings did nothing but give him whiplash.

"We're waiting on DNA to come back," DC Nicoll said stiffly. "But you know how long that can take."

Melissa nodded sympathetically. "Maybe we can do something to speed that up."

"Can we get back to the situation at hand," Drew said impatiently. "We've got a missing eleven-year-old boy out there, and you lot have actually spoken to him. What can you tell us about him that his mother can't or won't?"

Ambrose raised his eyebrows and rocked back on the heels of his boots. "To be honest, he seemed like a good lad. Shocked him to find the body like that, even if it was just a skeleton. I'd have been only too happy to pull something like that outta the ground when I was his age, but he was one of them quiet types."

DC Nicoll nodded. "The geeky type," she said. "And a bit of a mummy's boy, who wasn't yet ready to grow up."

"What makes you say that?" Melissa asked.

"I don't know, just something about him felt very young. Maybe naïve, even. You know how most young blokes nowadays are always far smarter than their parents. They know everything, and can't wait to cut the apron strings, so they can get out there into the big wide world?"

"Yeah," Drew said.

"Well, I don't think Oliver was like that. I got the impression he would have been happier to stay at home watching telly, or playing video games rather than go out messing with others his age."

Drew nodded. "So, running away isn't likely then is it?"

Ambrose shook his head. "I'm going to agree with Nicoll on this. He didn't feel like the running away sort."

"Shit," Drew said emphatically.

"Well, he got hurt out in the woods once," Melissa said. "Maybe he went back there for something."

Drew nodded. It was as good a lead as any they had, and considering they currently had nothing at all, he was willing to grab it with both hands. "Fine, get some of our uniforms together, and can you take them to the place where the body was found." Drew directed his question to the DS and DC in front of him. "Have the SOCOs cleared that scene yet?"

Nicoll nodded. "They finished yesterday. So there won't be anyone up there tonight. I can show the uniforms the spot." As she spoke she tilted her head in the direction of DS Scofield as though to get his silent approval.

Drew's smile was grim. "Good, at least we don't have that to contend with too. If I remember rightly, Dalby forest is a lot of ground to cover." He turned to Melissa. "See if Gregson will sign-off on our use of the helicopter."

"What are you going to do?" Melissa asked.

Sighing, Drew pushed his hand back through his hair. "I'm going to ask Mrs Poole why she didn't bother to tell me about her son and his accidentally stumbling onto a dead body in the woods."

CHAPTER TWENTY-ONE

THE LIGHTS on the Christmas tree in the corner of the room blinked in random succession, making Harriet feel a little seasick. She had never been a fan of the out of control feeling it invoked in her because it reminded her too much of her mother. "You must be very proud of your son," Harriet said, gripping the photograph Mrs Poole handed to her.

"He's such a good boy," the distressed mother said, dabbing at the corners of her eye with the shredded tissue she held in her hands. "He wouldn't stay away like this. He knows how much I worry about him."

Harriet glanced down at the picture of the shy boy who smiled timidly up out of the photograph at her. "And it's not like him to lose track of time with his friends, or--"

"No!" Mrs Poole said, shaking her head vehemently. "He knows the rules. And if he was going to be late, he'd have rung home by now."

"Oliver has a mobile phone?"

Mrs Poole sighed. "We didn't want him to have one, but everybody does nowadays. We thought by letting him have one he could use it to stay safe." She sighed. "But it's become an extension of him now. He doesn't go anywhere without it."

Harriet smiled kindly at the woman beside her. "I can imagine. In today's world, everything is always so busy. We've all discovered an innate need to be connected to everything all the time."

Mrs Poole nodded. "Exactly, and I just can't say no to him." She looked tenderly down at the photograph. "I think we spoil him a bit, but he deserves it."

Harriet thought it was an odd thing to say, but kept her thoughts to herself. After all, spoiling a child wasn't an unusual thing for a parent to do, but it felt odd that Mrs Poole would describe it as she had.

"Does he ever have any problems at school?"

Mrs Poole shook her head absently stroking the edge of the photograph with her thumb. "No, at least not anymore. He's a smart boy. Oliver has always done well in his exams. Says he wants to be a doctor when he grows up." She looked up at Harriet then, and her eyes glistened with unshed tears. "He's coming home, isn't he?"

"DI Haskell, and the rest of the team will do their utmost to get him back to you."

"That's not really an answer though, is it?" Squeezing her eyes shut, Harriet watched as a tear slipped from beneath Mrs Poole's lashes, and snaked its way down her cheek. "If I tell you something, promise you won't think I'm an oddball?"

Harriet patted the other woman's hands. "There's nothing you could tell me that would make me think that." It was the truth, when it came to confessions, Harriet was confident she'd heard nearly everything. And the depth of depravity of some things Harriet had heard during her time working in forensic psychology made it almost impossible for this reserved mother from North Yorkshire to shock her.

"I'm afraid to say it out loud, because when I do I know it'll be true," she whispered. When Mrs Poole opened her eyes, mascara had smudged on the papery, almost translucent skin beneath her eyes. There was a frantic expression in her eyes that hadn't been there a moment before, and Harriet felt a sense of foreboding rise in her chest. "I think he's gone."

"Why would you think that?" Harriet asked. She kept her voice level, and devoid of emotion.

"A mother knows these things," she said, and her voice broke over the last word. "They tell you not to lose hope. That where there's life, there's always hope." There was a twisted bitterness to her voice now, and Harriet knew there was something the other woman wasn't telling her.

With Mrs Poole's gaze pinned on the

photographs in her lap, Harriet took a second cursory glance around the room. From her vantage point on the couch, she couldn't see anything that might indicate the other woman's point of view, but there was a niggling in the pit of Harriet's stomach that told her Oliver wasn't an only child after all.

"You have another child?" Harriet asked, noting the way Mrs Poole's mouth tightened almost imperceptibly.

"Amy would have been fourteen last weekend," Mrs Poole said quietly. "Leukemia. An aggressive form of it. She passed when she was nine."

"I'm so sorry to hear that," Harriet said, but her words felt hollow. "Did Oliver remember much about his big sister?"

Mrs Poole nodded. "He does, probably not as much as he says he does, but I know he remembers enough of her. They were very close, and when she got sick, even though he was so young, they seemed to grow closer. When she passed he got so quiet, so introverted. It made him very vulnerable..." She trailed off. Harriet noted the subtle stiffening in the woman's shoulders, and the dark blotchy colour that crept up the side of her neck.

"You say it made him vulnerable," Harriet said. "What do you mean by that?" Alarm bells were chiming in her head, but she needed to hear it from the woman sitting next to her before she jumped to any kinds of conclusions of her own.

"It was nothing, really."

"I don't think that's entirely true," Harriet said, keeping her voice kind, but firm. "We need as much information as you can share with us, so we can bring your son home."

Mrs Poole swallowed hard and glanced down at the pictures. "There was a caretaker at the school," she said hoarsely. "Oliver didn't tell us, because he couldn't, his grief it made him mute."

Harriet nodded sympathetically. "I've heard it can happen in young children who undergo trauma."

"And losing his sister. It was a trauma for Oliver. He didn't understand, I think he blamed us for her passing." She sighed.

"What happened with the caretaker at Oliver's school?" Harriet pressed. As much as she hated to do it, she knew it was necessary for Drew to have all the facts.

"The police at the time said he'd been grooming Oliver. He maintained it was nothing more than a friendship, but there were some pictures on his hard drive." A look of revulsion rolled over her face as she spoke. "Oliver refused to talk about it with us, and he wouldn't say anything to the counsellor so we never got the full story. We let him down, I should have known..."

"This man," Harriet said. "Do you know where he is now?"

"I don't actually know," she said. "He received a

custodial sentence, and we were told he'd be placed on the sex offenders registry--" She cut off as a thud from the hall broke her concentration. "Oliver, is that you?"

"Karen, it's me." The man who stepped into the living room was tall, his receding hairline made him appear older than Harriet supposed he truly was. There was something about his eyes that seemed familiar to her, and when she glanced down at the photograph of the shy Oliver, she realised where the resemblance had come from. "He's not home yet?"

Mrs Poole shook her head and fell into the man's arms. "What if something has happened to him, Carl? What if something awful has happened to our boy?"

Harriet stood awkwardly, watching the meeting unfold. Mr Poole's eyes fell on her, and there was a darkness that seemed to sweep up through him as he manoeuvred around his wife.

"What are you lot doing hanging around here? Why aren't you out there searching for my boy?"

"I can assure you, Mr Poole, we're doing everything we can."

He snorted derisively and shook his head. "Doing everything would be you out there!" He jerked his thumb in the direction of the hall. "Not in here, hassling my wife, and upsetting her further."

"The last thing we want to do is upset you, or your wife further, Mr Poole," Drew's voice cut through the tension in the room. And Harriet instantly felt more at ease. Having him at her back made it easier to ask the inevitably more difficult questions she needed to get answers to.

"DI Haskell is correct," Harriet interjected. "Unfortunately, some questions we have to ask will make you feel upset, and uncomfortable." From the corner of her eye she caught Drew's interested glance, but Harriet kept her gaze firmly fixed on the couple in front of her. "We need to know the name of the man who groomed your son."

The tension in the room skyrocketed. Clenching her hands into fists by her side, Harriet kept her expression impassive.

"You told them about that?" Carl asked, incredulity lacing his voice.

"What did you expect me to do? I couldn't very well ignore it, and anyway, it's not as though it isn't true."

"Oliver said nothing happened." Carl sounded apoplectic as he pushed away from his wife and paced about in the small living room.

"He wasn't ever the same after it," Karen said, a noticeable tremor in her voice. "He used to be so happy, and then..."

"I'm sorry, can somebody catch me up here," Drew said, his usually calm tone seemed—to Harriet —a little more frayed than usual.

"After we lost our daughter Amy, well, Oliver--"

"We didn't lose her, Karen! She died," Carl interrupted angrily. "Amy wasn't some kind of sock lost in the wash. She was our daughter, and she died. Why can't you ever say that? Why can't you admit it?"

"Mr Poole, I don't think this is going to help anyone," Drew said. "Least of all Oliver. We need you both to remain as calm as possible, so we can do our job."

Karen sank into the nearest chair, her face pale. "I--"

"Perhaps it would be best if I took Mrs Poole into the kitchen, and we got a cup of tea," Harriet said, moving to the side of the distraught woman. Karen's lips were pale, and Harriet crouched down next to her. "Karen, can you make it onto your feet?"

The sound of frenzied action from the doorway pulled everyone's attention in that direction. A uniformed officer popped his head in the door. "Sir, could we have a word with you outside?"

"Have you found something?" Carl asked, pushing Drew out of the way before the other man could block his path effectively. "If you've found something, then I need to know."

"They've found him, haven't they?" Karen's voice was little more than a whisper.

"We don't know anything for certain yet," Harriet said, aiming for reassurance, but even to her it sounded weak. She couldn't imagine what the woman next to her was going through.

"We need you to stay here, Mr Poole," Drew said firmly. "When I know more, you will be the first to know." Drew escaped, leaving Harriet in the room with the uniformed officer, and the Pooles.

From the corner of her eye, Harriet was only vaguely aware of Mr Poole's behaviour as he paced back and forth inside the door like some kind of caged animal. Harriet chose instead to keep her attention fixed on the woman beside her.

"I've wrapped all of his Christmas presents," Karen said. "He never asks for much, but this year we wanted to make things special for him. Try and give him back some of what he'd missed out on in previous years..." She glanced over toward the tree.

"I'm sure he'll appreciate the effort you've gone to," Harriet said, touching her fingers to the other woman's. Karen's skin was cold, almost stony, and apprehension knotted itself in Harriet's stomach.

"Fuck this," Carl said, making a second attempt on the door. The uniformed officer made a valiant effort to keep him contained, but he was no match for the father's determination. Ramming him out of the way, Carl escaped out into the hall, allowing the chilly evening air to slip into the room and curl around Harriet's legs like an overly friendly cat.

Harriet caught the eye of the officer Carl had knocked down, and she shook her head subtly as he made a move for the door. "Could you stay here with

Mrs Poole and maybe fix her a cup of tea? I'll check on Mr Poole."

The PC looked Harriet up and down before he shrugged and stepped aside. "Be my guest. I've had enough of being out there for one night."

HARRIET HEADED for the door and found Drew arguing with Mr Poole out in the street. "What's going on?" She caught the attention of the nearest police officer.

"They found what they believe is Oliver Poole's coat."

"But no sign of Oliver?" The officer shook his head, and Harriet shivered despite the coat she wore. The temperature had taken a dramatic downturn, and she wouldn't have been surprised to see snow begin to fall from the sky. This wasn't the kind of weather for a child to be out in, especially one who was no longer in possession of a coat. "Have they found anything else?"

The officer shrugged. "I don't know. The DI is keeping it all pretty close to her vest." Harriet glanced over in DI Appleton's direction and was surprised to find herself the object of Appleton's attention, despite the almost physical altercation brewing between Drew and Mr Poole.

Making her way through the group, Harriet

approached DI Appleton. There was an almost imperceptible narrowing of the other woman's eyes, which Harriet found more than a little interesting. As far as she was aware, she had done nothing to upset, or offend the Detective Inspector, so it didn't make sense that that there would be any kind of animosity between them.

"Is there something you want, Dr Quinn?" There was an unmistakable frostiness to Melissa's voice that did nothing to make Harriet feel at ease.

"I heard you found a coat you think belongs to Oliver?"

"Those little birdies don't know when to keep their mouths shut, do they?" Sarcasm dripped from Melissa's words, and she shook her head.

"So that's a yes?"

"We found a coat."

"Anything else?"

Melissa shrugged. "I'm not sure it would be helpful right now for me to go blabbing to just anyone about the inner workings of this particular MISPERS." Before Harriet could reply, Melissa nodded her head toward Drew and the aggrieved father. "I need to sort this out before the two of them are brawling in the road. Wouldn't the press have an absolute field day with that?"

Harriet scanned the crowd and found Maz coordinating with a group of uniformed officers. He glanced up as she approached, his smile fleeting. "I didn't know you were here, Dr Quinn," he said, making a note in the pad he held.

"I heard you found a coat."

His expression turned grim, as he directed the officers to join the others who were conducting a grid search down on the path that entered the woods. "We did," he said. "DI Appleton directed us to begin the search down on the path where Oliver was last seen."

"And that's where the coat was?"

"It was nearby, dumped in some undergrowth a couple of feet into the woods."

Harriet sucked in a sharp breath and fought to ignore the shiver of apprehension that tracked down her spine. "Oliver wouldn't have just left his coat there like that."

"How do you know?" Maz asked. "I mean, when I was a kid, I did all sorts of crazy shit with my clothes. The number of times my mum gave me an earful for losing my coat, or my jumpers." He shook his head, a wry smile curling his lips. "I once even managed to lose a pair of brand-new trainers. I thought she was going to kill me." Maz's smile had lost some of its lustre, and Harriet wondered just how truthful he was being with himself regarding his memories.

Harriet returned his smile. It wasn't her place to question him. But his explanation regarding young boys and their ability to lose items of clothing didn't explain Oliver's coat being found in the undergrowth. "When you say dumped in the undergrowth, could it have been blown in there, or was it hidden from view?"

Maz's expression turned thoughtful. "I didn't find it personally..." He turned his attention toward the uniformed officers who milled around. "Oi, Barry, get your arse over here for a second." Maz's voice carried across the small cul-de-sac, drawing the attention of several of the other officers from nearby.

The officer Harriet assumed was Barry jogged over to them. "What's up?"

"When you found the coat, was it hidden from view, or dumped in plain sight?" Maz folded his arms over his chest.

"It was under some downed branches near the entrance to the woods."

"Did that seem odd to you?" Harriet jumped in before Maz could dismiss the man standing opposite them. She pushed down the irritation that surfaced in her when he glanced at Maz for what Harriet perceived to be permission.

"I wouldn't say it was odd per se," he said. "Maybe a little weird. We thought maybe the boy had hurt himself and crawled in underneath the branches, but there wasn't anything there."

"Have they searched the body dump site from the weekend?" Maz asked. Harriet tried to conceal the surprise that rocked her. She hadn't heard about anything about a body being found in the area at the weekend, but it seemed a little too coincidental to her, and if there was one thing she didn't believe in, it was coincidences.

"They're up there now, but so far there's no sign of the boy."

Maz nodded. "Cheers, mate."

"You still up for a pint at the weekend with the lads?" Barry asked, and Harriet tried to stifle her smile as Maz shuffled awkwardly.

"Now's not really the time, mate."

Barry nodded. "I'll give you a bell about it later on." And then Barry was gone, jogging back to the other officers who had gathered to receive instructions on the search groups they were creating.

"What's wrong?" Maz asked, turning his full attention to Harriet.

She shook her head. "The more I learn here, the more concerned I am that this isn't just a child who has run away or forgot to tell their parents where they were going."

"You think somebody took him?"

"Why would Oliver hide his coat, DS Arya?"

Maz pursed his lips. "He wouldn't."

"No, but somebody who was trying to conceal an abduction, or something worse, might."

"Why not take it with them?"

Harriet shrugged. "I don't know. Maybe they want us to know he's been taken. Maybe they panicked..."

Maz glanced over towards Dalby forest. "You think he's in there?"

Harriet shrugged. "I have no idea. But I know if we want to bring him home safely, then our window is rapidly closing."

Drew raised his hand, indicating for her to come over. "You going to tell the boss man your theory?"

Harriet nodded. "I've got to. It's the reason I'm here after all."

Maz smiled sympathetically. "No offence, doc, but I hope in this case you're wrong."

"So do I," she said, before she turned on her heel and crossed the road to where Drew stood with the others.

"WHERE IS MR POOLE?" Harriet got the question out before Drew could ask her what she'd been discussing with Maz.

"I managed to persuade him to return to the house; that his wife needed him."

Harriet dropped her gaze to the ground and was unsurprised to see frost beginning to glisten on the tarmac. "There's something you need to know," she said quietly. When he didn't reply, she glanced up only to find him watching her intently. "As you know, they found Oliver's coat."

"We won't know for certain it's his coat until we

can have one of the Poole's look at it, and forensics confirm it."

"One of the uniformed officers said when they found the coat it seemed as though somebody had made an attempt to conceal it."

Drew had raised his hand to his jaw to scrub his hand over his day-old stubble, but as Harriet spoke he halted. "What?"

"It was found beneath some branches. It frames this situation in a whole new light, and it's not a good one."

Drew swallowed. "You think somebody took him?"

"And you don't?"

He shrugged miserably. "I was hoping it wouldn't amount to that," he said. "Most kids who go missing are just runaways, and by all accounts that home hasn't exactly been the happiest."

"I think that's a little harsh," Harriet said a little more fiercely than she'd intended. "They love their son."

"Right, but Mr Poole has a temper on him that would make me want to run away if I was his son."

"You don't mean that," Harriet said sharply.

Drew dropped his gaze to the ground. "Probably not, but you know how I have to look at this, Harriet. I can't afford to show too much sympathy, at least not so much that it clouds my judgement of the situation."

"You mean the Poole's might be suspects?"

"Most abductions involve people who are known to the victim. And we haven't been able to verify any alibis yet."

"I know you're right, but I'm just not getting that feeling from them."

Drew raised an eyebrow speculatively at her. "Since when do you base your theories on feelings?"

"Not everything I do is based solely on statistics," she said. "Instincts play a part in it, along with empathy. And all I see when I look at the Poole's are a family who are grieving."

Drew nodded. "You can think that, but I'm going to hold on to my suspicions a little longer."

"What makes you suspicious of them?"

"There's something they're holding back. I don't know what it is, but it's there. And Oliver stumbled over a dead body at the weekend, broke his arm in the process, and Mrs Poole never bothered to inform us of that little fact."

"The body in the woods." Harriet said, sounding unsurprised.

"Wait, how did you know?"

"Well, for one it was on the news. But Maz mentioned it a few minutes ago."

"I'm not saying it's connected, but--"

"But it's too much of a coincidence?"

It was Drew's turn to nod. "If we are looking at a

stranger, what should we expect regarding bringing Oliver home alive?"

Harriet's shoulder's tightened as tension coiled its way around her spine. "Most kidnappings as you said are done by somebody known to the victim. In the case of children we get around a thousand abductions a year, and of those roughly a hundred of them are by strangers." She swallowed hard around the lump in her throat before she continued. "If Oliver was taken by a stranger, we're looking at something already quite uncommon. Most are failures, because the child escapes, but around half of the children taken in a stranger abduction never return home."

"Shit," Drew said harshly. "I thought we'd have better odds than that."

Harriet shook her head. "It's not an exact science because that number is skewed by the simple fact that children who are cared for in the first place are much more likely to be reported. Many children go missing, but because of their background they are never reported to the police."

"Don't social services notice when a kid goes missing?"

"Sometimes," Harriet said. "But social services are already overworked, and understaffed. There is only so much they can do, but mistakes are inevitably made, and children slip through the cracks."

Drew blew out his cheeks, his expression thunderous.

"But Oliver was reported. His mother called as soon as she realised something wasn't right."

"I know that," Drew said. "But we don't even have a clear timeline on when he went missing."

"We know he never met up with his friend," Harriet said thoughtfully. "I think it's safe to assume he disappeared almost as soon as he left home. And there's something else I think you need to know."

"The caretaker from the school," Drew said.

"Mr Poole told you?"

He nodded. "I got it out of him, eventually; wasn't easy, mind."

"And you still want to hold on to those suspicions regarding the family?"

Drew smiled wryly at her. "It's my job, Harriet. I have to keep everyone in the frame until I can tick them off the list. This case is too important to miss something, that boy's life depends on it. But the caretaker is definitely an angle worth pursuing." He sighed and closed his eyes. "I've got one more question," Drew said. "And I'm almost certain I'm not going to like the answer."

"Ask it."

"If a stranger took him, what's the likelihood that we're going to bring him home, versus us looking for his body?"

Wrapping her arms around her body, Harriet rocked back on her heels. "I can't tell you that, Drew."

"Just give me a rough guide."

Closing her eyes, Harriet pulled in a slow breath. When she opened her eyes again, it was to find Drew peering down at her intently. "If a violent, or predatory offender took him, then the odds are not good."

"How not good?"

"Around 74% of children are dead within the first three hours."

"So he's probably already dead?"

"The statistics would suggest that's true," Harriet said. She watched as Drew's expression twisted into one of anger. As much as she wanted to go to him, to offer some kind of comfort, Harriet knew it was impossible. There was nothing she could say to him that would cushion the blow of what she'd just told him.

"I don't care what the numbers say," Drew said fiercely. "We keep looking until we bring that boy home safely."

Harriet nodded, but they both knew Drew's bravado was just that. A front to keep hope alive, when the truth of the matter was too dark to handle.

CHAPTER TWENTY-TWO

TURNING over in her bed the next morning, DC Martina Nicoll closed her eyes against the shaft of sunshine that cut through her blackout curtains. Ten more minutes, that's all she needed. Ten more hours would have been preferable, but that wasn't going to happen considering everything that was going on. She broke away in the early hours of the morning when the physical search had been called off. Some of the uniforms had decided to stay on and send a drone up with heat seeking equipment to scan the area from the air. As far as Martina was concerned, they should have done that sooner, instead of letting them traipse around in the darkness of the trees.

Not that she minded. There was something about children that sent them all off the deep end. She didn't have children, but that didn't stop her from feeling compelled to find Oliver safe and well.

The phone next to her bed buzzed quietly, and Martina sat bolt upright in the bed. She smacked her hand against the locker next as she searched for the phone. Finding it, she answered the call and pressed it against her ear.

"DC Nicoll."

"Just me," Ambrose said.

"Any news on the boy?"

"Nothing yet. They're checking CCTV for the area so they can try to retrace his movements yesterday evening. And they're going through ANPR to see if there are any hits from cars in the area. And the rest are speaking to people who knew him."

"That's good, we can't keep going in circles."

"That's not why I'm calling," he said. Ambrose sighed, and Martina could practically see him leaning back in his chair, a cup of Yorkshire builder's tea on the desk in front of him as he swiped his hand down over his face. "Jackson said he has an ID on our body. And the forensic anthropologist wants us to come in for a word. How fast can you be ready?"

"Ten minutes," Martina said, and she was already out of the bed and stumbling around the room.

"I'll be there in fifteen," Ambrose said. "That'll give you chance to get a cuppa down you." The line went dead, and Martina tossed it onto her rumpled duvet cover as she raced for the bathroom.

Twenty minutes later she stood in the kitchen sipping a black coffee from her favourite mug. She'd have preferred tea but she needed the caffeine. Her damp hair clung to her neck, sending icy droplets of water down the back of her shirt. Mum had always told her not to go out with wet hair or she'd only get sick. As she'd got older, Martina had learned that not everything her mum told her was the god's honest truth.

The kitchen door swung open, and her father stepped into the small room. "You got in late again last night," he said, his tone icy as he moved to switch on the kettle.

"Something came up." She sighed, guilt swimming in the pit of her stomach as she sipped at her coffee before glancing surreptitiously down at her watch. Why was it every time she needed Ambrose to be on time, he was late? If she didn't know better, she might have thought he planned it that way.

"Something always comes up," he said stiffly from the other side of the kitchen. "Your mum was upset is all."

"Dad, I don't want to get into this right now. I really did want to come home early yesterday, but I couldn't." She finished the coffee and moved to the sink. Rinsing the cup under the tap, Martina could feel her father's gaze boring into her.

"Do you think this is easy for me?" The question took her by surprise, and the cup almost slipped from her hand, but she caught it before it could hit the bottom of the sink.

"Of course not."

"Then why do you behave as though it is?"

Exasperation ripped through her as she set the cup on the draining board. Before she could reply, there was the blare of a horn outside.

"Saved by the bell," her father said bitterly.

"I have a job to do, dad. I can't just drop everything."

Another blare of the horn. "Go, before he wakes your mother."

"How is she?"

"Go, Martina."

Emotion burned in her chest as she headed out the back door. Her father could always do that to her, make her feel like she was eight years old again and in trouble. Tears pricked at her eyes, but she swiped them away as she hurried down the footpath, and slipped into the passenger seat next to Ambrose.

"Bad morning?" His tone was amicable, but talking was the last thing she wanted to do.

"Just drive, Ambrose."

"Got it."

Martina settled back into the seat and closed her eyes. She needed to concentrate on the day ahead and leave her problems at home. It was easier said than done, but the further Ambrose drove her from her house, the easier it was to crush the lump that burned in the back of her throat.

CHAPTER TWENTY-THREE

"I WANT A WORD WITH YOU, HASKELL." The monk's voice carried over the chatter in the office, drawing Drew's attention to his boss stood in the doorway. The monk at least looked like he'd managed to get a full eight hours. By comparison, Drew had caught a glimpse of his reflection in the metal paper towel dispenser in the gents and was horrified by what he'd seen.

Pushing away from the desk he'd commandeered, he made his way slowly toward Gregson's office. As he knocked on the door, Gregson beckoned him inside, his eagle eyed gaze scanning over Drew's appearance.

"You look like shit," Gregson said finally, folding his hands over one another on the desk's surface.

"I feel worse," Drew said, scrubbing his hand down over his rough stubbled cheeks and chin.

"From where I'm sat, I'm not sure that's possible." Gregson arched an eyebrow. "You're the face of this operation. Well, you and DI Appleton. And Melissa is doing an admirable job of looking like someone who has her shit in order." Gregson indicated to the other Detective Inspector who was at that moment moving purposefully through the desks. She slipped into her office space and disappeared from view. "The public need to know that we've got a handle on this, Drew."

"Of course, sir," Drew said. "We contacted the NCA and had them put out a CRA last night." The Child Rescue Alert system was the responsibility of the National Crime Agency, but it was at the disposal of any force in the country, and for that Drew was grateful. Right now they needed every bit of help they could get.

"That's why I called you in here," Gregson said, his expression sombre.

"I thought it was regarding my appearance, sir."

"Unlike you, Haskell, I'm capable of multi-tasking." Gregson spoke drily. "The NCA have offered to send us over some help if we need it."

"That's very generous, sir, but I think we--"

"Sorry, perhaps I wasn't quite clear; the NCA are sending over some analysts to sift through the data coming in." There was no mistaking the edge to the monk's voice as he spoke, and Drew had the distinct impression that they'd all been manoeuvred into a corner that would undoubtably come back to bite them in the arse at a later date.

"That was very generous of them, sir," Drew said, managing to keep his voice measured and devoid of any kind of emotion.

"It was." Gregson sighed. "It's no harm. We're sorely lacking in computer analysts. I've been looking for some new blood to liven this place up, but so far I haven't found anyone who meets the criteria for what we need. With any luck, the NCA will send us someone we can entice to our side of the fence."

"Aren't we all on the same side, sir?"

The derisive noise Gregson made in response took Drew by surprise.

"We should be, but I haven't always had the best of luck with their sort," Gregson said darkly. "Anyway, I wanted to let you know they were arriving—"

"When?"

"Now," Gregson said. A wicked grin curled the other man's lips as he inclined his head in the direction of the office. The sound of a commotion pulled Drew's attention back toward the space he shared with the rest of the team and was surprised to see several people carrying boxes of equipment pour into the office. "I expect you'll get them all squared away here," Gregson said.

"What do you expect me to do with them, sir?" Irritation coloured Drew's words. The last thing he needed was to waste his time babysitting a lot of analysts. Oliver was out there somewhere, Drew needed to be out there searching for him.

"Get them settled and start feeding them the information they need. I want backgrounds on everyone in the area. And we need to know about any offenders who might have moved to the area. They're good at ferreting out information like that."

"But, sir--"

"Make use of them, Haskell. I might not be particularly fond of them and their tactics, but they are useful. At the end of the day, the sooner we get that boy back to his parents, the better for everyone involved."

Drew knew when he'd been managed. Sighing, he pushed to his feet and made his way to the door.

"What does Doctor Quinn think of us getting the boy back safe and sound?" Gregson's question brought Drew up short. He paused with one hand on the door handle and contemplated his options before he answered.

"She's concerned, sir, like we all are."

"So she thinks he's already dead?" Drew was accustomed to his boss' usual blunt manner, but even that took him somewhat by surprise.

"She didn't say that."

"Just because she didn't say it aloud, doesn't make it untrue," Gregson said sadly. "We know the statistics, Drew. The chances are in a case such as this, we're looking for a body, and not a young boy we can bring home safe to his parents."

He was right, but that didn't mean Drew had to accept it. "I prefer to keep an open mind on these things, sir. I find people are far more motivated in these situations when they think we can have a happy ending."

Gregson's smile was tinged with melancholy. "You keep that optimism, Haskell, if it's what helps you sleep at night. But I've seen too many happy endings soured by reality to be so naïve. I'll still call this a win if we manage to bring this boy back to his parents so they can at least say goodbye."

Drew fought back the desire to ask his boss just what he was talking about. They were all too aware of the many sad cases of missing children who were never returned alive to their loved ones. Their names were seared into the memories of everyone who had ever heard a whisper of their cases, their smiling faces instantly recognisable every time they appeared on a true crime documentary about predators. Gregson might consider it to be naïve optimism that allowed him to sleep at night, but as far as Drew was concerned, to think of it any other way was too much like giving up. And that was something he wasn't willing to do.

Stepping out into the main office, Drew headed toward a vivid-red-haired woman who seemed to be in charge of the others who had arrived with her.

"DI Drew Haskell, we're glad to have you here," he said, holding his hand out toward her. She glanced down at it, before returning her attention to his face. She took his hand swiftly, her grip fleeting before she withdrew her hand and curled her fingers into a fist at her side.

"My name is Jodie Meakin. I'm an analyst with the NCA." She paused and surveyed the space. "Is there somewhere we can set up our computers? Perhaps somewhere a little more private?" She raised an eyebrow at him speculatively. Her rich brown eyes sparkled with intelligence behind her blue framed glasses.

Drew nodded and gestured for her and the others to follow him across the hall. The floor they'd been assigned as part of the new task force came with extra square footage that they hadn't found any use for, but Drew had a feeling that Jodie and her cohorts would appreciate it.

She appraised the room on the opposite side of the corridor. "We can use this entire space?" The question was framed casually, but Drew could sense the underlying tension that coloured her words.

"Of course. Like I said, we're grateful for your assistance. We want to bring Oliver home as quickly as possible, and I know we'll do that all the more smoothly with your help."

She gave him a once over, but seemed almost disappointed when she couldn't find the least hint of dis-ingenuity in his demeanour. "I'll be in charge of the others here, at least until our boss can make his way over from headquarters." Drew noted the way she said the word boss, as though in that one word alone she could adequately describe her loathing for the person she worked for.

"And they'll be here when?"

"He'll be here in about an hour, and he'll expect us to have set everything up here." Her gaze flickered shyly to Drew's face, but she never met his gaze. "If you could have someone send over all the files we need to get a head start on, I can put everyone to work on this end."

"Of course," Drew amicably. He gave Jodie a wide smile, which seemed to cause a bright flush to spread beneath her tawny complexion. He paused in the doorway, watching her work to organise the desks and space to her particular liking. When she caught him studying them, the flush returned, spreading up the back of her neck before it crept into her cheeks and she ducked her attention back to a large black box she'd opened.

Leaving them to prepare, Drew returned to his own office. "Olivia," Drew called the DC over to his side. "Can you liaise with the NCA analysts that are setting up in the spare conference room? Get them everything they need to get started."

She nodded, her smile brightening as she caught sight of the hive of activity in the room opposite. "Got it, Guv. Oh, and we've got some people coming in later for a chat." She glanced down at a notepad in her hand. "A Mr Andrews, he's a teacher from the local school where Oliver goes. According to Mrs Poole he has quite a good rapport with the boy. And we've got a Tilly Mayhew due in the next hour. She works with the scouts and Oliver was a member of the troop."

"That's good work," Drew said. "Think you and Green can handle it?"

Olivia's grin grew wider. "Of course, Guv."

"Sir, I've got the name of the caretaker from Oliver's school," Maz's voice tugged Drew's attention from Olivia with a jolt.

"Then we should pay him a visit, see what he's been up to."

"Sir, what should I do with the people coming in for interview?"

"I'm sure you can handle them," Drew said. "Get some background on them and bring Green with you." Olivia nodded and took off towards the NCA group.

Maz's expression was eager as he pushed up from his chair, and slipped his jacket on, and Drew didn't have the heart to tell him he'd have preferred to bring Harriet along for the conversation. He tossed the keys to Maz, who had beat him to the door. "I want to pick up Dr Quinn." The irritation that flashed across Maz's face wasn't lost on Drew, but he chose to ignore it. Arya was a good cop, but he still had a lot to learn, and some things you could only learn through experience. The more time he got to see Harriet in action, the more he would benefit from her astute observations, and if that made him a better detective then Drew could see no downsides to the situation.

CHAPTER TWENTY-FOUR

FAT SNOWFLAKES HAD STARTED to fall, coating everything in their path in a fluffy white blanket. Harriet sat behind the steering wheel of her car, watching as the flakes gathered on the windscreen, obscuring her view of The Hermitage Hospital where her mother resided. The last time she'd called to see her, she'd been turned away on Dr Connors' orders.

But that was then. She wasn't going to allow him to keep her at arm's length. Pushing open the car door, she discarded her phone on the passenger seat before she dropped her paperwork on top to conceal it. Clutching her bag to her chest, she paused, allowing the heavy flakes to settle on her face and in her eyelashes, as she scanned the windows of the white building before her. Apprehension caused her heart to pick up its pace in her chest. The building had always reminded her of a prison rather than the hospital it was. The more times she was forced to return here, the image became cemented deeper into her mind.

Of course, it wasn't just a prison for those who lingered within its walls. For Harriet it was just as much a mental prison, as it was a physical one to those who were forced to stay against their will; for no matter how often Harriet left, she couldn't shake the feeling that she was leaving little pieces of herself inside the walls to linger with the lonely souls trapped inside.

It would be easier to turn away now. To simply slide back in behind the wheel and drive away from here. But that would only make it all the more difficult to come back. Over the years, she'd slid into a kind of routine in visiting her mother. It was easier to do something when you didn't have to think about it first. And she'd spent a lot of time not thinking about her mother, and all the traumatic baggage that her existence inevitably brought to the surface in Harriet's mind.

Some people found solace in abandoning all ties with those from their past who had hurt them; both physically and emotionally. Others felt it was necessary to their recovery to face their tormentors. So which category did she fall into? The mere fact that she stood here precluded her from being in the first group, but Harriet was also fairly certain she didn't belong to the second set either.

Sucking in a deep breath, she tucked a strand of dark hair behind her ear before she started up toward the front door. The reception was empty when she pushed inside, Harriet wasn't sure if she should feel relieved or disappointed by this fact. Perhaps if there had been others around it would have made it easier to slip away under the pretence that she would be disrupting the hard won equilibrium in the hospital.

The door behind the reception desk clicked open and a familiar woman appeared with a cup of steaming tea clutched in her hands. The receptionist glanced up, and Harriet noted the way in which the familiar woman's expression hardened.

"I didn't think you'd come back here," Clara said, her voice abrupt.

"Why would you think that?" The question slipped out before Harriet could stop it. There were all manner of possible answers, but Harriet had the sneaking suspicion that whatever Clara's reasoning happened to be, it wouldn't be something pleasant.

"You know he's been suspended because of your lies?"

Harriet shook her head and squared her shoulders. "I hadn't heard."

"He never did anything but good in this place. It's not just the staff who miss him, but the patients do as well. You're supposed to be a doctor, you should know the damage that can be done to such fragile mental states."

"I'm here to see Allison. I didn't come here to debate whether Dr Connors was fit for purpose or not."

"She's not here," Clara said. There was a cold glint in her eyes that suggested she was more than happy to be the bearer of such shocking news.

"I don't understand," Harriet stumbled over the words. Dr Connors had threatened to have her mother moved, but she'd never thought he would genuinely achieve his goals. "If she's not here, then where is she? And why wasn't I informed?"

Clara glanced down at the keyboard in front of her; her fingers moved quickly over the keys, her merlot gel-nails reflected the overhead lighting and served only to enhance the sensation of nausea that grew within Harriet. A couple of keystrokes later, and Clara glanced up at her. "She's in the hospital for a routine appointment."

Relief flooded through Harriet's body, and her shoulders sagged as she leaned against the edge of the reception desk. "And when is she due back?"

"It doesn't say here," Clara said. "But you know how these things are."

Harriet nodded. "I still don't understand why I wasn't informed of her appointment."

"She opted not to inform you," Clara said smartly.

"The patients here are entitled to their privacy, and you are not a physician on staff here."

"Can I have the name of the doctor in charge of her care now that Dr Connors has been suspended?"

Clara's expression soured, and for a brief moment Harriet wondered if perhaps the other woman would refuse to give her the information she'd asked for. Instead, Clara sighed dramatically, and her fingers flew over the keyboard a second time. "Dr Joseph Parvin." Clara leaned back in the chair and eyed Harriet over the top of the desk. "Would you like me to arrange an appointment for you to see him?"

Harriet nodded and held her bag a little tighter as she waited for Clara to pass the information over to her. "Fine. Friday afternoon at 2pm. He'll see you here, in his office. I've sent the relevant information to you in an email."

"Thank you," Harriet said, feeling somewhat at a loss now that she knew she wouldn't be getting in to see Allison. Dejected, Harriet made her way from The Hermitage. As she stepped out into the cold, brisk December air, she drew her coat in around her body tightly as the snowflakes fell steadily around her. She hurried across the car park and slipped into the driver's seat in time to hear the last pathetic bleep of her phone as a message came through.

Ignoring the sound, she chaffed her hands together in an attempt to bring some warmth back to her icy fingers. It seemed Dr Connors' wish to keep her from her mother had--at least for now--been granted.

Reaching over to the passenger seat, she scooped her phone up and without looking at the screen she hit redial.

The phone rang for a moment before Drew's gruff voice greeted her. "Where are you?"

Harriet felt a smile tugging at the corner of her lips as she watched her footprints disappearing steadily beneath the snowfall. "I'm out at The Hermitage Hospital," she said, slipping smoothly into the flow of conversation.

"How long will it take you to make it to Darkby?" There was an eagerness in Drew's voice that caught Harriet's attention.

"You've found something?"

He sighed, the sound drifting down the line. "We don't know yet, but it's definitely something worth looking into. I'd like your opinion if you're up for it?"

"Of course," Harriet said, sliding the keys into the ignition. "I might take a little longer because of the snow, but I'll be there as fast as I can. Can you send me the postcode?" Her phone bleeped as she spoke.

"Already done," Drew said briskly. "We'll wait for you." The line went dead. Harriet scrolled through the messages, her emotions electrified as she typed the postcode into her SatNav. Perhaps she was wrong to be so sceptical about finding the Poole boy safe. With that in mind, she pulled out of the car space and turned the car in the direction of Darkby.

AN HOUR LATER, Harriet parked in front of a small house on the outskirts of Darkby. Drew stepped out of the car ahead of her as she killed the engine and gathered her belongings from the passenger seat. His expression was grim as she stepped out of the car and met him on the road.

"Are you going to tell me what we're doing here?"

Maz had followed Drew's lead, and he stood back from them, his hands behind his back. Despite being the picture of ease, Harriet could feel the tension that rolled off him like mist rolling off a lake in the summer heat.

"This is the last known address we've got for a John Taylor."

Harriet raised an eyebrow at Drew. "Should I know who that is?"

"The caretaker from Oliver's school," Drew said. "He used to look after the grounds surrounding Darkby Primary school."

"I was under the impression from Mrs Poole that he was in prison." Harriet couldn't keep the surprise from her voice.

Shaking his head, Drew glanced up at the house. "No. Maz checked it up, he never served any jail time. He received a community order, mandatory therapy, and was placed on the register for ten years."

Harriet sucked a sharp breath in through her teeth. The work she had done when she'd started out her career in forensic psychology had put her face to face with a number of sexually motivated criminal offenders. The most complex of which had always been the paedophiles and child molesters, and those who preyed on the young and the vulnerable. The interviews she'd conducted with them still haunted her; their crimes, the stuff of nightmares. But the nature of her work dictated that she not sit in judgement, no matter how abhorrent their crimes were to her. After all, it was the duty of the legal system to pass judgement over them. But as much as she'd tried to remain neutral, she'd found it difficult to wrap her mind around the seemingly lenient sentences they received.

It seemed John Taylor was one of many to benefit from an overwrought and under funded system.

"Are you all right?" Drew's voice cut through her thoughts, pulling her back to the present.

"Sorry, I'm fine. I was miles away."

"Anything you want to share?"

Harriet shook her head. "Not right now." She smiled to soften her words.

"Right, this is just a chat," Drew said, addressing Harriet and Maz. "We don't have any evidence to suggest he knows anything regarding Oliver Poole's disappearance."

"But come on, sir. Are we supposed to just ignore his history with the victim?" Maz's interjection was something Harriet had already thought of herself. In her line of work, the experiences of the patient were vitally important. It allowed you to create an overall picture of their mental state.

"He was tried and convicted for it," Drew said. "He did his time. It's not our job to question that."

"But--"

"No buts, Maz. We're here to follow up on the current case. Sure, his past has some bearing on the situation, but we can't allow that to cloud our judgements."

Harriet could tell from Maz's expression that he was less than impressed with his SIO's orders. But if he had any other objections to the matter, he kept them to himself.

Drew led them through the small, rickety front gate. The path to the front door was strewn with weeds, and grass that sprouted up between the cracks in the paving slabs which lent the place an overall unkempt air. As she followed Maz, the familiar prickle of being watched started up, but she fought the urge to glance up at the windows at the front of the house.

Pausing next to Drew, she waited as he rapped roughly on the front door. From their position outside, Harriet could make out the sound of a television playing some kind of daytime game show from within the bowels of the building. Drew knocked again, this time a little more forcefully so that the door rattled in its framework.

The sound of the television disappeared and a couple of moments later the net curtain covering the glass on the front door twitched aside to reveal a face creased with age. The woman's mouth turned down in a moue of distaste as she raked her gaze over Drew standing directly in front of the door.

"What do you lot want?" The irritation in her voice was only slightly muffled by the door that stood between them.

"I'm DI Drew Haskell, and these are my colleagues DS Maz Arya, and Dr Harriet Quinn," Drew said swiftly. "We're looking for John Taylor." There was no denying the note of authority in Drew's voice. Harriet admired his ability to turn it on and off as the situation dictated. Perhaps it was something they taught in police training, although Harriet had her doubts about it. As far as she was concerned, it was something entirely unique to Drew and his abilities as a police officer.

"He's not here," came the gruff reply. The net dropped back into place, and Harriet felt the tension knot in the back of her neck as Drew glanced over his shoulder at them.

"Can you tell us where he is?" Drew raised his

voice, ensuring it would carry through the partially rotted door. He got his answer in the form of a bolt sliding open before the door swung inwards to reveal the woman they'd been speaking to through the door. She stood framed in the doorway, leaning heavily on a metal cane.

"What do you want with John?" She threw a cursory glance in Harriet and Maz's direction before she narrowed her watery blue eyes at Drew. "He hasn't done anything." Mrs Taylor shifted from one foot to the other and a look of discomfort passed swiftly over her face.

"We just want to speak to him," Drew said amicably.

"That's what you lot said last time, and then you destroyed his life. He lost his job, you know?"

Drew nodded. "I can imagine he did. But you need to remember your son was found guilty of a very serious crime."

She snorted derisively, but Harriet caught sight of whitening of the other woman's knuckles as she closed her creased fingers over the cane. Despite appearances to the contrary, it seemed John Taylor's mother was in fact perturbed by the crimes he'd been convicted of.

"I suppose you're here to accuse him of something else he didn't do?"

"Would it be possible for us to come inside and have a chat?" Drew gave her his most winning smile, but from where Harriet stood she could tell it had no effect.

"I don't suppose I can say no, can I?" She moved aside slowly, allowing Drew to step over the threshold and into the house.

Mrs Taylor huffed as Maz followed Drew, and when Harriet moved into the hall, she found herself the object of the other woman's attention. "Two coppers and a doctor, well aren't I the lucky one."

Harriet bit her tongue and allowed Mrs Taylor to shuffle ahead into the lounge. The house was in a state of disrepair. A large yellow water mark marred the far corner of the ceiling, causing the plaster to sag downwards. The faded floral wallpaper had begun to peel in places, but Harriet could see where somebody had made an effort to repair the damage. Despite outward appearances—the dated decor, wear and tear—Harriet could tell that Mrs Taylor took pride in her home. There were several small mahogany tables in the room with small trinkets and knick-knacks covering every inch of surface space in the room. Family pictures adorned the walls. The smiling faces of their children at various ages grinned down at them, spoke of happier times.

"Don't stand around," Mrs Taylor said. "I can't spend my time looking up at you, my neck doesn't work like that anymore." She pointed an arthritic finger toward the couch. Drew took a seat on the end of the couch nearest Mrs Taylor, and Harriet settled onto the opposite end, leaving Maz to stand awkwardly near the door.

"There's a chair in the other room," she said to Maz.

"I'm fine," Maz said. Mrs Taylor glared at him, and Drew nodded subtly, letting Maz know that he should do as he was told.

A couple of moments later, and all three of them were settled in the living room. It took Harriet a moment to realise just how strategic Drew's position was on his end of the couch. From the vantage point he'd taken up, he could see out the front window which meant anyone who came up the path would be instantly visible, and with his back to the wall it meant no one would sneak up on him without him knowing about it. Drew had many little habits and quirks, but this one in particular had become more pronounced since his run in with the Star Killer.

Mrs Taylor cleared her throat, her attention seemingly riveted to the television screen, but Harriet could feel the tension that radiated from the other woman. "You lot going to tell me what you want with John, or do I have to guess?"

"Are you aware of the boy who went missing yesterday?" Drew wasted no time in getting straight to the point. Mrs Taylor's jaw tightened, and she swung her gaze towards Drew.

"My John had nothing to do with that."

"How can you be so sure?" There was no

animosity in Drew's voice that Harriet could tell, just a gently curiosity.

"Because he wouldn't harm a hair on anyone's head," she said vehemently. "He's a good boy."

"How much has John told you about his prior conviction?"

She shook her head. "You're not going to trick me, DI Haskell. He didn't do anything wrong."

"He was accused of a very serious crime," Drew said. "He'd been grooming a boy at the school where he worked. When they picked him up, he was found with indecent images of children on his laptop."

Mrs Taylor shook her head, but Harriet could tell that the colour had drained from her cheeks. "He was kind to a boy who'd lost his sister, that's all. And as for images on a computer, John never said anything about that."

"How much does John share with you, Mrs Taylor?" Harriet interjected before Drew could say anything else.

"He tells me everything. I know it's not what you're used to hearing, but it's the truth." She sighed. "When I got sick, he moved back in here with me to make sure I was safe." There was a wariness to her eyes that told Harriet to press the issue.

"I'm sorry to hear you were ill," Harriet said swiftly.

"I had a fall and broke my pelvis," Mrs Taylor

said. "After John went to court, and they found him guilty, a couple of local lads came here and broke in."

"Was it connected to John's trial?" There was an edge to Drew's voice.

"They thought they could intimidate me; said they wanted to send John a message, so they pushed me down the stairs. But I won't be bullied by no-one, especially not a bunch of local thugs." There was a level of gritty determination to her voice that took Harriet by surprise. "I called the ambulance myself. And even though I told John I'd be fine to live here on my own, he insisted on moving in."

Harriet had a feeling that her son opting to move home wasn't entirely for altruistic purposes, but she wasn't going to say anything.

"Do you know what John was doing yesterday?" Drew asked, smoothly changing the subject.

"He was at work." There was a smug satisfaction to Mrs Taylor as she settled back into the faded, floral printed armchair.

"John doesn't have a job," Drew said gently. "We checked before we got here."

"That's not true," Mrs Taylor shot back. "He found a job a few months back…"

Drew's smile was sympathetic. "You're correct, he did. But he lost that job two weeks later."

Mrs Taylor sucked in a pained breath. "You're lying. You're just trying to trick me into saying something--"

Drew shook his head. "I'm really not, Mrs Taylor. All I want is the truth. I want to know where John is, so we can have a chat with him. The boy who went missing is the same boy John was accused of grooming."

Drew's words took their toll. "He's supposed to be at work," the other woman said miserably.

"And when is he due back?"

Mrs Taylor's face crumpled. "He should have been back already."

"Would it be possible for my colleague and I to have a look at John's room?" Drew asked.

Mrs Taylor nodded. Her face was chalk white, and she'd wrapped her fingers around the top of her cane as though it could protect her from the truth if only she clung to it hard enough.

"I'll stay here," Harriet said to the unasked question on Drew's face. He nodded and pushed onto his feet, allowing Maz to go first out into the hall. Harriet waited until the sound of their footsteps on the creaky stairs filtered through the house.

"Tell me about John," Harriet said, her gaze never left Mrs Taylor's face.

"He was such a quiet boy," Mrs Taylor said. "Everybody was surprised at how quiet he was. Today they'd call it introverted." She stared at the contestants on the television screen, before she glanced over at Harriet. "Do you have children?"

"No."

"Oh well, I suppose nowadays it's all about getting on in your career. People don't view marriage and children in the same way anymore."

"I'm just not in the right place," Harriet said diplomatically.

"Perhaps you're right. John has only brought me heartache..." She glanced down at her gnarled hands. "He lied to me."

"About his job?"

Mrs Taylor shook her head sadly. "Not just about his job. He lied to me about everything. DI Haskell said there were some images on a computer?"

Harriet nodded. While she hadn't found the opportunity to take a look at John Taylor's criminal record, she could already imagine what she would find there once she did.

"He promised he wouldn't lie to me."

"Why would he make a promise like that?" There was something in Mrs Taylor's tone of voice when she said it that made Harriet think there was more to the statement than met the eye.

The other woman sighed. "His father was a liar. Every second thing from that man's mouth was a lie. It was a compulsion. He lied to me, to John, to everyone who ever met him. One exaggeration after another." Anger tinted her words. "John promised me he wouldn't ever lie to me the way his father did."

"Perhaps he didn't tell you because he didn't want to hurt you?"

Mrs Taylor's laugh when it came was brittle, and it hurt Harriet's ears to hear the sound. "If he didn't want to hurt me, then he wouldn't have done such terrible things."

"Do you think he's capable of taking Oliver Poole?" The question slipped out before Harriet could stop it.

Mrs Taylor shrugged. "Before you told me the truth, I'd have said no."

"But now you're not so sure?"

"How can I be certain of anything anymore? The apple didn't fall far from the tree with him it seems." The sound of a key turning in the back door pulled Harriet's attention from the woman in front of her.

"Is that him now?"

Mrs Taylor shrugged. "Probably... John, is that you?"

"Yeah, Sylvia, sorry I'm late, I--" John Taylor appeared in the doorway, his broad shoulders blocking out the light that streamed in from the kitchen behind him. The moment his gaze fell on Harriet, his expression twisted into a grimace of distaste. "What do you want?"

"Mr Taylor, my name is Dr Quinn, I--"

The sound of footsteps on the stairs broke John's concentration, and he swung away from Harriet and turned toward the stairs.

"Hello John, fancy a chat?" Drew's voice was

amicable, but Harriet was acutely aware of the underlying tension as he raced down the stairs.

"Fuck this!" John bolted back in the direction he'd come from.

"Don't run, John. You'll only make this worse!" Mrs Taylor shouted, her voice drowned out by the slam of the door. Instinct caused Harriet to move after John. He couldn't be allowed to get away. A young boy's life depended on it. She reached the doorway in time for Drew to block her path.

"You stay!" He barked the order at her, as he manoeuvred past her into the kitchen. Maz clattered down the stairs clumsily and followed hot on Drew's heels. Harriet reached the kitchen in time to see Maz disappearing out the backdoor.

"Is there somewhere John would go? Somewhere he would feel safe?" Harriet turned to face Mrs Taylor, who had shuffled out into the kitchen.

"How would I know? We've established he's been lying to me the whole time. Why would I know where he'd go to ground?"

"Because you know your son, Mrs Taylor."

The older woman glared at Harriet before she shook her head and ambled over to the kettle. Leaning heavily on her cane, she lifted the kettle with one hand and carried it over to the sink. Letting it drop into the sink with a resounding clatter, she pulled off the lid roughly and turned on the tap. Water gushed into the receptacle, as Mrs Taylor stood over it, her gaze fixed on something beyond the window.

"I don't think I ever knew him," she said flatly.

A few seconds later, Maz appeared in the doorway. His cheeks were flushed, and his eyes bright from the chase.

"Did you get him?" Harriet asked.

"No. He had a motorbike. Drew followed him in the car."

"And you didn't go with him?" Harriet couldn't keep the irritation from her voice.

"He didn't give me the chance," Maz said sheepishly. "You know what the boss is like. Before I knew what he was doing, he was in the car."

Closing her eyes, Harriet pressed her fingers against the bridge of her nose before she turned back to face the woman who was at that moment hobbling back to the counter with the kettle.

"You must know where he'd go," Harriet said. She crossed the kitchen and took the kettle from Mrs Taylor. Setting it down on the base, she turned it on, before facing the indignant woman. "This is far too important. I need you to be honest with me."

"I have been honest." Mrs Taylor's voice crept up, as two spots of colour mounted her cheeks.

"No. You're telling me what you think I want to hear. You want me to believe that you had no idea what your son was capable of, when we both know that's a lie."

"How dare you come into my house and accuse me of lying?" Mrs Taylor tried to slip past Harriet as she spoke. "I've been nothing but cooperative."

"You've known all along what your son was like," Harriet continued. The front door flopped open with a thud, and Drew appeared in the kitchen.

"He got away."

"You can't speak to me like this," Mrs Taylor said.

"You knew what your son was, and you turned a blind eye to it all, just as you did with your husband..." Silence descended on the room as though she'd dropped a grenade into the centre of the room. Cringing inwardly, Harriet knew she had to push onwards. As much as it was distasteful to her to question Mrs Taylor in this way, the fact that there was a young boy missing seemed to warrant a more direct approach to the situation.

There were all sorts of reasons why people tried to pretend they knew nothing of the truth, especially when it came to something as shocking and disturbing as paedophilia. And in some cases it was entirely believable. Nobody wanted to believe the worst of their loved one. But in light of the conviction he'd received there was no way Mrs Taylor hadn't known what was going on where her son was concerned and considering the way she'd spoken about her husband Harriet knew it wasn't such a stretch to think she knew exactly what he'd done to their son. She might not have known at the time, but she certainly at least had her suspicions.

"I think you need to leave," Mrs Taylor said. Her voice shook with emotion, and she gripped the edge of her cane so tightly Harriet wouldn't have been surprised to see it warp beneath her strength.

"Protecting him now, won't fix the past," Harriet said softly.

Mrs Taylor flopped back against the counter as though all the strength had left her body. Before Harriet could move, Drew was there to catch the elderly woman before she collapsed entirely. Wrapping his arm around her, he helped her over to a chair at the table. The woman dropped into the chair and buried her head in her hands.

"I think we should go," Drew said. Harriet caught his eye and was surprised to see his face white with rage.

"If he'd told me, I would have done something," Mrs Taylor said, breaking the silence finally.

"If who'd told you what?" Drew paused.

"John. If he'd told me what his father used to make him do when he was a boy, I'd have put a stop to it. I would have done something..." She trailed off. Her hands shook as she placed them on the table in front of her. "There's a shed. It's over near Darkby Primary school... It's where he'd go to feel safe." Her voice was half-choked with emotion.

"You go, I'll stay," Harriet said.

Tight-lipped, Drew nodded. "Fine." He was gone before Harriet could say another word, leaving her alone in Mrs Taylor's kitchen.

"How do you take your tea?" Harriet asked, moving to the kettle.

"You think I'm a monster, don't you?" Mrs Taylor asked, causing Harriet to turn back.

"No. I think you're a mother who loves her son... no matter what he's done."

Tears gathered in the corners of Mrs Taylor's eyes, causing the blue to brighten. She closed them as she nodded. "God help me, but I do still love him. I never wanted this for him, but I know now it was my fault."

Shaking her head, Harriet reached out and covered the other woman's hand with her own. "This is not your fault."

"I wish I could believe you."

CHAPTER TWENTY-FIVE

"HOW DO you want to handle this?" DC Green asked. Olivia kept her gaze trained on the papers in front of her. Every time she glanced up at the DC he became flustered and while it was funny to mess with him under normal circumstances, she needed him on his game now. Drew had trusted her with and she wasn't about to let her boss down.

"We've just got two coming in for a chat, a Mr Andrews and a Ms Mayhew."

"And do we know how they knew Oliver Poole?"

Olivia risked a sneaky glance up at her colleague. "Didn't you read the notes I gave you?"

Timothy lifted his gaze to hers, and colour suffused his face. "I didn't get any notes. Shit, when did you leave them there?" He started to turn away, but Olivia shook her head.

"Don't, it's fine. I'll catch you up here. We don't

have time now, anyway." She glanced over at the clock on the wall. "They'll be here any minute. Andrews is a guidance counsellor at the school, so he knows all the kids. But by his own admission he knows Oliver quite well because of what happened to his sister." She let her eyes travel down over her own notes. "Oliver's mother said Mr Andrews developed a close rapport with her son. And that only seemed to strengthen after the incident involving John Taylor." She glanced up and found Timothy nodding, his attention locked onto her as though she were the only person left in the world.

"And Ms Mayhew? How does she fit into the Poole boy's life?"

"She's a volunteer with the scouts. Oliver didn't stick with the scouts for very long so I'm not sure what use she'll be, but we still need to talk to her."

DC Green nodded. "Want me to stick the kettle on?"

A genuine smile cracked Olivia's cool facade, and she nodded. "That'd be great."

Colour swept up over Timothy's face for a second time, and he practically bounded away toward the kitchenette. Sighing, Olivia watched him go. Ever since he'd arrived on the team, he'd been somewhat awkward around her, and she hadn't been able to figure out why. But it was rapidly getting to the point where she was going to have to confront him about it. They were a team; they didn't need any kind of weirdness, especially when they were working such an important case.

She caught sight of one of the uniformed officers in the door waving her over. Over his shoulder she could see the guidance counsellor. Mr Andrews was younger than she'd expected him to be; early thirties at most, and his face was smooth and freckled. He wore his greying strawberry blond hair swept over to one side; a bad attempt at covering a prematurely bald spot, she surmised. Sighing, she pushed onto her feet and caught Tim's eye as he worked in the kitchen. He nodded his understanding and carried on with the kettle. It would have been easier if Maz had been doing the interviews with her, at least with him she knew exactly where she stood.

"Please don't shit the bed on me," Olivia muttered as she gave Green one last look before she crossed the office.

A FEW MINUTES LATER, Olivia sat across from Mr Andrews. He was taller than she'd thought. His lanky frame didn't fit into the tweed jacket he wore; almost as though he'd bought it when he'd been larger and just hadn't got around to buying a new one.

She glanced down at her watch, her smile apologetic. "I'm sorry for the delay. My colleague will be here in a minute."

Mr Andrews' smile never reached his eyes as he crossed his legs and leaned back in his chair. "I tell my students that punctuality is the height of manners." He clasped his hands on his knee.

Olivia nodded. "As I said, I'm sorry for the delay, but we are running an investigation here regarding one of your missing students. I've always found that things don't always run to time." There was something about the man that instantly put Olivia's teeth on edge, but she couldn't for the life of her put her finger on what it was.

DC Green chose that moment to shove open the door to the interview room. His face was flushed and he looked flustered. Definitely not the start Olivia had been hoping for.

"Sorry," he said, setting three cups down on the table. "I couldn't find the sugar."

Mr Andrews' smile was a little more brittle than it had been. "Don't worry about it. I just want to help in any way I can."

"Great," Olivia said, flipping open her notepad. "Can you tell us about your relationship with Oliver Poole?"

"My relationship?" Mr Andrews sounded a little taken aback. "I wouldn't say we had a relationship."

"Then what would you call it?" Timothy asked, settling into his seat. The directness of his question took Olivia by surprise, and she cast him a quick glance before she returned her attention to the man in front of them.

"He was a student of mine. I met him once or twice, but that was it. I wouldn't call that a relationship."

Olivia made the pretence of flipping through her notebook. "According to Mrs Poole you worked quite closely with Oliver after the incident regarding the school's caretaker."

Mr Andrews straightened up and fidgeted with the knot on his tie before he brought himself up short. "We were all shocked to learn about that," he said. "I wanted to help Oliver, but he made it clear that he wanted nothing to do with me or the help I offered him."

"And why do you think that is?" Olivia asked. "And why would Mrs Poole think your connection to her son was more than what you're making it out to be here today?"

Mr Andrews flushed and reached for the cup of tea Timothy had brought him. "I suppose for a parent in her position she has latched onto every little detail in her son's life in the hope that something will come of it." He raised his gaze to Olivia. "But I assure you, my connection to Oliver is tenuous at best. He came to see me a handful of times and trying to get him to open up, well I may as well have been trying to get blood from a stone for all the good it did." He huffed out a breath and lifted the cup to his lips.

Olivia dropped back into her chair. "Would you say Oliver was a happy child?"

Andrews seemed to mull the question over before answering. "He introverted. I wouldn't say he was unhappy, but I always got the opinion that he was still grieving the loss of his sister."

"Did he tell you that?"

Andrews smiled, and this time it was genuine. "He didn't have to DC Crandell. I'm a trained counsellor and I'm capable of reading between the lines. He put on a brave face, but deep down Oliver had not dealt with the loss of Amy. And that monster who groomed him, never gave him a chance either."

"You come from the area, is that correct?" DC Green asked. It was an innocent enough question, but Olivia had the sudden feeling that his delay hadn't been caused by him searching for sugar at all. Had he gone and found the notes she'd left on his desk, after all? And if that were true, then what was he getting at now?

"Lived here all my life," he said proudly. "Generations of my family have come up in the same area. We can trace our lineage all the way back." His smile grew warmer. "My mother was an amateur genealogist. She went to great pains to create an accurate picture of our family tree."

"And you'd have been how old twenty years ago?" Green asked, his tone suggested nonchalance.

"Twelve." Mr Andrews shifted uncomfortably,

and Olivia had the sneaking suspicion that he knew exactly where Tim was going with his line of questions.

"So you remember the case of the children who went missing from the area twenty-odd years ago?"

"Twenty-one, to be precise," Mr Andrews said coldly. "I'm not sure what that has to do with Oliver's disappearance."

"You must have known the three children who disappeared then too?"

"What of it?" Andrews folded his arms over his chest.

"I'm just trying to get a little background, is all," Tim said, his smile pleasant. "You don't think this feels too much like history repeating itself?"

"What happened to those children has nothing to do with Oliver," Andrews said, his voice harsh.

"How can you be so sure?" Green asked. "It seems a little coincidental that four children disappear from the same small village in Yorkshire."

"Twenty-one years apart," Andrews said. "They're not connected."

"You sound awfully sure," Olivia said gently. "For all we know the same person who took those children--"

Andrews was already shaking his head. "It's not possible."

"And why is that?"

"Because my parents said it had been dealt with. Everyone at the time knew it."

It was Olivia's turn to feel confused. "I don't understand. They never found the children?"

Andrews shrugged. "I was never privy to the story, but I believe my parents and they said the parents of those three poor children got the closure they needed."

"Why would they say that?" Tim asked. He leaned his elbows on the table and leaned forward.

"How should I know? If you're so interested, go and ask them. But I doubt you'll get much from them on the subject. I came here to give you my statement regarding Oliver Poole and I think I've done just that." Andrews stood abruptly, causing the untouched tea in the cups to slop over the sides and out onto the table. "I'm sorry I can't help you further, but I really think I'm wasting both of our time here."

"Mr Andrews," Olivia said, trying to keep her tone level. "There are a few more--"

The other man held up his hand. "I don't know anything about Oliver's disappearance. If I did, I would tell you. And if I knew who took him, I would definitely tell you. The only thing I can say is that the monster who targeted Oliver to begin with, I'd look to him. He might have said nothing happened and Oliver wasn't in any fit state to dispute it, but we all know that's simply not true."

Tim opened his mouth, but Olivia gave him a

subtle shake of her head and he stopped. "Thank you for your time," Olivia said, pushing onto her feet. She held out her hand and Andrews took it, his grasp sweaty and limp.

He left without a backwards glance. "What did you make of that?" Tim asked, as soon as he was out of earshot.

"He was a little cagey regarding the past," Olivia said thoughtfully. "But he's not wrong when he says they likelihood of this case being linked to Oliver's disappearance is little more than coincidence."

"Come on, you didn't think what he said about the parents wasn't weird?"

Olivia nodded and chewed the top of her pen. "It's worth having a chat with them. If only because of the coincidence." Glancing down at her watch, Olivia pushed onto her feet. "I'll see if Ms Mayhew is here."

Tim nodded. "If she knows as little as Mr Andrews then these interviews were a complete bust."

Olivia didn't argue with him. But in an investigation like this background interviews were a lot like panning for gold in that everything helped. While Andrews hadn't told them anything particularly useful, there were still traces, and she wasn't going to dismiss them as a waste of time just yet.

CHAPTER TWENTY-SIX

SLIDING into the driver's seat, Drew waited for Maz to hop in before he gunned the engine.

"Should I call for back-up?" There was no escaping the edge of excitement in Maz's voice.

"We don't even know if he's going to be there," Drew said thoughtfully as he manoeuvred the car around the narrow roads. "We might be better off waiting to see if there's a hit on the partial plate I called in. We can always check the school."

Maz slumped back against his seat. "I suppose."

The wheel shuddered beneath Drew's hands as the tyres slid on an icy patch on the road. Swearing broadly, he clung to the wheel as got the car back on track. A few moments later, they entered the heart of the village. The Christmas lights strung overhead glittered and blinked in the evening light. From the corner of his eye, Drew watched Maz grip the door as the car took a corner a little faster than he'd anticipated.

Cresting the hill, Drew spotted the primary school up ahead. There was no sign of John Taylor's bike, but that didn't mean he wasn't hiding somewhere on the grounds. Drawing to a halt, Drew killed the engine.

Maz was already out of the car and surveying the scene. "With all due respect, guv, I really think we should call in for back-up. What if the Poole boy is here, and--"

Drew nodded. "Fine. You're right. It's better to be safe." If Maz thought he was going to hang around and wait for the uniformed officers to arrive, then he was sorely mistaken. Maz was right about one thing, if Taylor was responsible for the abduction of the Poole boy, then hanging around here would only give him the opportunity to harm the boy. And that wasn't something Drew could allow.

"Wait here," Drew said.

"But--"

"DS Arya, just do as I ask. If he comes back this way, then I need to know about it."

Maz looked apoplectic, but he nodded. "Right." There was a mutinous tone in his voice that irritated Drew, but he didn't have time to hang around and argue the correct protocol.

Drew hopped the low gate of the school and took off towards the side of the small squat grey building.

The evening light had begun to close in around him, and sleet was drifting down from the sky, coating the ground in an icy slick which made every step treacherous. Rounding the corner of the school, Drew spotted tracks across the grass at the back of the building. Excitement thrummed in his veins as he scanned the area before he set off in the direction the tracks led.

He followed them up to the back of the school where there was a large bottle green shed tucked away. Taylor's bike was propped up against the side of the building, and Drew could see light from beneath the bottom of the door. Sliding his phone from his pocket, he called Maz and in hushed tones told him what he'd discovered. With his free hand, Drew pulled his cuffs from his belt and approached the shed cautiously.

"Mr Taylor, John, my name is DI Haskell, I just want to have a chat with you."

There was a muffled noise from within the shed, followed by a half strangled noise that caused the hairs on the back of Drew's neck to stand to attention. Reaching the door, he tugged it open and found John Taylor suspended from a beam in the middle of the building. His legs kicked and thrashed beneath him, hands clawing at the rope wrapped securely around his throat. Taylor's face was turning an unnatural colour, blotchy and purple as he was slowly strangled by the ligature.

"Fuck!" Drew swore vehemently as he dropped the cuffs and crossed the small floor space. The stool which Taylor had stood on was knocked aside, and Drew wasted no time in standing it upright. Grabbing Taylor's legs, Drew fought with the flailing man who seemed determined to remain suspended from the rope.

He finally managed to get Taylor's feet on the stool, and he glanced up at the man who towered above him. "What the fuck are you doing?" Drew's breathing was ragged, adrenaline zinging in his veins as he kept the large man steady. "Take the rope off."

Taylor shook his head, but Drew was pleased to see his colour slowly returning to something that resembled a normal hue as he kept him in place. "Leave me be."

"I just want to talk to you," Drew said, exasperation colouring his voice.

"Well, I don't want to speak to you lot. I know what you're going to do, and I'm not going to prison."

"Nobody said you were," Drew said. "Look, come down so we can talk about this sensibly."

Taylor shook his head and made a futile attempt to kick Drew away. "No. I'm not going to prison. I didn't touch that boy, but you lot never listen. I can't go to prison. I won't let you send me there."

"Come down, please. We can talk about this."

"Guv?" Maz's voice broke through the panic.

Relief flooded through Drew as he turned in time to see the other man appear in the doorway.

"Help me."

Maz moved into the space and reached up to steady Taylor, allowing Drew to push up onto a box. Taylor tried to push him away. It took a couple of minutes to get organised, but Drew managed to pull the rope from Taylor's neck. They collapsed onto the ground in a heap of limbs.

"Fuck!" Drew huffed, sucking in large mouthfuls of cold air. "Get him up. You do not have to say anything. But it may harm your defence if you do not mention when questioned something which you later rely on in court. Anything you do say may be given in evidence." Drew pulled in a deep breath as he sought to get his heart rate back under control.

Between them, they managed to get Taylor onto his feet. The other man seemed to be more irritated rather than injured, but the last thing Drew wanted was to find a negligence case on his hands if Taylor turned up later with some mysterious injuries. "We need to get an ambulance here," he said, urging Taylor over to the edge of the room where he could sit.

John Taylor tried to shrug free, but after everything Drew was in no mood to be denied. "Sit. Maz get an ambulance out here."

Taylor took the hint and dropped onto the stool

he'd used only moments before in his attempt to end his life. He rubbed at the red ring around his neck. The skin was reddened and angry looking. Drew glanced away. The sight of the bruising which was beginning to appear brought back too many unpleasant memories that he would much rather not be reminded of.

"Why would you do that?" Drew asked, pausing in front of Taylor.

"Why not? Like I said, it's not as though you'll actually listen to me." Taylor's gaze strayed to the rickety floorboards under foot and he shifted on the stool. The squeal of its legs as it slid across the damp, moss covered ground hurt Drew's ears, but he ignored it.

"Why wouldn't we listen?"

"I know what you think of me." There was a hoarseness to Taylor's voice as he fixed his gaze on the wall opposite. "I know you think I'm scum."

Maz snorted derisively, and Drew shot him a withering glare. "We just wanted to speak to you, John. Nobody was accusing you of anything."

Taylor's laughter was brittle, and he glanced up at Drew. "You really believe that, don't you?"

"Why wouldn't I? I'm a man of my word."

"Given half a chance, you'd string me up, just like everyone else would."

"It's not my job to pass judgement, John. I'm just looking for Oliver Poole."

"And your first thought was that I had him?" The colour leeched from Taylor's face.

Drew opened his mouth to argue, but Taylor cut him off before he could get a word out. "Don't lie to me. There's no point. You thought when you followed me here that you'd find the boy? Come on, at least admit that I'm right."

Shaking his head, Drew glanced down at the oil stained floor. "It crossed my mind."

"Hah, see that wasn't so hard now, was it?"

"But you can understand why we'd want to talk to you?" Sirens split the air, apprehension spiralled in Drew's gut as he realised he was rapidly running out of time to ask Taylor all the questions he had. And if he did have Oliver, then Taylor going into hospital would be a delay they could ill afford.

"Aye, I can understand it. Don't mean I have to like it."

"Do you know where he is?" Drew blurted the question out and watched as Taylor's expression closed.

"I never hurt him."

"But do you know where he is, John?" The sirens grew closer, and the cold fingers of dread gripped the back of Drew's neck. "Please."

"I don't know where the lad is. I haven't seen him, not since..." Taylor trailed off as Maz popped his head around the door.

"Sir, ambulance is here."

"Since when?"

"Since before I was arrested. I didn't touch him then, neither. Not that you lot would believe me."

Paramedics in high-vis jackets appeared in the door carrying their bags of medical equipment.

"Fine." Drew let go the breath he'd been holding onto.

"You believe me then?" Taylor asked, as the paramedics began setting up.

"You said you haven't seen him, what choice do I have?" There was a hard glint in Taylor's eyes as Drew spoke, which sent a chill down his spine. Taylor might not have Oliver, but there was something he wasn't telling Drew, and that made him uncomfortable. "But when you're done in hospital, you and I are going to have a chat."

Taylor shrugged, his expression one of ease as though Drew had just wished him a merry Christmas. Drew left the paramedics to settle the blood pressure cuff on the other man. He stepped outside the shed, one eye on the proceedings taking place inside.

"Do you really think Taylor had nothing to do with Oliver's disappearance?" Maz asked, his voice hushed.

"Honestly, I have no idea," Drew said, the strain of the case evident in his voice. "But right now, all I can do is take Taylor's word for it. At least where that's concerned."

"So we just sit around twiddling our thumbs, and in the meantime Oliver is god-knows-where?" Anger laced Maz's words, which took Drew by surprise.

"Nobody is going to sit idly around, Maz. In the meantime we get a warrant for Taylor's communications, his computers, his house. I want you to go to the hospital with him, make sure everything is above board."

"We don't have a lot of evidence to get a warrant."

"We'll get it," Drew said, determination hardening his resolve as he watched the paramedics lead Taylor from the shed and back in the direction of the ambulance.

"There's something he isn't telling us, and I want to know what it is."

CHAPTER TWENTY-SEVEN

TILLY MAYHEW WAS a mouse of a woman, at least in demeanour. She sat on the other side of the table, her shoulders rounded over so that she appeared smaller than she truly was. Her handshake had been warm, the palms of her hand calloused and her grip strong; the antithesis to Andrews, Olivia thought. Her brown hair was scraped back from her face, revealing wide, honest brown eyes. She was attractive, but nobody would ever call her beautiful. Her nose had a bump that suggested it had been broken in the past, and her complexion was a little too rosy a testament to the amount of time she spent outdoors.

"Thanks so much for coming in," Tim said. "We just have a couple of questions."

"Of course, anything I can do to help," Tilly said,

her voice a low burr. "I don't know how much use you'll find me. Oliver wasn't with the scouts very long."

"But you were a scout leader at the same time?"

Tilly nodded. "I led the troop. He came out on two trips with us, but dropped out shortly after."

Olivia glanced down at her notes. "According to his mother, he went on at least five trips. Three overnights camping in the woods."

Tilly shook her head, her smile apologetic. "I'm sure what you want me to tell you, DC Crandell, but Oliver only came out on two trips with us, neither of which were camping trips." Tilly looked genuinely confused. "I keep records, I brought them with me."

"You keep your records from three years ago?"

"I have records that go back ten years," Tilly said. "I don't like to get rid of them because I don't when that knowledge will prove useful." She shrugged and slipped a folder from her bag on the floor.

Olivia took it gratefully and flipped through the contents, giving everything a cursory glance. "This will be very helpful," Olivia said.

"Why would Mrs Poole think Oliver had gone out five times with the scouts?" Olivia asked as she noted the calendar dates in the file Tilly had shared with her. "Honestly, I have no idea. We don't have that many camping trips away. At least not at that age. We do a few, but never in such a short period of time. She has to be mistaken."

Olivia nodded. "I suppose that could be true."

"Is there anything else I can help you with?" Tilly asked.

"When did you last see Oliver?" Tim asked.

Tilly glanced down at her hands. "The afternoon he went missing."

"Excuse me?" Olivia asked, straightening in her chair.

"I don't just work with the scouts," Tilly said. "A group of us do the safe crossing for the children going to school. The last time I saw Oliver was the afternoon he disappeared when he crossed on his way home."

"How did he seem?"

Tilly shrugged. "Normal, I guess. He was with his pal Darren. They both waved, and that was it. I was distracted because Chrissy fell as she ran over the road and I had to go and help her..." Tilly trailed off. "I wish now I'd paid more attention to him."

"Why is that?" Olivia asked.

Tilly shrugged. "Maybe if I had, I'd have more information for you." Her eyes glistened with unshed tears. "I can't imagine what his parents must be going through. It's a good parents worst nightmare, not knowing if their child is safe, or..."

"Is there anything else you can remember from that day?" Tim asked. "Anything at all."

Tilly shook her head. "I wish I could."

Olivia nodded. "Thanks for coming down here."

"I just hope you find him safe."

Olivia nodded. "We'll do our best to bring him home."

Tilly stood, and Olivia and Tim did the same and saw the other woman out of the interview room.

"Well, that was a bust," Tim said once they were alone. Olivia sighed. She couldn't argue with him. They had nothing to go on, and Tilly Mayhew had just proven that Mrs Poole's accounts couldn't be entirely relied upon to be accurate. If she could misremember information regarding Oliver attending scouts, then what else had she got wrong?

"I just hope Drew and Maz are having better luck with John Taylor, because as it stands right now we have no leads on Oliver Poole's whereabouts."

Tim nodded. "Want me to run the details of the two people we spoke to over to the analysts?"

Olivia nodded. "Good idea. Have Jodie run backgrounds on them both. And anyone else, including the information Andrews gave us about the other three missing children."

Tim took the files and took off like an overly excited puppy. They might not have had very much to go on, but at least the interviews had run smoothly. Despite it all, Olivia had a sinking feeling that their best efforts would be for nought. Oliver had been away from his family for too long now and they would soon all have to admit that they were no longer searching for a living missing boy, but a body. But she wouldn't let that thought intrude... Not today, at least. They would find him and they would bring him home. They had no choice.

CHAPTER TWENTY-EIGHT

"I DON'T WANT to talk about it, Ambrose," Martina said, raising her voice to be heard over the sound of the trolleys clattering up the hall.

"All I'm saying is, if you need somebody to talk to, I'm here."

"Thanks, but I don't need your pity." Her voice was razor sharp. Guilt swelled in her chest as she watched Ambrose swallow down the hurt, but he didn't say another word about it, and for that she was grateful. He was well meaning and all, but she didn't need him poking his nose into her business.

Sighing, she stared down at the take-away cup of coffee she'd picked up from the vending machine. While it wasn't the worst coffee—that dubious honour belonged to the old filter machine they had in the office—it certainly wasn't the best, but it would just have to do. Taking a swig of the contents, she grimaced as the bitter taste of lukewarm coffee flooded her mouth. Swallowing it, she glanced over at Ambrose, who at that moment had taken a keen interest in the tile pattern on the floor.

"Did they give you any kind of hint as to who the body belongs to?" She was aiming for amicable, but there was still an underlying hint of the harsh tone she'd used earlier.

If Ambrose noticed, he didn't give anything away. Sighing, he straightened up and fiddled with his crooked tie. "Not really. Jackson said he had an ID, and that we needed to speak to the anthropologist." Ambrose shrugged. "After that, your guess is as good as mine."

"I've never spoken with a forensic anthropologist before," Martina said. "What do you think they'll be like?"

"I've always found us to be just like everyone else." The statement took Martina by surprise, and she swung around to find a petite woman, with large dark eyes, and greying blonde hair standing behind her with a bemused expression on her face. "Of course, I suppose that depends on your view of the world."

Heat swept up Martina's neck and rapidly climbed her cheeks. "I'm sorry, I didn't--"

"No need to apologise. I've got this terrible habit of sneaking up on people. And you didn't say anything bad, I've certainly heard much worse in my time. My mother was right when she said eavesdroppers never heard anything good about themselves, but in this instance she was incorrect."

Her smile was inviting and warm. "I'm Dr Grieves." Martina noted that she didn't offer her hand, opting instead to keep them down at her sides. "If you're ready to come in, we can begin. Dr Jackson said he would join us shortly."

Martina cast a sideways glance at Ambrose—who studiously avoided her gaze—as he clambered to his feet and followed the woman into a small room off the corridor. Drawing in a breath, Martina tried to quell her embarrassment. After all, it wasn't as though she'd actually said anything bad. Then again, that wasn't really the point. If the forensic anthropologist could sneak up on her like that, then she was clearly off her game, and she knew why. But knowing the reasoning behind her behaviour didn't give her a path toward fixing said issue.

Pushing the thoughts aside, she followed Ambrose and Dr Grieves into the examination room. The smell of formalin was stronger in here. Reaching into her inside jacket pocket, Martina felt around for the tub of Vicks she normally carried there, but her fingers came up empty. Wrinkling her nose in disgust, she swallowed the saliva that flooded her mouth. *Don't you dare up-chuck here, and now, Martina. Just focus on Dr Grieves words.*

Catching the anthropologist's eye, Martina did

her best to plaster a smile on her face, but judging by the surprise that crossed Grieves' face, Martina assumed she'd failed in her attempt to appear unperturbed. The poor woman probably thought she was some kind of nutter. Once they were suitably attired, and gloved up, Dr Grieves took them into the main room where the skeleton lay on a metal examination table. There was an oddness to the manner in which the skeleton had been displayed that surprised Martina.

"What can you tell us?" Ambrose said. How he could appear so at ease in this place of death never failed to take Martina by surprise.

"As you know, your skeleton belongs to a young male. 6ft 2inches in height. Originally I placed his age range in the region of 18-30--"

"Dr Jackson had us looking at people mid to late twenties," Martina interjected. She half expected the other woman to be irritated by the interruption, but Dr Grieves instead seemed to be unperturbed by it.

"There was a little disagreement between myself and Dr Jackson, but now that we have an ID we can say with some degree of certainty that the young man in question was twenty-four."

"So who is he?" Ambrose said.

"I'll leave the formal identification to Dr Jackson. He has the report from the forensic odontologist. We have however established a CoD."

Despite feeling ill, Martina perked up at the

thought of getting a cause of death. When it came to skeletal remains, she knew from studying past case files that it wasn't always possible to determine one definitively.

"So, go on," Ambrose urged. "You've got us on tenterhooks here."

"I'd prefer to show you," she said, directing them over to the skeleton. The pieces of the skull were gathered together to form an approximation of its original shape. The other bones which had been recovered from the crime scene had been laid out in what Martina assumed was anatomically correct positioning, but the overall picture was a disturbing one. The spinal column had been laid out with a distinctive 'S' shape curvature, which seemed to throw off the rest of the skeleton.

"It's not all here," Martina said, more to herself than the rest of the room.

"Good eye, detective," Dr Grieves said, sounding particularly pleased. "Despite combing the area, we weren't able to recover a complete skeleton."

"Did the killer remove some of the body?" Ambrose's question brought a sickening image to the forefront of Martina's mind.

"It's a possibility. It seems more likely some of the smaller, more delicate bones simply decomposed over the years. And there's evidence of animal predation which could be attributed to some of the missing pieces too."

"But it is possible," Ambrose pressed.

Dr Grieves sighed. "Of course. At this point in the investigation, anything and everything is fair game."

"Is the spine placed like that because of the missing bones?" Martina asked, unable to tear her eyes away from what remained of a once living, breathing human being.

"No, they're all here and accounted for," Dr Grieves said. "This young man had scoliosis, which is what has given the spine that shape, but that isn't a contributing factor to his death. If you look here, you'll see there has been extensive trauma to the parietal bone." As she spoke she indicated a large rounded piece of skull that to Martina's unqualified opinion looked like the back of the skull. "There has been fracturing to the maxilla, the mandible, orbital, and superciliary arch, and the zygomatic arch--"

"I don't mean to interrupt," Ambrose said. "But we didn't spend years in university studying obscure bones."

Dr Grieves smiled indulgently. "Sorry, I get carried away sometimes." She sighed and glanced down at the skull. "This young man sustained some very serious blunt force trauma to his skull, probably received in the form of a severe beating."

"How can you tell? I mean, the skull was in pieces when it was recovered," Martina asked.

Dr Grieves nodded. "Yes, that complicated

matters." She picked up a piece of the skull, and indicated a large hole, with several spider-web style fractures which spread outwards from the injury. "This is the parietal bone, it sits at the back of the skull above the occipital, or base of the skull. This kind of injury wasn't caused by natural predation, or even the incident which occurred during the recovery of the body. This is a blunt force trauma. Obviously I can't tell you exactly what it was that he was struck with, but I can tell you that from the fracturing that occurred this injury alone is not congruent with survival. When you look at this particular injury along with the fracturing which has occurred in the bones of the face, it paints a very disturbing picture." She sighed and set the bone back down on the metal table gently.

"There is extensive damage to the rib bones, several fractures of the lower arm bones, and legs, which are also in congruence with my hypothesis that this young man received a sustained and vicious attack directly before and leading up to his death. Staining on the bones indicates he suffered substantial internal haemorrhaging directly preceding his death."

"Please tell me he was already dead, or at the very least unconscious for it?" Ambrose asked.

"There's honestly no way to know if he was awake, or unconscious. The staining on the bones, along with some evidence of repair suggest he was still alive for a time after the attack."

Dr Grieves words settled over them like a mantle of sorrow, determined to weigh them down.

The door at the back of the room swung open and Dr Jackson hurried inside, snapping on gloves as he moved. "Have you given them the cause of death yet?"

Dr Grieves nodded. "I was just explaining it to them."

From beneath his arm, Dr Jackson produced a file which he handed off to Ambrose without any preamble. "The odontologist's report. There was a full x-ray on file of the victim because he'd been to hospital to have some teeth removed."

"Why hospital?" Ambrose asked, as he flipped open the file. "Jack Campbell, twenty-four. Reported missing in 1999 by his next-of-kin, a Marjorie Campbell."

"According to the report from the dentist who treated him, and subsequently referred him onto the hospital he was a young man with a complicated medical history including a congenital disorder, and intellectual disability which required him to have precautionary measures taken when undergoing the dental procedure." Dr Jackson glanced down at the report. "He had DiGeorge syndrome." He raised an eyebrow as he scanned the notes. "Definitely a significant medical history. He had a repair on a cleft lip, and palate when he was quite young but it left him with quite extensive hearing loss."

Martina glanced back over at the skeleton. "Christ, this just gets worse, and worse." From the corner of her eye, she noted the look of sadness on Dr Jackson's face. In all the times she's seen him give reports on post-mortems, she'd never once known him to be affected by the situation. Until now.

"I've got a feeling this one is going to get worse, before it gets better," Ambrose said, as they headed for the door.

Martina kept her thoughts to herself. She didn't need to say anything else, her silence was enough agreement.

CHAPTER TWENTY-NINE

HOURS LATER, and what felt like a million cups of tea later, Harriet made it back to the operations room. It had taken time to get Mrs Taylor to calm down, and by the time she'd managed that, Drew had returned with a veritable army of personnel to turn the elderly woman's house upside down. In the end, Harriet had persuaded her to contact her daughter so she could take her to stay with her sister, who lived in Staithes.

"He's in a right mood," DC Olivia Crandell said as soon as Harriet walked in the door. "Please tell me you can put a smile back on his grumpy-arse-face."

Surprised, Harriet tried to keep her smile to herself, but it proved impossible as Olivia grinned at her as she headed for the kitchen area. "You fancy a cuppa?"

"I'd loved one," Harriet said. "Let me help."

Olivia started to shake her head, but Harriet followed her anyway. Her motivations weren't entirely altruistic, getting the inside scoop from a friendly face would give her the upper hand in her dealings with Drew. And considering the sensitive nature of the case they were dealing with, Harriet had the distinct impression that she needed all the help she could get.

Olivia swung open a white cupboard door and removed a box of tea bags from inside. She dropped it onto the black faux granite counter next to the kettle. Catching Harriet's eye, she shrugged. "Gotta be Yorkshire tea," she said, as she set about setting out two mugs.

"You'll hear no arguments from me," Harriet said. Coffee would always be her preference, but she'd been struggling to sleep, so tea seemed like a good idea. "What happened with John Taylor?"

Olivia chewed her lip as she prepped the cups. Finally, she folded her arms over her chest, and leaned back against the counter, the picture of ease. Harriet couldn't help but notice how far she'd come since she'd first met her. It seemed getting out of uniform suited the young DC.

"The hospital is keeping him overnight," she said. "Haskell is furious, as you can imagine. We spoke to some people from Oliver's life today, but nothing that moves us forward." She sighed.

Harriet nodded. She could imagine. The last

thing Drew wanted was something getting in the way of him finding Oliver Poole. Although, as the clock ticked down the hours, Harriet was beginning to lose faith that they would find the boy alive, not that she would ever say that to Drew. He needed to cling onto the remnants of his hope. It was an integral part of his being, and she wouldn't ever take that away from him. The job would do enough damage without her interference.

The boiling kettle clicked off, and Olivia turned to pour the water into the cups. "Can you pass me the milk?" Olivia asked.

Harriet busied herself with the small fridge in the corner of the room.

"Is there anything you can give us to help maybe speed up the process of finding Oliver?" Olivia's question took her by surprise, and Harriet froze, fingers wrapped around the handle of the milk carton.

"What do you mean?"

"Isn't there something you can tell Drew that will crack this thing wide open? Anything at all?"

Straightening up, Harriet placed the milk on the counter before she shook her head. "There's really nothing I can say. Until we have more information, I have nothing to go on."

"But the fact that our guy has taken a child, that must mean something, right?"

Sighing, Harriet tucked a non-existent curl

behind her ear. This was the problem when it came to mixing what she did with policing. Hollywood had a lot to answer for. At least in the movies, or on the tv there was always an easy answer, a quick fix that led them to the perpetrator. The same could not be said when it came to reality. Quick fixes, and easy answers played no part in the job they did. But it seemed that wouldn't stop people from wishing it were true.

"It means exactly what you think it means," Harriet said. "There is a predator out there who had the capability to snatch a child in broad-daylight without anybody noticing."

Olivia stared at her with an eager expression, as though she were waiting for Harriet to bestow some kind of life-changing wisdom. It made Harriet uncomfortable, and she regretted following the DC into the kitchen.

"So that must mean that we're dealing with somebody particularly smart and organised?"

"Possibly," Harriet said. "You cannot rule out the possibility that there was luck involved, and opportunity. Oliver took the shortcut into the forest. For all we know the person who took him, would have snatched just any child who happened to stumble across their path."

Olivia's expression fell, and Harriet knew she'd disappointed the young detective. "You think this a wild-goose chase, don't you?" Olivia lifted the milk carton, and topped up both cups with a generous amount, before she slid Harriet's mug towards her. The milk swirled outwards, lightening the almost black depths to a rich tan colour.

"I wouldn't say that," Harriet said carefully. "Unfortunately, it's one of those situations where I need more information to be of any real assistance."

"So you don't think it's strange that twenty years ago three kids went missing in the same place?"

"What?" Harriet snapped her attention up from the cup in front of her. "Nobody said anything to me about others going missing in the same area."

Olivia nodded before she took a large mouthful of tea. "Yeah, twenty years ago, three other children, of a similar age to Oliver Poole disappeared in the woods near Darkby. Drew had me look into it because of the body they found in the woods over the weekend."

"Can I see the files?"

Olivia nodded. "I don't see why not. They're three cold-cases now. It was a terrible blow to the village when they couldn't find the kids. And now with Oliver going missing, I think it's only a matter of time before the press latch onto the history of the place and spin it up into some Bermuda-style-triangle thing for kids."

Harriet nodded absent-mindedly, her thoughts already awash with the possibilities. It was too much of a coincidence, and she'd always found that coincidence had a terrible habit of stretching the limits of credibility. No, there had to be a connection, and perhaps if she could figure it out then they would stand a chance of getting Oliver Poole home.

"You're not listening to me anymore, are you?" Olivia asked. Her question brought Harriet up short, and she glanced over at the other woman.

"Of course, I am." Heat climbed into her cheeks, as guilt twisted her stomach.

Not that she needed to have bothered with the emotion. Olivia it seemed was either made of sterner stuff, or she was all too used to those around her following their own thoughts down more interesting rabbit-holes. She grinned and shook her head before indicating the now tepid tea Harriet had set down on the counter earlier. "Come on, I'll get you set up with the files I've managed to dig out so far."

Happily Harriet followed Olivia back into the office. It was then she noticed the space across the hall was occupied. "I didn't know you had more officers seconded to the task force?"

Olivia shook her head. "Nope. Those are the analysts, and forensic digital experts sent over by the NCA." Harriet pulled a face, and Olivia smiled. "The National Crime Agency. I've got a feeling they're here to assess performance."

"Why would it matter to them?"

"Because they're always looking for the best and brightest to join their team."

"But aren't we all working for the same goal?"

Olivia shrugged. "You'd think so, but I sometimes wonder if anybody has told them that." She indicated the others in the room across the hall. "Well, here you go." Olivia slapped the top of a large box that took up most of the space on her desk. As her hand connected with the lid, it caused a plume of dust to rise off the cardboard surface.

"Is this everything?" Harriet asked, unable to keep the surprise from her voice. She'd grown accustomed to large files and reports that filled numerous boxes for even the most straight-forward of cases.

"God, no," Olivia said. "This is just what I managed to gather as a brief overview of the facts. The rest of the files, and exhibits are still over in the storage facility. If I tried to check those out, we wouldn't have any room to run our own investigation."

Harriet smiled sheepishly. "Of course."

"You can take over one of the desks in the corner if you like. Most of us here hot-desk, so we don't have any specific workspace."

Picking up the box, Harriet strained beneath the weight of the files within. If this was just a brief overview of the case from twenty-years ago, then she didn't dare imagine how many more files she would find if she was forced to get them from storage. She carried them over to the desk and set the box down before taking a seat. The hustle and bustle of activity around her faded into the background as she pulled off the lid and took out the first file on top. Flipping it open, Harriet was faced with the pictures of three children. They smiled up at her from the front of the file, two boys, and a girl; their open expressions and trusting eyes sparkling with so much joy it caused her stomach to clench painfully.

Twenty-one years, and they had never come home. It was a bitter agony for any parent. But perhaps, if she was lucky, the Poole's story would have a happier ending and they would see their son returned to them. Setting the images to one side, Harriet positioned their pictures so they were at the edge of her vision; never out of sight. It seemed important that she not lose sight of them as she started to pull other files from the box. As though by keeping them there, and always visible, they would somehow guide her to the truth. It was a fanciful notion, but with another child missing, Harriet was willing to try anything; no matter how much of a long shot it might seem.

CHAPTER THIRTY

MARTINA SETTLED her shoulders as Ambrose rapped his knuckles against the wood front door. The silence stretched around them and Ambrose scratched at the stubble growing along his chin. "I told her we were calling around," he said, sounding a little bewildered. "Why would she go out?"

"Somebody's here," Martina said, jerking her head in the direction of the car parked in front of the garage. "Engine is still warm."

"How can you tell?"

"You can hear the tick of it cooling down," Martina said. "Maybe I should go around--" She cut off as the front door swung open to reveal a man in his late thirties.

"DS Ambrose Scofield, and this is my colleague DC Nicoll," Ambrose said, a warm smile curling his lips up at the corners. "We spoke to a Marjorie Campbell about an hour ago, is she in?"

"You found him, didn't you?" There was no preamble in the man's question.

"I was hoping maybe we could come in to have a chat?" Ambrose said. "Can I ask your name?"

"Sorry, I'm Greg Campbell, Marjorie is my mother." Martina ducked her gaze and felt her chest constrict. As she stood there and listened to the murmur of her partner's voice as he spoke to Jack Campbell's brother, she found herself wondering how strong of a resemblance there would have been between the two men had Jack lived.

She followed Ambrose into the house as Greg directed them through to a cosy living room. The floral print couches were worn, but comfortable. The dark green patterned carpet underfoot looked brand new, although Martina had a feeling that it was anything but. There was a matte black wood burner set back into a fireplace in the corner of the room. The orange glow of the flames inside cast odd shadows across the floor. Martina's gaze trailed over to the woman who sat next to it. A small bird of a woman, fine-boned and delicate, but the expression on her face was anything but delicate.

Marjorie Campbell met Martina's gaze head on. Her shrewd hazel eyes were like two chips of granite, and Martina dropped her attention to the carpet rather than find herself locked into a battle of wills.

"You found him, didn't you?" Marjorie's unwavering voice belied the woman's more fragile appearance, and Martina's respect for the mother who had lost her son twenty years ago climbed even higher.

"We spoke on the phone," Ambrose began to speak, but Marjorie's gaze withered him where he stood.

"Just tell me, did you find my son, or not?"

"We did," Martina said finally, breaking her silence.

Marjorie's gaze shifted to Martina, the momentary flicker of hope extinguished almost immediately, and Marjorie slumped back into the chair. She shrank in on herself, her small shoulder's rounding over. She exhaled harshly as though Martina had punched her straight into the solar-plexus.

"Mum." Greg pushed past them and rushed to his mother's side, placing his hand on hers.

She pushed him away, turning her hard expression on him. "Don't." That one word carried with it so many years of hurt and anguish, and Greg flinched, withdrawing from his mother.

"Where?" Marjorie's voice was husky with emotion, but there were no tears that Martina could see in her eyes.

"Dalby Forest," Ambrose said.

Marjorie nodded. "He liked to walk the trails there." She spoke as though she was only one in the room. "He loved everything to do with wildlife, always off birdwatching, or looking for fox tracks." She glanced down at her curled hands in her lap. "Who killed my son?"

"What makes you say that?" Ambrose asked.

"My son didn't just wander off one day and forget to come home. Somebody stopped him from coming back to me, there's no doubt in my mind."

"Did he have enemies?" Martina could tell from the tone of Ambrose's voice that he felt as off kilter by the entire situation as she did.

"Only the ignorant fools who didn't understand him. They thought he was weird, odd. The children used to make fun of him because he liked to go out on the nature walks with the scouts..." She glanced over at Greg, and for a moment Martina was almost certain she caught sight of something bitter in the other woman's expression. "They thought he was unnatural. That he behaved inappropriately for a man of twenty-four." Marjorie turned her attention back to Martina. "How did he die?"

"I'm not sure that's—" Ambrose started to speak, but Marjorie shook her head.

"I've waited twenty years to know what happened to him. I deserve to know the truth."

"It's our belief that he was murdered," Martina said.

"I figured that out for myself," Marjorie said. "I want to know how."

Martina shook her head. "My colleague is correct, I—"

"I don't need your pity," Marjorie snapped. "I don't need it, and I certainly never asked for it. I want to know the truth. I let him down all those years ago because I wasn't with him. I need to know what happened to him. Maybe if I know the truth, I can take some of the pain—some of the fear he must have felt —" Her voice cracked over the words.

"I really don't—"

"He sustained a serious head injury," Martina said, cutting her partner off. "According to the post-mortem, it's the belief of the pathologist that he took a beating. He has broken bones, it would have caused some severe internal injuries."

Marjorie remained dry-eyed, but there was no denying the tightening around her mouth, and she closed her eyes as she drank down every detail Martina shared with her.

"And would he have known what was happening to him?" Marjorie asked. "Did he call out for me?"

"Mum, please—" Greg said hoarsely, the grief he felt evident in his face.

Martina swallowed hard. "There's no way to know..." It was a lie of omission, but to her at least it felt necessary.

Marjorie nodded. "He knew. My boy knew what they were doing to him. He would have called out for me."

"Can you tell us what happened the day he went missing?" Martina asked, edging a little closer.

"Why, so you can lie and pretend I'm just overreacting? You know, they told me he was a grown man, that he was entitled to leave if he wanted to..." She choked off angrily, and lifted her eyes to Martina. "But I was right, wasn't I?"

"You were," Martina said gently. "But we need your help, Mrs Campbell. I want to find the person responsible for your son's murder." Martina glanced over at Ambrose, who nodded almost imperceptibly.

"Perhaps you could show me where I can make some tea," Ambrose said brusquely. "The wife said the only thing I'm good for is boiling a kettle."

Marjorie kept her attention riveted on her hands in her lap as Greg pushed onto his feet and followed Ambrose from the room. As the door clicked shut, Martina turned her attention to the woman across from her. "Do you mind if I sit?"

"Go ahead," Marjorie said tightly. "I don't know what you expect me to tell you that I didn't already say when he first disappeared."

"Did your son have many friends?"

Marjorie scoffed loudly. "Friends? He thought they were his friends, but they weren't..."

"Who are they? Can you remember their names?"

She nodded. "I wrote it all down," she said, reaching down the side of her chair. "When I spoke to your colleague, I got this out..." She clasped a small notepad in her hand, the edges of which were dog-eared and stained from age and usage. "I knew one day I would need it all, and I was worried I might forget." She glanced over at a framed picture of a young man on the table next to her. "I never wanted to let him down."

"You didn't."

Her smile was a bitter twist of her lips. "I wasn't there when he needed me. He died alone and afraid, and I wasn't there for him. I should have been there to protect him, to hold his hand..." Her voice broke over the last sentence and she dashed the back of her hand over her eyes. "If that's not letting somebody down, DC Nicoll, then I don't know what is."

There was a pit in the bottom of Martina's stomach as she took the proffered notebook from Marjorie. "You said people thought your son was behaving inappropriately," Martina said hesitantly. "What did you mean exactly?"

Marjorie glanced down at her weathered hands. "He was twenty-four, but that was in body only." She drew in a deep breath. "He was born with a severe form of DiGeorge syndrome, which made his life difficult," she said. "He had a cleft-lip and palate that he received surgery for, but not before it damaged his hearing. Those two things alone were enough to single him out as different. But there were complications even before he was born that made his life harder. The umbilical cord prolapsed prior to birth, and he was starved of oxygen resulting in a severe brain injury." She glanced over at the picture on the table. "He was such a handsome young man, and so bright." She closed her eyes. "Physically he was twenty-four, but Jack had the mental age of a very young child. He had difficulty tying his shoelaces and writing his name, but people don't see that. Instead, they saw a grown man wanting to play hide-and-seek with their children. As far as Jack was concerned, he couldn't see the difference between himself and who he thought were his friends..."

"The parents complained?"

Marjorie nodded. "A few months before he went missing there was an altercation..." She drew in a shaky breath.

"Would this altercation have been around the same time as the three children who went missing in Dalby Forest?"

Marjorie lifted her gaze. "I told them he would never have hurt those children. They were his friends. But one of the fathers wouldn't listen to reason and demanded to know what he'd done to them. Somebody threw a punch, and Jack wound up losing a tooth. He had to have surgery. I remember how much he cried because he couldn't understand why I wasn't taking away the pain. I reported the incident, but nothing came of it."

"Jack was actually friends with the three children

who went missing?" Martina asked, unable to keep the edge of excitement from her voice.

"He was, among others. They had all been part of the same scouts' troop. The people who ran it allowed Jack to tag along, but after the three disappeared that all stopped."

"They stopped Jack from going?"

Marjorie shook her head. "No, I put a stop to it. I had a chat with one of the scout leaders, Graham I think his name was. It's all in the notebook anyway. I spoke to him and told him my concerns and we agreed it was better for Jack to stay away."

"You thought someone would go after him when he was with the troop?"

Marjorie's smile was tinged with sadness. "I was partially right. But maybe if I'd let him stay with the group he'd have been safer."

"The day he went missing, where was Jack?"

Marjorie leaned back in her chair. "We'd gone to York earlier in the day, and when we came back, I asked Greg to take him along the forest trail, but Greg came home without him. Said he'd popped into the shop because Jack wanted ice cream."

"And where was Jack when Greg was in the shop?"

"Greg told me Jack wanted to wait outside, and he thought it was safe."

"How old was Greg?"

"Fifteen..." She closed her eyes. "I don't blame

him," she said. "I know that's what you're thinking." She paused and closed her eyes. "I know it's what he thinks too. But, the truth is, I don't blame him at all. He was young and I put far too much responsibility on his shoulders. No, I don't hold my son accountable, it's my fault. I should have been there, and I wasn't. I let them both down that day."

Martina kept her thoughts to herself.

"And when did you call the police?"

"I went out myself but I couldn't find any sign of him, so I can home and called the police. I told them everything, but I don't think they took it seriously."

"And you told them he was vulnerable? That he wasn't like other twenty-four-year-olds?" Martina couldn't fathom the idea that Marjorie's reporting of her vulnerable, missing son wouldn't have been taken seriously.

"I told them, but they thought I was a helicopter parent. And they were preoccupied with the missing children's case." She sucked down a shuddering breath. "I think maybe you should go," she said. "I'm not feeling very well, and anything else you need is in the notebook."

Martina climbed to her feet. The heat in the room seemed almost overwhelming now. "I'm sorry for you loss," she said, but before she could say another word Marjorie shook her head.

"Don't. Just find the person responsible."

"I'll do my best," Martina said.

"I hope your best is better than mine was," Marjorie said, as she picked up the smiling photograph of her son. Martina watched as the older woman drew a shaking finger down over his cheek. "I'm sorry." Marjorie's voice was little more than a whisper. Martina crept from the room, leaving the other woman to her grief.

CHAPTER THIRTY-ONE

PULLING the fur-lined hood of his short puffer jacket up, AJ Wilson leaned back against the school wall. Bending his knee, he propped his foot behind him, ignoring the sound of his Nike Air-Max trainers as they scuffed along the bricks he jammed his hands down into his deep pockets. Out here, with the other lads from the years below him, he was king of the heap. And he'd earned his position at top of the food-chain, the other boys knew it too. The younger ones were all afraid of him. He'd had to break a few noses to gain the respect that he now possessed, and, well, the years ahead of him liked him because of what he could offer them.

His dad getting the job as a supplier for Game-Stop had been a stroke of luck that he had leveraged to his advantage. It didn't hurt that his parents got him whatever he asked for. He'd once overheard his aunt Jackie telling his mum that he was, 'nowt but a spoilt-brat,' but mum had given her what-for. Aunt Jackie just had a stick up her arse, probably because she was nothing more than a barren bitch.

From the corner of his eye, AJ spotted Darren hurrying across the open grass. His eyes were red-rimmed, his pale skin blotchy. The news that his best mate Oliver had gone missing was all over the school. The dozy teachers had even offered them all counselling. He'd managed to get out of maths because of it, but the counsellor was just the school's guidance counsellor Mr Andrews and he was nothing more than a creepy bastard who spent his time adjusting his crotch. Barry had once asked Andrews if he was suffering from some kind of crotch rot. It had landed him in detention for a week, but as far as AJ was concerned, that was a small price to pay for being a legend. Part of him had even wished he'd thought of it himself, and he'd been jealous of Barry and the attention he'd garnered.

"I think he got him," Darren said, as soon as he'd drawn level with AJ.

"Who got what?"

"The Owl-Man," Darren said. His blood-shot eyes were like flying saucers, and AJ half expected to see them bulge out of Darren's head any moment.

"Stop chattin' shit, yeah. The Owl-Man is nothing but a story we tell little kids like you lot to scare you."

"He's real," Darren said defiantly. AJ contemplated clipping Darren around the back of his head—just like his dad did to him—but changed his mind. Darren was having it rough, and while AJ was tough, he was fair. "We saw his eyes in the woods."

"You saw nothin'," AJ said, turning away from Darren. From the opposite side of the school Barry was ambling towards them both and AJ pushed away from the wall.

"I'm telling you, AJ, we saw his eyes on Saturday night. He was there, I know he was. And Oliver saw him too."

"Well, if you saw him, then I guess Owl-Man must have taken Oliver." Derision dripped from each one of AJ's words, but the strangled noise that left Darren's lips told AJ that the younger boy didn't know when he was the butt of a joke.

"You really think he took him?"

"Prolly," AJ said. "And if he did, then he ain't coming back, so stop banging on about it all the time, yeah?" Darren sniffed and AJ caught sight of the tears that glistened in the younger boy's eyes, and for a moment he felt the briefest flicker of guilt.

"It's all my fault," Darren whispered. He scuffed the back of his hand beneath his nose and sniffed loudly.

"You comin'," Barry called from the other side of the marshy lawn.

"Yeah!"

"What am I supposed to do?" Darren asked, but AJ ignored him and started onto the grass.

He immediately regretted his decision as the mud from the lawn squelched up around his pristinely white trainers. AJ's foot slipped, and he windmilled his arms, barely managing to stay on his feet. "Shit," he swore vehemently as he righted himself.

Barry's laughter drifted across the air, causing heat to mount AJ's cheeks. He watched Barry double over, his already straining buttons on his white school shirt gaping against his rotund belly. The guilt AJ had felt moments before fled as humiliation burned in his chest.

"I don't fucking know, or care, Darren. Why don't you piss off and cry at someone who gives a shit?"

"But you're my friend--" AJ's laughter cut Darren off before he could finish his sentence.

"Who gave you that fucking idea? I'm not your friend. Your only friend is prolly dead. Maybe you should go and join him." With that final parting shot, AJ started off across the grass leaving Darren to sniffle loudly behind him.

CHAPTER THIRTY-TWO

"WE'RE GOING TO HOLD A PRESS-CONFERENCE," the monk said, his voice carrying over the murmuring in the room. It was enough to bring silence to the conference room, and Drew felt a frisson of tension race down his spine. Press conferences were never a positive sign, he knew it and so did everybody else present.

It would open up Oliver Poole's family to all sorts of responses; both negative and positive. If they weren't suitably emotional, or often if they were too emotional, many people would see red-flags that simply weren't there. Too many armchair detectives believed they could solve a case simply by watching something on the television. It was never so simple. True, there had been a number of high-profile cases that had involved liars who were only too happy to shed their crocodile tears in front of the nation. But more often than not, at least in Drew's experience, those who resorted to the ordeal of a press-conference were simply too desperate and distraught to care about the implications of the public turning against them.

"Are you sure it's a good idea?" Drew asked the question he knew the rest of the team were thinking.

"You know as well as I, that if we could keep the press out of it, we would. But we need to reach a wider audience and the media is the fastest way to do it." From where he sat, Drew could see the strain the case was beginning to take on his DCI. He'd never been a conventionally handsome man, but the toll of the case had seemingly robbed him of what little youth he had left on his side. The monk's usually pallid complexion was washed out under the harsh strip lighting and the dark circles ringing his already too-small eyes caused them to practically disappear beneath his heavy brow.

"We can set up some alerts through social media." A somewhat familiar voice from the back of the room piped up, and Drew turned in his seat and scanned the people who stood against the back wall. He snagged his gaze on the red-haired analyst who had come down with the others from the NCA. She didn't see him, her attention instead riveted on the front of the room. What was her name again? Jamie, Jessie? Jodie. The name popped into his head and Drew was pleased to know his lack of sleep hadn't completely turned his brain to Swiss cheese.

"And what good will that do?" Gregson asked, managing to sound both dismissive and irritated at the same time. "People join places like that to look at videos of cats, not missing kids."

"That's not entirely true," Jodie said. "We've seen some excellent responses through social media to previous investigations. The public like to see their local police forces reaching out through the arenas they're already familiar with. It gives them a greater sense of security. Not to mention people like to think they can make a difference."

"Great, so it's a morale boost," Gregson muttered beneath his breath. "I thought your lot were supposed to help with CCTV and the likes, not turn this into a popularity contest. Oliver Poole needs action, not likes on a post."

As Gregson spoke, colour flooded up into Jodie's face, travelling up her neck until it reached the tips of her ears, turning her a becoming shade of pink.

"Actually, I think Ms Meakin is correct." Harriet's support took Drew by surprise. Not only had he not realised she'd been invited to the meeting, but he hadn't actually seen her arrive. "People are most likely to get their sources of news from social media these days. There have been a number of studies done to reflect this, it's actually one of the reasons we've seen an uptick in false narratives flourishing.

People like to think they've discovered something for themselves, and the more unscrupulous among the general population who feed on sowing anarchy and discord are only too happy to use this medium for their own benefit. And it's because of this base that we're having a corresponding rise in the 'fake news' rhetoric among populations."

"I don't need to know why people believe the bull-shit spouted on the internet as fact, Dr Quinn. What I need is action. There's a young boy missing and as every hour passes our chances of finding and bringing him home to his parents alive decrease."

"Then social media is one of the best tools to utilise in the search," Jodie said. There was still a slight pink tinge to her cheeks, but she'd mostly managed to recover her composure.

"Just get the word out there," Gregson said irritably. "Dr Quinn, I'd like you to help the parents prepare for the press conference. Everyone else you know what you're supposed to be doing. I expect results."

Drew was on his feet and moving before the DCI had managed to step away from his position at the top of the room. He spotted the monk's attempt to catch his eye but quickly sidestepped his boss as he made after Harriet, who seemed to be in deep conversation with the analyst as they left the space.

He managed to catch up to them in the hall and was a little chagrined to find himself somewhat out of breath; too many bacon stotties, he reasoned. He'd have to do something about the almost constant barrage of junk-food before he turned into the Pillsbury Doughboy's brother.

"Are you all right?" Harriet raised an eyebrow at him.

"I wanted to know if you'd found anything in the old files?"

"Olivia told you I was looking over them?" There was the briefest flicker of accusation in Harriet's voice, which took him somewhat by surprise. It wasn't like her to overreact to something so innocuous as the sharing of information amongst the team.

"She said you were engrossed, I just wanted to know if you'd discovered anything that might help us? Is everything..." He trailed off, suddenly unsure how to finish the sentence.

"Sorry," Harriet said. "I've just not been sleeping too well. The case, and I've got a few things on my mind."

"Lavender is supposed to help with that," Jodie interrupted, reminding Drew that she was there.

"With the case?" Harriet asked, managing to look suitably confused. Drew was used to her being a little scattered but if she wasn't keeping abreast of the conversation enough to know what Jodie was referring to then she really was distracted.

Jodie's smile was indulgent. "No. I meant with

your insomnia. Lavender is supposed to help. You can get all sorts of pillow sprays and things nowadays. I can bring you in one if you'd like?" There was an eagerness to Jodie's voice, and Drew found himself in the unusual position of being on the outside looking in, a position Harriet herself was normally placed in.

"I'm not suffering with insomnia," Harriet said, although she didn't sound particularly convincing. "But thanks for the tip."

"It's the least I could do," Jodie said. "At least now I can go full steam ahead with using social media to cast a wider net."

"You really think that's going to help?" Drew asked. He was mostly being polite, but he was a little curious to know the answer.

"Do you have a smartphone?" Jodie's question didn't seem particularly relevant, but he decided to play along.

"Yeah. Although sometimes I wish I didn't."

"And what's the first thing you look at when you wake in the morning?"

Drew opened his mouth to answer, the automatic answer practically tripped off his tongue. But he was forced to bring himself up short as he realised it would be a lie. He shuffled awkwardly, his sudden realisation made him more than uncomfortable. He'd been about to tell them that the first thing he looked at when he woke in the morning was the last picture he'd taken of Freya, but if he was honest he hadn't done that in months. When had it changed?

"I'm sorry," Jodie said. "I didn't mean to put you on the spot like that. My boss is always telling me I need to learn to read the room before I open my mouth."

"No, it's fine," Drew said. "I guess I look at my Facebook app first thing." As he spoke he was acutely aware of Harriet's attention, which was fixated on his face. Her uncanny ability to read his mind wasn't something he particularly wanted right now. But when she didn't say anything, he found himself letting go of some of the building tension in his shoulders.

"You see, that's exactly what most people do. If we can leverage our social media accounts to get the general public's eyeballs where we want them to be, we might begin to uncover some useful information. I can even stream the press-conference live through the accounts, and--"

"Guv!" There was a note of excitement in Maz's voice that pulled his attention away from the conversation at hand. "Can I have a word?"

Drew stepped away, leaving Harriet and Jodie to continue their conversation. "What is it?"

"It's Taylor. The hospital phoned. They're sending him straight over."

"That's great news," Drew said, his mind already

beginning to spin with the possibilities. Perhaps this was the break they'd been waiting for all along.

"Get the interview room prepped," Drew said. "And I want you to keep this quiet. We don't need the world and his wife knowing we've got Taylor in here for questions. Once that press-conference goes out this place will be crawling with people and I don't want someone getting it in their heads to go after Taylor before we have the chance to give him a thorough going over."

Maz nodded and was gone before Drew had to say another word.

When he returned to Harriet's side he discovered Jodie had already left.

"What was that about?" It never ceased to amaze him that Harriet could keep her curiosity so well contained.

"Taylor is coming in the next few minutes to have a chat with us," Drew said, feeling the familiar feeling of excitement bubble in his chest. "The hospital has given him a clean bill of health, aside from a few bruises he's no worse for wear after his suicide attempt yesterday." Drew caught Harriet's eye. "Do you think it was a legit attempt?"

Harriet pursed her lips. "Given that he couldn't have known that you would figure out where he'd escaped to, I have to believe there was at least some sincerity in his actions."

"But?" Drew asked shrewdly. He always seemed

to know when she was hedging her bets and now was no exception.

"There is always the possibility that he intended for things to work out as they did. It's possible he heard you coming and in a moment of panic thought taking matters into his own hands would be a preferable scenario. Maybe he was even trying to hide something from you. Anything is possible. I should know more once you've had a chance to speak with him."

"You're sitting in, right?"

"I'd much rather observe if possible," Harriet said. "The moment I walk in there, Taylor is going to get his back up, and I'd rather we give him the opportunity to cooperate."

Drew's expression turned thoughtful. "That's a good point. From all accounts he's spent quite a bit of time talking to psychologists."

Harriet nodded. "I read his file. He's not exactly a fan of the people in my profession."

"Well, who do you suggest I take in there with me? Melissa would be the obvious choice of course."

Harriet let her gaze sweep hastily over the squad room. "Perhaps going with someone who might show a little more empathy might be safer," Harriet said.

"You don't think Melissa is empathetic?" Harriet knew the moment she heard the surprise in Drew's voice that she'd plunged straight into the trap he'd set for her. "I take it you're not exactly keen on her then?"

She shook her head. "I'm capable of keeping my personal feelings separate from my professional opinions," Harriet said archly. If there was one thing she disliked, it was being made to feel as though every one of her choices was somehow reliant on her personal thoughts when that couldn't have been further from the truth.

"That's not a no," Drew said, a lazy smile playing around his lips.

"She has a forceful personality," Harriet said, attempting to keep her tone of voice as diplomatic as possible. "And while that is an excellent trait to have for the job she does, it won't serve us well in this situation. Taylor needs to feel as though somebody is on his side and you're not capable of that." Drew's smile faltered, and Harriet knew her words had hit home.

"That's a little harsh."

"You don't keep me around here, Drew, so I can pander to your ego. You keep me here because I can provide insight into situations that you cannot. If both you and DI Appleton go into that room together, you stand zero chance of getting anything useful from Taylor."

"Then who?"

Harriet pursed her lips. "Olivia would be my first choice," she said. "And DC Green would be my second, but Olivia has more experience working with the team. Also, from what I've read of Taylor's file he seems to believe he can appeal to women more easily. You could use that to your advantage in there."

"I'm not sure I want to appeal to him, Harriet. I just want answers."

"And you'll catch more flies with honey," Harriet quipped back. "Look, you asked my opinion and I'm simply giving it to you."

Drew nodded. "I'll take it under advisement." There was a clipped tone to his voice that made Harriet uncomfortable. She'd obviously said something wrong when she hadn't agreed with him on DI Appleton, but if he couldn't see the truth, then it wasn't her problem. Of course, for Harriet, that was easier said than done. She hadn't wanted to cause friction between them. It was the last thing she wanted, and yet here they were.

"Good," she said, sharing a tight smile with him as the tension in the hall mounted.

"Fine." Without another word, Drew turned on his heel and strode away, leaving her to stare after him.

She hadn't meant to cause friction between them, but her time as a psychologist had taught her in most cases the road to Hell was paved with good intentions.

CHAPTER THIRTY-THREE

DREW HAD MULLED over Harriet's concerns regarding Melissa, but as he settled in next to his fellow DI, he felt certain he'd made the right choice. Harriet didn't know everything. And she was only human, and people made mistakes. She'd obviously made a mistake where Melissa was concerned. As far as Drew was concerned, there was no other officer he'd rather have by his side in the interview.

He settled back in his seat and studied Taylor's hunched over form. The grey tracksuit he wore only served to highlight the dark bruising around his neck, and the fluorescent lights overhead washed him out; making him appear pasty and unhealthy.

"Feel like telling us where Oliver Poole is?" Melissa's question cut straight to heart of the matter, and Drew shifted uncomfortably in his seat.

"I didn't do nothing to the lad," Taylor mumbled,

keeping his head down, gaze trained on the table in front of him.

"We know you had an inappropriate relationship," Melissa interjected before Drew could even open his mouth to respond. "Do you really expect us to believe you don't know anything when he's mysteriously upped and disappeared?"

"I don't care what you lot believe," Taylor said, finally lifting his gaze. He fixed Drew with a rage filled glare. "I told you already. I don't know where he is. As for what happened, that's in the past. I never touched him then and I definitely haven't done anything to him now neither."

Melissa scoffed. Drew sat up a little straighter. "Help us to understand, Taylor. Why did Oliver single you out as a friend in the first place?"

"He was a quiet lad, and I remembered being that age. I remember how tough it was when others picked on you and there wasn't anything you could do about it. I felt sorry for the boy, but that was all."

"Taylor, we know that's not true. There's more to this story that you're not telling us." DI Appleton cut in. "You're not fooling anyone with this act you've got going."

"I knew this was a waste of time," Taylor said. "You lot are never going to believe anything I tell you, so why should I tell you anything. You're just going to screw me over like you always do." There was an edge to Taylor's voice that Drew recognised. He was a man with nothing left to lose as far as he was concerned, because he'd already lost everything worth having. A man on the edge like that was dangerous, and if he did have something to do with Oliver's disappearance, then it would end in only one way.

"Taylor, we want to hear your side of things," Drew started to say, but Taylor shook his head.

"I didn't kill that boy."

"Who said anything about murder?" Drew asked.

"It's what you're all thinking," Taylor said, brushing his hand over his face nervously.

A knock on the door stopped Drew before he could finish. Pushing back from his seat, he allowed Melissa to make a note of the time they'd suspended the interview for the benefit of the recordings. Crossing the floor, he pulled open the door and came face to face with Maz.

The young DS' expression was haunted, and the sinking feeling Drew had been getting in his gut only got worse.

"What is it?"

"Can I have a word in the hall?" Maz asked, keeping his gaze studiously fixed on a point on the floor.

The tone of Maz's voice caused the tiny hairs on the back of Drew's neck to stand to attention. He closed the door softly and turned toward his DS, before the detective sergeant could even utter the words, Drew knew the truth.

"They've found a body."

"Oh god," Harriet's utterance reached him, he hadn't noticed her come into the hall and from the corner of his eye he watched as she placed her hand over her mouth.

"Is it the Poole boy?" Drew's voice was rigid and unyielding.

"We don't have confirmation yet," Maz said.

CHAPTER THIRTY-FOUR

THE MOMENT the word had come that a body had been found, the place had erupted into a hive of activity.

But now that they were out here in the woods, Harriet couldn't help but feel utterly useless. Drew's expression was practically unreadable, but Harriet had grown accustomed to his almost chameleon like ability to hide his true emotions. And she could tell from the grim set of his jaw that he was affected by the discovery.

"Forensics have said the body matches the description we have on file of the young boy." The glimmer of hope that ignited in the centre of Harriet's chest quickly guttered and was finally quenched as Maz's words sank in.

"Who found the body?" Drew's voice was clipped with an emotion Harriet couldn't quite pinpoint.

"The local community had arranged for searches of the area."

"Please tell me it wasn't a member of the family who found him?" Harriet jammed her hand into the pocket of her coat, clenching her fingers tight enough to cut off the circulation.

Maz shook his head. "No, the group was made up of a teacher from the school, one of the neighbours, and another local resident who just wanted to help out. They're all pretty shocked, they definitely got more than they bargained for. We're keeping them all back for statements."

"What do we know about the scene so far?" Drew asked. He looked pale in the shadow of the trees that surrounded them, and Harriet found herself wondering if she wasn't the only one struggling to sleep at night.

"Well, that's the weird bit," Maz said. He shuffled, his shiny black shoes scuffing through the leaf mould beneath their feet. "Sick bastard left him in the exact place where the other body was found."

Silence stretched around them, and Harriet's stomach clenched uncomfortably. "Well, that's good news, right? Somebody must have seen something?"

"We've got nothing," Maz said.

"How is that possible?"

Maz started to shrug, but Drew's apoplectic response cut him off mid-movement. "Don't give me that," Drew said, his voice rising over the din of their surroundings. "How could somebody get in and out without being spotted? The place has been crawling with people searching for the missing boy, not to mention the fact we were supposed to have people up here since he went missing."

Colour suffused Maz's cheeks. "DI Appleton pulled them out of here after the arrest of John Taylor. Everyone seemed so sure it was him, and..."

"For fuck's sake!" Drew swung around and slammed the palm of his hand against the bark of the tree.

"Was she not supposed to do that?" Maz asked.

"I told her I wasn't sure about him. There was something not quite right... Fuck!"

Harriet stepped forward and started to reach for Drew, but pulled up short as she caught the ever-watchful eye of DS Arya. "He could still be involved," Harriet said. Drew responded with a rough bark of laughter that caused her to cringe.

"You really think that? You're a lot of things, Dr Quinn, but naïve is not one of them. He's been in hospital, he couldn't kill Oliver and dump his body without somebody noticing he was missing from his bed."

"I don't need to be naïve to know Mr Taylor could be working with another."

"And you really believe that?" Drew asked, swinging around to face her. His anger radiated from him and Harriet knew he needed a target for his rage, but she would be damned if she let him make her it.

"What I know of this case, DI Haskell, is that it's far more complicated than you want it to be. Not everything is clear cut, and this is definitely not one of those situations where everything will get tied up into a neat little bow that gives everyone involved a happy ending. I understand that you're angry, and that you feel responsible--"

Drew started to answer, but Harriet cut him off with a wave of her hand. "Don't interrupt me, please. How could you not feel responsible? You're a good police officer and you want to protect those in your community; it's the reason you joined the force. It's the reason you all did," she said, adding the latter to remind Drew that he worked within a team of dedicated individuals. She half expected Drew to storm off, but when he didn't, she decided to continue. Sucking down a deep breath, she plunged ahead. "I don't think it was a coincidence that Oliver went missing so soon after the discovery of the body. I'm loathe to believe it was even a coincidence that he was the one chosen to consider the fact that he was the one to find the body in the first place. It all feels too perfect, too staged."

"So you think whoever left him here is trying to send a message?"

"It's definitely a possibility. Further to that, I

think whoever left him here is intimately familiar with the area itself."

"Somebody local," Maz mused aloud. "No one is going to like that."

"If this was an opportunistic predator, they would never have brought the body back here knowing the risk of discovery. Bringing the body here is a statement."

"And what are they trying to say?"

"Well, I don't know yet," Harriet said. "I need to see the scene. And we need to know how he died."

"As soon as forensics are done, they've said they'll give us a preliminary report."

"The two detectives investigating the discovery of the other body, have they been informed of this development?" Harriet could feel the germ of an idea forming in her mind, but it was far too tenuous and delicate to even think about sharing it with the others.

"As far as I know, not yet," Maz said.

"I think they should be brought in." Harriet fought to keep her voice emotionless as thoughts whirled in her mind. There were far too many variables, to make a pronouncement at this early stage would be reckless. But they would look to her for information, anything she could give them to help potentially move the investigation forward would be invaluable at this time. And if she was right, then taking the correct steps now would prevent further tragedy from befalling this small village.

Maz cocked his head to the side and opened his mouth. Harriet could practically see the cogs turning in his mind, but thankfully Drew cut him off before he could form his first question.

"You heard Dr Quinn. If she thinks the others should be informed, then do it. It won't be long before this reaches the media, and when that happens this place will be crawling in reporters desperate for the shot that'll make their career."

Maz didn't need to be told twice by Drew, and Harriet tried to keep her smile under wraps as the younger DS scurried off to do his superior's bidding.

"What's so funny?" Drew asked, catching her eye.

"He really looks up to you," she said, choosing the diplomatic route.

Drew shifted uncomfortably, his expression taking her by surprise. "That bothers you?"

His mouth formed a moue of distaste. "Where are you going with this?"

"Which part?"

"Why involve the others?" His gaze searched hers, as though the answers he sought were right there in her face.

"Drew, you need to give me time. I know you want answers, but this is too important and I don't want to get it wrong."

"You think both cases are connected, don't you?"

"I--"

"Just answer that one question, Harriet. I need something from you if you want me to just go along blindly. As much as you don't want to get this wrong, neither do I. And at the end of the day, I'm the one with the duty of care."

She sighed. He was right, of course he was right. She couldn't just ask him to blindly follow her without giving him something to cling to. "You're right, I think the cases are linked. But what's bothering me more, is that I think the case involving the kids who went missing twenty-one years ago is somehow connected to all of this too."

"But why? It wouldn't make sense to take three kids twenty years ago and wait all of this time..."

"And that's why I need time to pull the pieces together," she said.

Drew took a moment before he nodded. "Fine, I'll buy you some time with the monk, but I can't keep him off your back for long. You know what he's like, and once he gets a bee in his bonnet, he won't stop until he has answers."

"Thank you," Harriet said. Drew started to speak, but they were interrupted by the arrival of a SOCO dressed head to toe in the white overall Harriet had come to associate with horrific sights.

"Are you DI Haskell?" The SOCO's serious expression was only barely visible over the mask he'd pulled down from his nose. Drew nodded briefly, his smile thin lipped and strained.

"I'm David Farley, the crime scene manager here. We've secured the scene."

"So soon?" Drew didn't bother to hide the surprise he evidently felt.

"There's not much here beyond the body itself. The scene is pretty immaculate, and considering we were here only a few days ago, it's difficult to identify disturbance caused by our own team and that caused by the perpetrator. It was smart putting the body out here. Whoever it is seems to be at least superficially aware of forensic counter-measures. If you suit up, I can take you through for a quick review before the pathologist has the body removed."

Harriet could tell from the look on Drew's face that the last thing he wanted to do was take a walk-through on a scene that belonged to a child. When Drew swallowed back his discomfort, Harriet caught a glimpse of the toll it took on him to appear so unaffected.

"If it's possible, I'd like Dr Quinn to walk through the scene too." He glanced over at Harriet as he spoke. "The insight might prove useful to her on helping us to find the answers we need."

The forensic manager gave her a once over before he nodded.

CHAPTER THIRTY-FIVE

A FEW MOMENTS later and Harriet found herself dragging on one of the uncomfortable Tyvek suits at the outer perimeter of the crime scene itself.

"Are you a medical doctor?" The crime scene manager's question broke through the deep well of thoughts she'd tumbled head first into.

Harriet shook her head as she dragged one plastic bootie on over her left shoe. "No. I'm a forensic psychologist. I help Drew—DI Haskell—and his team on some of their more difficult cases."

The SOCO nodded, his blue eyes serious as he held out a box of gloves towards. "You must see a lot of crime scenes then?"

Harriet smiled politely. "Thankfully, no. I'm much more accustomed to viewing the scene through the photographs taken. Actually getting out here to see it in person is testament to the unusual nature of the crime."

"It's not an easy scene," he said softly. In such a simple statement he managed to convey a depth of feeling that Harriet hadn't honestly been expecting and she felt a lump form in the back of her throat.

"I'm sorry," she said. The words felt woefully inadequate but necessary none the less.

"Thank you," David said. "I try not to think too much beyond what we're dealing with. It's important to have some distance, I couldn't do my job without it. But there's just something about cases that involve children that makes that impossible." He smiled ruefully as he brought himself up short. "Look at me being all morose. You're clearly very good at your job, Dr Quinn."

"What makes you say that?"

He grinned at her. "Because five minutes in your company and I'm practically blubbering all over the place with my feelings. Next you'll ask me whether my mummy took my favourite teddy-bear away when I was very young."

"Are you a killer?" Harriet asked, her expression deadpan. The question seemed to bring David up short, and he shook his head a little more vehemently than was strictly necessary.

"Well, no, I--"

"Then I'm afraid I'm not much use to you,"

Harriet said. "I'm much more comfortable delving into a deviant mind."

He stared at her for a moment before he started to laugh. "You know, I'd heard you lacked a sense of humour. But that's just not true." He continued to laugh as he led them beyond the perimeter.

Harriet glanced over at Drew. "I wasn't trying to make a joke," she said. "I'm genuinely more comfortable speaking to people with a deviant mindset."

"I know that," Drew said gently. "But there's no point trying to explain that to him. He won't understand."

With a curt nod, she slipped the mask on over her face as she followed Drew along the path. If Bianca could see her now and the unintentional joke she'd just made, she'd find the entire situation hilarious. Harriet sighed, her warm breath stifled beneath the heavy mask she wore. Every time she thought she had a handle on the personalities that made up the team, she found herself confounded with another. It was definitely easier to deal with killers and psychopaths. At least with them, she knew exactly where she stood.

HARRIET PAUSED on the embankment and took stock of her surroundings. Despite the forest itself being popular with tourists, the particular area they found themselves in seemed almost untouched by the outside world. Leaf litter covered the ground beneath her feet, and even through the protection of her mask she could detect the damp scent she associated with a forest.

Some of the trees were bare, their branches reaching upwards so that they intertwined over head like the hands of a priest clasped together in prayer. The scene was abuzz with activity but the atmosphere that lay over it all was that of a deep, bone aching sorrow. In the deep hollow beneath her, Harriet was only too aware of the white forensic tent which had been set up to preserve as much of the scene from the elements as possible.

With the information she'd gleaned from Oliver's parents, she had an inkling that he wouldn't have enjoyed camping. He'd gone to great pains to assure his mother after his excursion into the woods the previous weekend that it had not in fact been his idea of fun, and it had been a point she had laboured to Harriet when she'd spoken to her. But the person who had brought him here had done so because the place meant something to them. The person responsible for his untimely end was comfortable in the woods, that much Harriet was certain of.

"What do you think?" Drew asked, his voice a low whisper.

"Tell me why you're whispering?" Harriet asked, her gaze tracking over the trees that surrounded them.

Drew shrugged next to her. "I don't know, I suppose it feels like the right thing to do."

"But why?"

He sighed and raised his hand as though he was about to jam it back through his hair, but the sight of his glove brought him up short. "Maybe I'm acutely aware of the dead child below us," he said, his voice harsh with unspoken emotion. "Why do you want to know?"

"Because everyone is behaving the same way." She glanced over at Drew, and even though his mask covered most of his face, she could tell from the expression in his eyes that he was struggling. "Are you all right?"

He shrugged. "Are you?"

Harriet smiled behind the mask. "I suppose it's a stupid question to ask given the circumstances." When he didn't answer, she inclined her head in the direction of the scene. "Shall we see if we can get a closer look?"

Drew answered by moving ahead of her. They followed the path laid out by the SOCOs and Harriet was at least relieved to reach the bottom of the hollow without once slipping on the uneven surface.

"Seems like the pathologist beat us here after all," Drew said. Harriet didn't need him to point Dr Jackson out, especially as he was the one barking orders to the others under his authority.

"Have you been in to see him yet?" Drew directed his question to the pathologist who stood outside the white tent.

"Who said you lot could come down here?" Dr Jackson asked. Harriet didn't need to see his expression to know his hostility was nothing more than a facade. It probably inured him against the suffering he witnessed on a daily basis. It was likely nothing more than an affectation he'd developed years ago as a coping mechanism.

"The same person who said you were free to move the body." Drew folded his arms over his chest, causing the material of his suit to stretch precariously across his broad shoulders.

"Well, I don't want you to touch anything," Dr Jackson muttered. "Give you lot an inch and you'll take a bloody mile."

"When have I ever come into a scene and touched things?" Drew's voice rose with incredulity.

"Do you want to see him or not?" Dr Jackson's question instantly brought Drew up short.

"Fine."

Harriet observed the exchange from a distance, and as Drew made a move toward the tent, she told herself to follow. In spite of her brain's instructions, she found her legs refused to cooperate.

"Are you coming?" Drew's question carried across the hollow.

"I just need a moment," Harriet said. She took a

deep breath as Drew shrugged and followed Dr Jackson into the tent. She'd been so careful to keep her distance from the case. It would be far too easy to become wrapped up in the intricate tragedy of it all. The death of a child was something most people would struggle with, and it made sense that she would fall prey to the same feelings as everyone else involved. But if she gave into it, then she would be more than useless to Drew and the team. She would be nothing more than a liability, and Drew deserved better than that.

"This is just like every other case." Her voice was little more than a whisper, the words sounding more and more like a murmured prayer rather than the pep-talk they were supposed to be. *What waits for you in the tent, you need to separate yourself from it. The little boy that was is gone, but the person responsible is still out there. Get a grip, Harriet.* It struck her as a little odd that the voice inside her head sounded suspiciously like that of Dr Connors; then again, he was certainly capable of compartmentalising himself from his patients. Protecting himself against the pain and suffering he was privy to. But it still didn't sit well with her that there were still things to be learned from a man like him.

Squaring her shoulders, she made her way over the plastic steps on the ground—laid out by the SOCOs to denote the safest route to the body. Her hands shook as she pulled the tent flap back. Her view of the scene was impeded by Drew, and she released the breath she'd been holding.

"From the discolouration I can see around the boy's mouth, it seems possible suffocation was the cause of death..." Dr Jackson glanced up, his gaze snagging on Harriet's as she stepped around Drew's frame.

Her eyes travelled down to the small shape which lay on the dirt. Harriet recognised him from the pictures Mrs Poole had shared with her when she'd spent time with the woman. He lay on his side in a foetal position, his arms wrapped around a brown teddy-bear that was clutched to his chest. Despite the unnatural pallor of his skin, and the eerie stillness of his body if they had been anywhere else, Harriet might have found herself convinced that the boy was merely sleeping instead of the terrible truth of the matter.

"DI Haskell, are you quite all right?" Dr Jackson's question pulled Harriet from her own thoughts and she glanced up at the tall man next to her.

"Drew?" She touched his arm gently, and he started. When he looked down at her, Harriet could see that his eyes were just a little too wide, the pupils dilated beyond what might have been considered normal. Harriet had seen it before in others who were suffering from a state of shock.

"If you're going to get sick, can you do it somewhere else?" Dr Jackson said, managing to sound both irritated and bored at once, which to Harriet's mind at least was somewhat impressive.

"Drew, do you need a moment?" Her question appeared to reach him, and Drew straightened up as he blinked rapidly.

He clenched his gloved hands, forming fists that hung uselessly by his side. "I'm fine, Dr Quinn." The coldness of his voice didn't surprise her. People reacted in all manner of ways when they were struggling to process a situation.

"I haven't been sick at a crime scene since my first day in uniform," Drew said sharply, directing his ire at the pathologist who was still crouched next to Oliver Poole's body.

"Well, it's nice to know I can still be surprised," Dr Jackson said drily. He returned his attention to the boy's body. "From the bruising visible on his wrists, I'd say it's consistent with ligature marks. And there's a residue around his mouth, while I can't be certain I'd hazard that it's possible he was kept bound and gagged. I'll have it tested, but I'd imagine it's going to come back as consistent with something like duct-tape or the like."

"Is there any signs of..." Drew said hoarsely before he cut off and coughed.

"If you're asking if there are any signs of a sexual assault, then I'm afraid I can't answer that at this moment, DI Haskell. Until I get the body back for a post-mortem, we won't know anything for certain."

"Oliver," Drew said sharply.

"Excuse me?" Dr Jackson seemed only half interested as he continued to examine the body in situ.

"He's not a body," Drew said. "His name was Oliver Poole."

Dr Jackson straightened up, the crack of his knees oddly loud in the veritable silence of the crime scene. "I'm aware that you feel a connection to this boy, DI Haskell. I won't tell you how unhealthy that is, but please don't lecture me on my job. If I want pointers from you, then I'll ask. Until then, I'd ask you to keep your thoughts to yourself."

Drew opened his mouth to continue the argument, but Harriet touched his arm. The expression in his eyes was one of utter betrayal before he turned on his heel and strode from the tent, letting the plastic flap shut behind him.

"I'd half expected you to be the one blubbering all over this scene," Dr Jackson said, his attention once again riveted on the boy.

"Why?"

"Well, you women get more involved in these things. It's simple biology."

Harriet smiled behind the mask she wore and chose to ignore the insult dressed up as a compliment. "Does the scene strike you as odd in any way?"

"In what way?" Jackson snapped to attention, and Harriet could practically see him bristling.

"It's all so careful."

"You mean the idea that our man is forensically aware?" Something in Dr Jackson's statement took her by surprise.

"You seem certain a man did this?"

Dr Jackson guffawed, the sound only barely muffled behind the white mask that concealed most of his face. "I think it's the only logical explanation."

"Why, because women are supposed to be more maternal, nurturing even? You don't think a woman, or another child would be capable of a crime like this? We only have to look at some of the most heinous crimes in recent memory to know that anyone is capable of murder, even children."

The expression in Dr Jackson's eyes was sympathetic. "Look at where we are, Dr Quinn. Do you really think anyone other than a man could have got the body in here? There are no drag marks. The nearest you can get a car to this spot is a mile and a half and I should know, I had to walk it."

She nodded thoughtfully. "I suppose you're right."

"Of course I'm right. You don't need to be a psychologist to know that it's men who commit crimes like this. And when you add the physicality of the crime to it, then it's more than clear. A woman, or another child couldn't be responsible for the murder."

She couldn't argue with him on that score. Even Drew had struggled to make it to the crime scene. If you added a body to the scenario, it became infinitely more difficult.

"I suppose you're right," Harriet said.

"You'll find, I'm correct about most things. Now, can you tell your partner that I'll call as soon as I have a report to share?"

Harriet knew a dismissal when she heard one. Nodding, she stepped out of the tent, the image of Oliver Poole clutching his teddy-bear imprinted on the inside of her eyelids like indelible ink. As she made her way from the hollow, Harriet knew it would be a long time—if ever—before she would be free of the horror of today.

CHAPTER THIRTY-SIX

HARRIET EMERGED from the clearing and quickly stripped out of the Tyvek suit. "Have you seen DI Haskell?" She caught the attention of the PC who had signed them into the crime scene, but he shook his head and she found herself back at square one.

From the corner of her eye, she spotted a familiar face among the small crowd which had gathered at the outer edge of the perimeter. Hurrying up the side of the embankment, Harriet caught up to the female officer as she prepared to leave. "You're DC Nicoll, right?" Harriet struggled to catch her breath, little clouds of cold air puffing out in front of her face and obscuring her vision. The cold air made her lungs burn, but she had no doubt that it was a blessing for the forensic team. However, traipsing around in the woods at any time of the year was definitely not her idea of fun.

The woman in front of her raised a quizzical brow in her direction. "And you are?" She had the familiar Yorkshire burr that meant she had grown up in the area.

"Dr Quinn," she said, holding her hand out. "Most people call me Harriet."

"I don't think Oliver Poole is going to need a doctor," DC Nicoll said gruffly. She wrapped her arms protectively around her thin frame, as though she expected a body blow.

"I'm not that kind of doctor," Harriet said. "I'm a forensic psychologist and I--"

"I've got nothing to say to you," DC Nicoll said brusquely, before she started to tramp back through the woods.

"Actually, I was hoping you could give me a lift back to the station," Harriet said, hurrying after the detective constable. "I came with DI Haskell."

"So you can go back with him then."

Harriet smiled and glanced down at the ground. "I think there was a little misunderstanding. I think he already left. And maybe this way we can have a little chat."

"I already told you, I don't have anything to say to you." DC Nicoll huffed out a breath and her shoulders dropped. "But I suppose I can give you a lift."

"Thanks--" The other woman didn't wait for

Harriet to finish speaking, and instead took off once more through the trees. Harriet followed a couple of steps behind and when the detective constable paused to examine one of the tree barks, Harriet followed suit.

"Is there something there?"

"Not anymore," DC Nicoll said. "I mean there was. When we were called out the first time, this whole place was covered in reflectors. You know, the kind you get on a bike."

Questions bubbled in Harriet's mind, but she bit her tongue. If she allowed her excitement to get the better of her here and now, she would lose any opportunity to question DC Nicoll about the body Oliver Poole had discovered.

"That seems a little odd," Harriet said thoughtfully.

"That's exactly what I said," DC Nicoll said, glancing back over her shoulder. "Everyone else thought it was just kids, but it's weird even by the standards of children. And then to find a body out here..."

Harriet smiled encouragingly. "It must have been quite a sight when you came out here that first night. The torches would have lit them all up at once."

"They looked like eyes," the DC said. "Lots of pairs of eyes."

"The reflectors were put up in pairs?" Harriet's curiosity was well and truly piqued.

"Yeah. Oliver mentioned something called Owl Man. We figured it was some kind of urban legend in the area. It was the reason they were out here that night. Thought they could track the Owl Man back to his lair..." DC Nicoll stared off into the distance. "Instead, Oliver found a body. And now he's dead and we have no leads."

"Owl Man, did that come about before or after the children went missing twenty years ago?"

The DC's gaze raked over Harriet. "You'd get along with my sergeant. He thinks it's all connected, convinced that it's one and the same case. Not that we've got anything to prove that."

"Did you get an ID on your body?"

Nicoll nodded. "Yeah, Jack Campbell." There was a haunted expression in the other woman's eyes that Harriet recognised only too well. "We went to see Jack's mother... Marjorie," DC Nicoll shook her head. "I don't know why I'm telling you this."

"Because we both want the same thing, and it helps to talk about these things."

The DC nodded before she jammed her hand into her pocket. "I suppose so. I don't really come from a family of talkers." She smiled apologetically.

"That's all right," Harriet said. "I didn't exactly come from a talkative family either. What did you learn when you spoke to Jack's mother?"

"I don't know how she has hung on all these

years." DC Nicoll closed her eyes. "She blames herself. Thinks her son died because of her."

"Why would she think that?" Harriet asked, unable to hide the interest from her voice.

"Jack Campbell had something known as Di George syndrome--" the DC paused as though waiting for Harriet to interject but when she didn't she continued, "--it made him vulnerable. Before he was born, he suffered a brain injury. His mother said he would have had the mental age of a very young child." She sighed.

"And you think there's a connection between Jack Campbell's death and the children who went missing?"

"I don't think it, I know it," DC Nicoll said. "And so does Jack's mother. You see, Jack liked going to scouts, the same scouts that the three kids attended. They went missing a short time before we now know he was murdered." Harriet couldn't help but notice the animated look on the DC's face as she spoke. "They were friends. And before Jack disappeared, there was an altercation between him and one of the parents of the children. It was how we were able to identify him. The parents of the missing kids at the time were certain Jack was somehow involved."

"And what do you think?" Harriet kept her voice level.

"Listening to Jack's mother, I don't see how it's

possible." DC Nicoll shoved a hand back through her hair. "He was vulnerable, maybe even more so than the kids who went missing at the time. And somebody took him out into these woods and they beat him to death." There was no escaping the passion in the DC's voice and Harriet fought not to get caught up in it. "Coincidence is one thing, Dr Quinn, but I'm not sure I can say this is just a coincidence anymore."

"Do you have an evidence to suggest everything is connected?"

DC Nicoll glanced down at the leaf mould beneath her feet. "I've got Marjorie Campbell's diary of events from the time."

"Would you mind if I took a look at it?"

"Shouldn't you be focusing on the Poole boy's case?"

"Who says I'm not?" Harriet said. "If you're right and these are all connected then by looking over the diary I am working on the case." She could see the hesitation in DC Nicoll's face. "I just want to help. And Jack Campbell deserves justice too."

Her words seemed to reach the other woman, and the DC nodded. "Fine. When we get back to the station, I'll let you look it over. But I need you to understand something."

"What's that?"

"I'm going to get to the bottom of this case, no matter what I have to do to get there."

"I can understand that," Harriet said. "You don't

need to worry about me. I'm not going to stand in your way. If we don't speak for those who can't, then who will?"

DC Nicoll nodded. "Good, I'm glad you understand."

Harriet smiled and followed her the last couple of steps back to the car. She did understand, but it also worried her. The DC was emotionally invested, and it was Harriet's experience that in a case such as this solving it wouldn't feel like a win. With so many lost lives, nothing would ever feel like a win, and that could so easily destroy a person. She just had to hope that it wouldn't take DC Nicoll down too.

CHAPTER THIRTY-SEVEN

SITTING behind the wheel of his car, Drew stared over at the primary school. His mouth and lips were dry, and he tried to run his sandpaper tongue over them to bring some relief, but it was a pointless endeavour. What was he doing here?

He'd left the tent, stripped out of the borrowed forensic suit and started walking, not stopping once until he made it back to the car. He'd abandoned Harriet in the middle of the woods, but despite the guilt he felt, it hadn't stopped him from coming here. Gripping the steering wheel, he flexed his fingers and stared past the school to the place where John Taylor's shed was tucked away in the trees. Something had brought him here, something niggled in the back of his mind. It had been that way from the moment he'd arrested Taylor that day. There was something that didn't quite sit right with him, but for the life of him Drew couldn't put his finger on it.

Until now.

Something so innocuous that Harriet had said when he'd asked her why Taylor would try to take his own life. He hadn't attempted it when he'd been arrested over his grooming of Oliver Poole before. So why now? Harriet had suggested that Taylor was potentially hiding something. It had certainly crossed his own mind, but they'd tossed Taylor's house after his arrest and they'd found nothing.

And then in the interview Taylor had known Oliver was dead before Maz had told them about the discovery of the body. Of course it could be chalked up to coincidence. Everyone knew the risks when a child was missing for a number of days. The likelihood of them turning up unharmed grew slimmer with every second they were gone. Taylor could simply have been saying what they were all already thinking.

Still, something had brought Drew here. Harriet was right. It was possible that Taylor was still involved. And if he was, then Drew was going to get to the bottom of it. Pushing open the car door, Drew stepped out. The temperature had taken a nosedive on the drive over, and Drew cupped his hands up around his mouth before he blew hot air against his chilled fingers.

Squaring his shoulders, he started across the grass. And with every step he took, he felt the feeling in his gut intensify.

CHAPTER THIRTY-EIGHT

AJ PUSHED OPEN the front door of his house and waited for the silence to settle around him. It was his favourite part of the day. He'd have the whole house to himself for three hours, maybe four if his parents worked late, and considering the closeness of the Christmas period, he was almost certain they would be late. Dropping his schoolbag in the hall, he shuffled through to the kitchen and spotted the note left on the counter. His mother's distinctive curly handwriting told him what he already knew, but he was pleased to see a twenty-pound note waiting beneath the sheet of white paper.

Takeaway pizza it was then. He crumpled the note and proceeded to ram it back into his pocket. Crossing to the fridge, he took out a can of pop and flipped it open. The contents fizzed against his upper lip as he took a deep swig. And he'd just closed his eyes when the letter box thudded. The noise made him jump, and he slopped fizzy liquid over his hand and down the front of his shirt.

"Shit!" He swore fluidly and swiped at the dark liquid already soaking through to his skin. Embarrassment brought heat to his face, and his heart thudded in his chest. Probably just one of those charity bag thingies his mother loved. And if it was, then the weekend would be a wash-out because she'd spend the time rooting in the wardrobes in search of something to donate.

Leaving the barely touched can of pop on the counter next to his mother's note, he pulled out of his phone and typed out a message to Barry. His stomach grumbled and he made his way back into the hall. He'd pop to the takeaway, get some grub and get back in time for the Fortnite Tournament.

His attention snagged on the white note haphazardly shoved through the letterbox. His initials were just barely visible, and he felt his stomach lurch painfully.

Slipping his phone back into his pocket, he fumbled to pull the paper free of the postbox and only succeeded in tearing the edge off the notebook page.

'Meet in woods. U know where. If U don't I'll tel everyone wot U did. JT'

The scrawled handwriting made the note almost illegible, but this wasn't the first time he'd got a note like this. Of course, he'd thought it was all behind him. He'd done as he'd been told, and John had told him he was finished with him. If that bastard thought he could go back on his word now...

It would serve him right if he didn't turn up. Leave him waiting in the woods. A smile crept over AJ's face as he imagined the other man waiting in the freezing woods. He glanced down at the note again and the threat killed his joy stone dead. If anyone knew what he'd done. If anyone knew what they'd done... The thought alone was enough to bring scalding bile racing up the back of AJ's throat. Humiliation caused heat to flood into his cheeks as his mind tried to bring the worst of the memories back to the surface.

John had said it was his fault, that he'd let it happen... That he'd enjoyed it. Squeezing his eyes shut, AJ shook his head. No. He wasn't going to let that fucker screw everything up. Not now. He wasn't the same scared kid he'd been back then, and he'd seen enough stuff on the net to know that what John had done was wrong.

"You're not the only one who can make threats," AJ said to no-one in particular. The silence in the hall closed in around him again. Nobody had to know what had happened. Nobody would find out so long as he did as he was told. But this was the last time, and he was going to make sure John knew it, too. Clenching his hand around the note, he balled it into his fist and snatched his schoolbag from the floor. He'd give that bastard what-for and make him regret ever coming to his house. Satisfied that he had a plan, AJ pulled the front door open and stepped out into the night without a backwards glance.

For a fleeting moment he contemplated leaving a note for mum, but quickly changed his mind. He'd be home before she ever knew to miss him. No harm, no foul. He slammed the front door after himself and slung his bag high up onto his shoulder.

He'd soon be home, tucked up in front of Fortnite with a pepperoni pizza. It was a comforting thought, and he held it close as he disappeared into the night.

CHAPTER THIRTY-NINE

DREW STOOD in the centre of the shed and stared at his surroundings. Everywhere he could think to look had turned up nothing more than cobwebs and pointless tools. Dropping onto the stool where Taylor had sat the day before, he studied his surroundings a little more closely. He raked his gaze over the lollipop sign and the old school projectors that lay discarded alongside tables and chairs that had seen better days.

He'd pulled everything out, searched through every scrap of paper he could lay his hands on. He'd even managed to open the toolbox Taylor had left out on the workbench, but it had turned up nothing. Had he been wrong to think Taylor was acting suspicious? Was there really nothing to find here?

It was hard to believe, but there was no denying the facts as they presented themselves. Burying his face in his hands, he sighed. It wouldn't be the first time he'd been wrong...

The image of Oliver Poole's body as it lay in the woods, his arms wrapped tight around the brown teddy-bear. It was a memory that would stay with him.

His phone buzzed inside his pocket, and Drew reached into the jacket and slipped it out before he could stop himself. He glanced down at the name on the screen and was surprised to see Melissa's name scrolling in time to the ringing tone. He contemplated letting the call ring out, but changed his mind at the last second. She would only keep calling. Melissa was like a dog with a bone and once she'd latched onto the idea of getting him on the phone, he knew she would stop at nothing to get it done.

"Yeah, go for DI Haskell," he said wearily.

"What the fuck, Drew," Melissa said. Her rage was palpable. "You didn't think to let me know where you were going?"

"There was something I needed to do," he said darkly.

"And?"

"And what?"

"Did you find what you were looking for?"

Drew shook his head and leaned back on the stool, causing the floorboards beneath his feet to groan. "No."

"Do you even know what it is you're looking for?"

"Is there something you need to tell me, Melissa, or did you just call me up so you could berate me?"

"Drew, I know you're finding this case hard. The fact that you left your pet psychologist at the scene is proof enough of that. But we need you back here at the station. The time is ticking down on Taylor and we need to have another chat to him, especially now that we've got Oliver's body."

Hearing her utter the words sent a chill down Drew's spine. "How can you be so cold?"

"Excuse me?"

"You make it sound like nothing at all. That a boy died, and it means nothing to you."

"That's not fair," Melissa said, and Drew was rewarded by the first stirrings of emotion in her voice. "I'm like this because I have to. Because it's my job. And if I don't keep my head then the person who did this is going to walk."

"I'm sorry," he said. Drew pushed onto his feet and the floorboards flexed beneath his boots. "I'll come straight back and--" He cut off as he realised Melissa had already hung up.

"Great," he muttered, his breath forming little puffs of white air in front of his face as he spoke. He'd pissed her off and now he would pay for his behaviour. He took a step forward and was rewarded with another squeak from the old boards beneath his boots. Glancing down, he noted the uneven surface of the floor. Taylor had seemed interested in the floor the day before, hadn't he? Was he just imagining things now?

Crouching down, Drew ran his fingers over the boards and found the spaces between the wood were wide enough to jam his fingers in. Try as he might, he couldn't get enough purchase on the board. Glancing up, he scanned the space and spotted the screwdriver that rested on the shelf over his head. It couldn't be a coincidence.

Grabbing the tool, Drew jammed it in between the boards and levered the wood out of place. It came up easily, sending a large black spider skittering for the darkness beneath the floor. Lifting the board free, he dislodged several woodlice, their grey shell bodies tumbled into the space left behind. Drew pulled his flashlight out and held it over the space, illuminating the contents that awaited him. He snapped on a pair of gloves from his pocket and set the torch on the ground next to his knees.

An old, rusted lunchbox sat in the darkness. The image on the front long since worn away by time, leaving only patches of the original red colour it had been. Next to the box sat a couple of plastic folders. Drew lifted them out first and flipped through the contents. His stomach flipped with disgust as his brain made sense of the images which had clearly been downloaded from the internet at some point in the not so distant past. Closing the first folder, he opened the next one and was confronted with pages of handwritten accounts. He scanned the pages briefly, his rage mounting with each word he digested. Oliver had not been the first child to fall victim to Taylor's predatory behaviour, it seemed.

Drew clamped his eyes shut and sucked a deep breath in through his nose. The urge to return to the interview room just so he could annihilate the man who had printed the images was almost overwhelming.

When he finally got himself under control, Drew reached back into the hole and lifted out the tin lunch box. The shiny new lock which had obviously been on the front of it remained in the hole, the clip of which had been snapped. Had Taylor lost the keys and been forced to cut the lock himself? It didn't make much sense, but Drew couldn't rule out the possibility. He set down the lunch box and pried open the lid, careful not to damage the contents within.

It took him a moment to realise that the box contained twenty to thirty Polaroid pictures. The grainy images were initially indistinct and Drew flipped through the pictures quickly until a flash of washed out purple caught the corner of his eye. He paused and raised the picture closer to his face so he could study it more closely.

Oliver Poole lay on a cement floor, his eyes closed, arms wrapped around the same brown teddy he'd been clutching when they'd found him in the woods.

Bile swept up the back of Drew's throat and he let the pictures drop back into the box before he half scrambled, half fell backwards into the corner of the shed. He closed his eyes, but he couldn't rid himself of the images. They crowded out his brain until he couldn't tell where the images started and the memory of what they'd found in the woods began. It made no sense, Taylor had been in hospital and yet there was no denying the fact that the photos had been found in the same shed he'd tried to hang himself in. He turned the pictures over and found a note scrawled across the back. It took him a moment to decipher the spidery handwriting, but when it did, it brought a fresh wave of nausea racing up his throat.

"This is our little secret."

His hands shook as he pulled the phone from his pocket and dialled DI Appleton's number. She answered after the first ring. "Are you--"

Drew cut her off before she could finish her sentence. "I need SOCOs down to the shed where Taylor tried to hang himself yesterday."

"I don't understand. Why would you--"

"Melissa, he has pictures--" Drew cleared his throat abruptly and fought to get his temper under control. "I came to the shed because I had a hunch. I've found some pictures here and a few other items that need to be processed by a forensics team."

"Done," Melissa said. "Drew, what kind of pictures?"

He knew what she was asking him and he contemplated lying, but changed his mind. She would know soon enough, anyway. "Exactly what you'd expect from someone like him." He squeezed his eyes shut and pinched a gloved finger to the bridge of his nose. "But that's not all. There are pictures of Oliver."

"Christ," Melissa swore. "He has indecent images of the Poole boy?"

"No. I can't be certain, but I'm almost sure that the pictures are of Oliver shortly before and directly after his death."

Silence swept down the line. "Drew, how is that possible?"

He shrugged and then remembered she couldn't see him. "I have no idea. All I do know is we need this processed ASAP, and then we need to sit down with that bastard again. And this time I'm going to have the truth of what happened to Oliver if it's the last thing I do."

He hung up before she could answer. He snapped off the gloves and pushed onto his feet and left the shed. He made it halfway across the grass before his stomach dropped him to his knees and he retched until there was nothing left inside. The icy ground seeped through his trousers, freezing him to the bone, and still it felt like something that was happening to someone else, someone far removed from the situation at hand. He'd witnessed horrors before, but this was different. This was a child, an innocent boy who had died, scared and alone at the hands of some lunatic. And that was after everything Taylor had done to him.

Drew's chest constricted. He would get justice for Oliver. No matter what it took, no matter the cost, he deserved that much, at least. Shakily, Drew stood. Taylor would pay for what he'd done, Drew would see to that much.

CHAPTER FORTY

SITTING at the desk in the corner of the office, Harriet flipped through the pages of the diary Martina had let her look through. She'd already jotted down some questions and as soon as Martina returned, she was hoping to persuade the DC to take her to Marjorie's house.

"You find anything useful?" Martina's voice made her jump, and Harriet straightened up in the chair.

"Maybe," Harriet said. "Would it be possible to visit Marjorie?" The moment the words left her mouth, Harriet could tell the other woman wasn't at all comfortable with the idea.

"I don't think so. Hasn't she been through enough? If we keep bothering her then--"

"It's just some of the names in the diary, well she never attached a surname to them and if we're going to get a complete picture, then we need to know all the people in play at the time."

Martina started to shake her head. "I just don't see how upsetting her again is going to push us further."

"That wouldn't be my intention--" Harriet cut off as the door to the office slammed open and Drew strode in. His normally dark hair was grey with dust and dirt. His jacket was the same, his hands blackened from whatever he'd been digging around in. Harriet pushed up from her seat and met his gaze head on. "What happened, are you--?"

"I'm fine," he said briskly. "I need to see Melissa. Have you seen her?"

Harriet shook her head. "Not since she went into her office. I've been a little preoccupied--"

"With what?" Drew's tone instantly made her bristle.

"The Jack Campbell case," she said, but Drew's blank expression told her he had no idea what she was talking about. "The other body found in the woods."

"The skeleton?" Drew asked, incredulity straining his voice. "You're telling me you've put aside the murder of Oliver Poole so you can work on a cold case?"

"It's an active investigation," Martina interjected coldly. "And Dr Quinn offered to assist me and I very gladly took her up on her offer."

Drew narrowed his eyes at the DC. "You're not even supposed to be here," he said. "Don't you have an office back in York?"

"Drew, I don't think that's appropriate," Harriet said, folding her arms over her chest. "My job is to consult, and that's what I'm doing."

"You work for our team," he said angrily. Harriet watched as he flexed his fists down by his sides.

"Tell me what happened?"

He shook his head. "If you think a twenty-year-old cold case is more important than the murder we've just had, that's your business," he said. "But I don't have time to explain to you the workings of a case you're supposed to know." He stormed off, leaving Harriet to stare after him.

"Shit," Martina said softly. "I'm sorry. I didn't know you'd get so much grief for helping me out."

Harriet shook her head. "I don't think it has anything to do with my working with you," she said.

"What then?"

"Something has happened," she said.

"Like what?"

Harriet shrugged. "I don't know, but it must be bad for Drew to behave like that." She sighed and levelled Martina with a hard stare. "Now, after all of that, are you going to let me help you with your case or not?"

Martina's smile was lopsided. "I suppose after that I can't exactly say no."

With a last glance over her shoulder at Drew, who'd stopped outside Melissa's office, Harriet grabbed her coat from the back of her chair. "Let's go then."

A SHORT WHILE LATER, Harriet sat in Marjorie Campbell's overly warm living room. The woman opposite her looked exhausted. The dark circles beneath her eyes only served to highlight the hollowness of her cheeks, and she clutched a picture frame in her birdlike hands. "DC Nicoll said you wanted to ask me some questions?"

"I'd like to if you're willing?" Harriet took the seat she'd been offered.

"You're here now," Marjorie leaned back in her chair. "I've waited twenty years for this and now that it's here I'm finding it a little more difficult than I thought it would be." She sighed. "That came out wrong. I always knew it would be difficult, but--"

"But there's too much finality in knowing the truth," Harriet said.

Marjorie nodded. "There's a kind of freedom in it too, you know? I now know where Jack was all this time. I never believed he would deliberately stay away, but if you hear that often enough it only adds to the anguish. You start to wonder if maybe you've been lying to yourself, if perhaps your memories are not as real as you once thought them to be."

"I can't begin to imagine how that must make you feel," Harriet said gently. "But if you're willing, I'd like to know a little about Jack and the life he led?"

Marjorie glanced down at the picture she held clasped in her lap. "Will it help you to find out who killed my son?"

"We hope so," Martina interjected before Harriet could get a word out.

Marjorie's smile was wan. "What do you want to know?"

"Did Jack have many friends?"

Marjorie seemed a little taken aback to begin with, and she stared down at the image of the young man with the bright eyes. "He made friends with everyone he met," she said softly. "But that's not what you're asking me."

Harriet shook her head. "No. From what I've read in the diary Jack was a wonderful young man, so full of love for everyone he met."

Marjorie's eyes glistened with unshed tears. "You got all of that from the diary?"

"I can see it here, in your home," Harriet said. "It shines out of him, out of every picture you have. And in the words you wrote about him. I could feel how much you loved him. He clearly brought you great joy."

"Do you have children?" Marjorie asked, never lifting her gaze from the picture.

"No." As she said the word Harriet couldn't help

but feel a pang of an emotion she'd never allowed herself to explore before and she pushed it away now too.

"They're a blessing--" Marjorie continued without looking up. "And a curse. They bring you the greatest of joy, create in you a love you never thought you were capable of, but they bring their own kinds of heartache too." She closed her eyes as though the memories were too much to deal with.

"Do you need a break?" Martina asked. "This was a mistake, we should--"

"No. I'm not some weak-willed ninny. I let my son down once before, I won't do it again. If this helps you to get closer to his killer, then I will happily help." She opened her eyes again and levelled her determined gaze on first Martina and then Harriet. "All this to say, Jack didn't have many friends, and that broke my heart. I tried to give my son everything he wanted. He'd suffered so much, so I wanted to give him as much happiness as I could. It was the reason I allowed him to go with the scouts in the first place. It made him happy, so I let him go."

She sighed and lifted the picture from her lap and set it down on the table next to her chair. "But the other children didn't see him in the same way he saw them. Children are so easily influence by their parents."

"You mention in the diary a girl," Harriet said. "I

was wondering if that was the same girl who went missing?"

Marjorie shook her head, the briefest flicker of a smile crossing her lips. "No. Matilda wasn't the same girl who went missing. She was the only one who treated Jack as a friend. She was good to him, invited him out into the woods for nature walks and the like whenever she could. But her father was kind, he was the one who allowed Jack to go out with the scouts in the first place."

"We were hoping to speak with him," Martina said, but cut off as Marjorie shook her head sadly.

"That won't be possible. Graham died a few years ago. Cancer, I think Matilda said. She dropped by after they found Jack's body. A sweet little thing. She said she'd wished there had been more she could have done for him. I was just so pleased to know he hadn't been forgotten..." Marjorie choked off as her tears spilled over her lashes and raced down her papery cheeks.

"What is Matilda's surname?" Harriet asked. "We'd like to speak to her too if at all possible."

"Of course," Marjorie said, swiping the tears away with the back of her hand. "Matilda Mayhew, I can give have Greg dig you out her number."

"That would be very helpful," Martina said.

"After Jack went missing, did anything unusual ever occur?"

"Such as?"

"Maybe phone calls, or..."

Marjorie was already shaking her head before Harriet had the chance to finish speaking. "No. Never anything like that." Marjorie's hands shook as she pulled a handkerchief from her pocket. "I know you probably don't want to hear this," she said. "The people working on Jack's case in the beginning certainly didn't want to hear it."

"Anything you can tell us will be helpful," Martina offered, as she gave Harriet a sideways glance. "Sometimes the smallest of details can crack a case wide open."

"I know who killed my son," she said finally.

Harriet felt her mouth drop open, and she stared at the woman opposite her.

"I'm not sure I understand," Martina said hoarsely. "If you've known all along who murdered your son, why didn't you say it the first time we came to see you?"

"Because nobody has ever listened to me before," Marjorie said, her voice a fierce whisper. "No one listened to me when Jack disappeared. Nobody believed me when I said something had happened to him. What am I supposed to think? How could I know you would be different?"

"Who was it?" Harriet asked.

"David Wilkes, Stanley Forder, and Gus Barre." She gripped the handkerchief so tightly Harriet could see the strain of it in the fabric.

"The fathers of the missing children?" Martina didn't bother to keep the incredulity from her voice. "You can't honestly believe..."

"You didn't see David Wilkes the night he punched Jack," Marjorie's voice dropped to a hoarse whisper.

"Mum, I think that's quite enough." Greg Campbell stood framed in the doorway of the living room. "You said you'd let this go."

"Let it go?" Marjorie's voice rose in pitch. "He's dead, Greg, and you want me to just let it go? You can't expect me to ignore the truth of the matter."

"I don't expect you to ignore anything," he said, sounding weary. "But you know those men didn't kill Jack. Deep down you know it."

"They attacked him. They threatened him," she said, fresh tears coursing down her cheeks. "Why wouldn't I think them capable of murder?"

"Do you have any proof of this?" Martina asked. Hearing how calm she seemed to be took Harriet by surprise.

"I know it in here," Marjorie said, as she thumped her fist against her birdlike chest.

"You know that's not proof, mum," Greg said. "And you know accusing those people of something they didn't do won't bring him back."

"I can't promise that anything will come of it," Martina said. "But we will look into it." She pushed onto her feet, and Harriet followed her.

"If I'm so wrong in all of this, then answer me this." There was a triumphant note in Marjorie's voice as she spoke. Harriet could feel her stomach sink as she waited for the grieving woman to drop her bombshell. "If those men are so innocent, then why is it Stanley Forder's grandson who was found murdered in those woods in the exact place where they put Jack?"

"How do you know this?" Harriet got the question out before Martina could say anything.

"This is a small area," Marjorie said. "Bad news travels fast."

"Mum, this is serious," Greg said, aghast.

"As far as we're aware there's no connection between the Poole boy and your son," Martina said.

Marjorie shook her head. "Then you don't know the full truth because Karen Poole is the older sister of Allison Forder. The little girl who disappeared all those years ago. She only became Poole when she married Carl."

Harriet had known it couldn't be a coincidence that Oliver Poole's body had been left in the same place they'd found Jack Campbell. But at the time when Drew had asked her what she thought, she didn't have the proof to back up her theories. But slowly the pieces of the puzzle were beginning to unravel, and there was no doubt in Harriet's mind that when the truth finally surfaced, the people of Darkby would wish it had stayed buried.

CHAPTER FORTY-ONE

"WE NEED to have a chat with Taylor," Drew said as he shoved open the door to Melissa's office. He didn't wait for her response before he started to pace up and down the small space in front of her desk.

"I had the crime scene manager send up some copies of the pictures," she said, her gaze fixed on her computer screen. Drew didn't need to ask her what she was looking at. The expression of horror reflected in her eyes was proof enough. "How could he have these?"

Drew shrugged. "That's what we need to find out," he said.

"What do you think the writing on the back of the images means?"

Drew shook his head. "I have no idea. But I know it gives me the creeps."

"It's on them all," she said quietly. He watched as

her eyes flickered back and forth on the screen. "This suggests he wasn't the one who murdered Oliver." She spoke the words he'd already been mulling over in his mind.

Drew snorted derisively. "He knew about these pictures," he said.

"How can you tell?"

"Because rather than get caught with them, he tried to hand himself," Drew said. "Harriet was right when she said he was probably hiding something."

"Drew, finding the pictures there isn't proof of anything. Chances are the minute we show these images to Taylor he'll say they're not his."

"He's not going to weasel out of this," Drew said.

"The shed doesn't belong to him," Melissa said. "It belongs to the school. He'll claim someone else put them there. You know this, Drew. We have to be prepared."

He nodded before he dropped into the seat next to the door and buried his face in his hands. "You don't think I haven't realised that already?" He groaned aloud, the sound animalistic and barely human.

"Are you all right? Maybe you need to go home and get some rest before we face Taylor?"

"No. I don't need rest. I need to string this bastard up by his balls," Drew said, his voice harsh. He glanced up at Melissa's concerned filled expression. "You didn't see the other pictures," he said.

"It's enough to make me want to rip my own eyes out."

Melissa looked pale, but she nodded. "This isn't my first child-abuse case," she said gently. "But it doesn't change the fact that we need something more substantial before we go in there and--" She cut off as Maz knocked on the door.

"What is it, DS Arya?" Melissa's tone had lost the gentle note and was back to business.

"It's Taylor," he said, sounding apologetic. "He's been screaming down the custody suite for the past two hours. He wants to speak to one of you."

"What does he want?" Melissa asked, and Drew caught the curious glance she threw in his direction.

"Says he wants to know what's going on."

Drew sighed and glanced over at Melissa. "We need to have a chat with him, DI Appleton." It sounded weird to call her by her formal title, but using her first name would have been too familiar. "I think it's high time Taylor came clean on the secrets he's been keeping."

Melissa caught his eye and Drew knew she'd understood his meaning completely and the relation it had to the message on the back of the pictures. She pursed her lips, and he half expected to have a battle on his hands. When she nodded instead and pushed onto her feet, Drew didn't bother trying to conceal the relief he felt.

"You're right. We need to know what he knows."

CHAPTER FORTY-TWO

"ARE you sure this is a good idea?" Martina asked.

Harriet studied the outside of the Poole house and steadied her breathing. If she was honest, she wasn't sure it was a good idea, but she was also certain she had no choice. They needed to know the truth, and if what Marjorie had told them was true, then it was important to explore the possibilities that it entailed.

"Maybe I should call Ambrose," Martina said, uncertainty colouring her words.

"If it would make you feel better," Harriet said. She pushed open the door without waiting for Martina.

She reached the front door and knocked gently as the first flurries of snow began to settle on the surrounding ground. The older woman who answered was oddly familiar, and she cocked her head to the side as she met Harriet's gaze. "Can I help?"

"I was hoping to speak with Karen. My name is Dr Harriet Quinn. I've been assisting on the case--"

The woman in the doorway shook her head. "My daughter has been through quite enough already," she said. "She needs time to rest and--"

"Mum, who is it?" Karen Poole's voice filtered through from the living room and a moment later she appeared in the doorway. She looked smaller and more frail. From where Harriet stood she could see that her eyes were a little unfocused, which made Harriet wonder what medication they had her on.

"I'm sorry, Mrs Poole," Harriet said, taking a step forward so that the porch light illuminated her. "I was just asking your mother if it would be all right if we could have a chat."

"Why?" Karen's voice was devoid of emotion and she moved out into the hall, her movements slow and jerky.

"New information has come to light," Harriet said carefully. "It might be helpful."

"You don't have to do this, love. You've been through enough already," Karen's mother piped up.

"It won't bring him back," Karen said. "It won't bring either of them back."

"No," Harriet said softly. "I'm afraid it won't, but it might help us understand who is doing this."

Karen's jaw tightened momentarily, and Harriet

half expected her to tell her to leave. Instead, the other woman exhaled, her shoulders rounding over, exposing her for the broken and vulnerable woman she was. "Come in."

"Karen--" Her mother started to speak, but was cut off by a determined shake of her daughter's head.

"Please, mum, don't. I don't want to hear it."

The older woman stepped aside, but Harriet could tell from the censorious look on her face that she wasn't happy. Harriet made it halfway into the hall before DC Nicoll caught up and made her apologies for her delay to Oliver's grandmother.

Harriet followed Karen into the living room. The Christmas tree stood in the corner of the room in complete darkness. The presents beneath the tree a painful reminder of everything that had happened.

Karen caught her staring at the tree and shrugged. "I haven't had the heart to take it down," she said shortly. "Part of me thinks if I leave it up, he'll come home and this will all have been a nightmare."

"That's understandable," Harriet said gently.

"Is it?" Karen raised her bloodshot eyes to Harriets. "Carl doesn't think so. He wants to rip the whole thing down."

"People handle things in different ways." It sounded woefully inadequate to Harriet's ears, but she wasn't here to help Karen navigate her relationship with her husband.

The woman across from her sighed and dropped into an armchair like someone whose legs had simply given up. "What did you want to speak to me about?"

"Your maiden name is Forder," Harriet said, keeping her tone gentle. Karen nodded and stared down at the tissue she'd pulled from the sleeve of her cardigan.

"What does that have to do with Oliver?"

"So your sister was Allison Forder?"

Karen met Harriet's gaze. "What has Allison got to do with any of this?"

Harriet sighed. "We don't think what happened to Oliver was a coincidence."

Karen stared at her. "I don't believe this," her mother said from her place in the doorway to the living room. "You can't be serious about this."

"Please, Mrs Forder," Martina said. "We just have a few questions."

"No," Mrs Forder said emphatically. Two spots of colour appeared high on her cheeks, and her eyes flashed with rage. "I won't stand for this. I won't."

"You think there's a connection between Oliver's death and Allison's disappearance all those years ago?" Karen spoke slowly, as though she were struggling to digest the words.

"We're exploring the possibility," Harriet said. "We spoke to Marjorie Campbell."

Karen's gaze flitted to her mother as the older woman stumbled in the doorway. "Mum?"

Mrs Forder's short gasp as she clutched her chest made Harriet think she knew something she wasn't saying.

"This is ridiculous," Mrs Forder said, but her words came out sounding strangled.

"As you know, Allison and the other two children weren't the only people to go missing at the time." Harriet studied the expressions of the women in front of her and was rewarded by the flash of guilt that crossed Mrs Forder's face. "Jack Campbell also disappeared a short while after the disappearance of your sister," Harriet said, directing her statement at Karen who was at that moment shredding the tissue in her lap into confetti.

"I don't know what--" Karen tried to speak, but Martina cut her off.

"Oliver was found in the same spot where Jack's body was discovered. In the same spot where your son found the body." The sentence hung in the air.

Karen looked over at her mother, whose colour had completely drained from her face. "Mum?"

"I'm getting your father," Mrs Forder said before she disappeared into the hall.

Martina glanced at Harriet before she followed the older woman out.

"Karen, I know this is painful, but I need you to tell me what you know."

Karen stared down at the tissue. "I'm not the one you should be speaking to," she said quietly.

CHAPTER FORTY-THREE

"THEN WHO?" Harriet asked, sitting forward on the edge of her chair.

"What's going on here?" The booming voice of Stanley Forder echoed in the hall and made Karen shrink back against her chair. Harriet glanced up at the man who stood in the doorway. He wouldn't, she surmised, have looked out of place on a rugby pitch. His broad shoulders brushed against the door frame as he stepped into the room and Harriet was fairly certain he would have to duck if he didn't want to bump his head on the low hanging light fixture.

"My name is Dr Harriet Quinn." She pushed onto her feet and extended her hand towards the man, who was rapidly turning an unnatural shade of cerise pink.

"I don't care who you are," he said. "You've upset my wife and I come in here to find you badgering my daughter, too? Are you all so inept at your jobs that you feel compelled to bother grieving families?"

"That's not what I'm doing," Harriet said mildly. "As I told your daughter, we've discovered some new information--"

"I don't care what you think you've found," he spoke over her. "I want you to leave my family alone."

"Dad," Karen said, her voice pitched low, but it was at least steady.

"Don't worry, sweetheart, I'll deal with this and then--"

Karen shook her head. "What you like you dealt with Jack Campbell?"

The large man took a step backward as though his daughter had struck him a blow rather that just ask him a question.

"What did you say?"

"You heard me. I might not know everything that happened in the woods that night. You and mum did a good job of shielding me from the worst of it, but I know something happened and now--" Karen's voice broke. "And now Oliver is dead because of it."

"You can't honestly believe..."

"All I know, dad, is that you did something to Jack Campbell, and he never got to go home. And now—and now Oliver. My Oliver." Karen's open palm slapped against the upper part of her chest, the sound echoing in the silence of the room like a gunshot. "Is gone. Dead. Murdered. My beautiful boy is gone and we both know it's because of what you did all those years ago." She squeezed her eyes shut against the tears that had started to course down her cheeks.

"Karen, love, I--"

"Just tell them. Do that much. Tell them what happened so they could find the person responsible for taking my baby away." Karen focused her attention on her father, who had gone deathly pale under the scrutiny of his daughter.

"I--" he started to speak and then shook his head. "We never meant for any of this to happen. We just wanted him to tell us what he'd done with Allison."

"You mean Jack Campbell," Harriet asked, who had until that moment watched the events unfold silently.

"That creep knew something," he said fiercely. "He knew something and he wouldn't tell us."

"He couldn't," Harriet said softly. "If Jack knew something, he wasn't keeping it from you deliberately. It was because he couldn't express it."

Stanley shook his head. "No, you don't understand."

Harriet nodded. "Actually, I do. Jack suffered a brain injury before his birth. He was diagnosed with DiGeorge syndrome which only exacerbated his underlying condition."

"He was a grown man," Stanley said. Horror crept into his voice. "He was a man."

"Physically he was a man," Harriet said. "But mentally, he was still a little boy. A frightened and innocent little boy."

Stanley shook his head. "No, we wouldn't have hurt a child. I would never have--"

"What did you do?" Harriet asked.

"We just wanted to scare him into telling the truth. We took him into the woods, but he wouldn't talk to us."

As Stanley told them what had happened to Jack, Harriet's heart constricted in her chest. It had been a monstrous act, that much she was certain of. But there was no denying that he'd truly believed Jack had been responsible for the disappearance of his daughter. Stanley finished speaking and for a long time, silence filled the space in the room.

"Stanley, why would you think Jack was responsible for Allison's disappearance," Harriet asked.

"I told you why," he said. "He was a creep... We thought he was."

"You keep saying we. Who was there?"

Stanley hesitated. "I'm not sure--"

"We'll find out anyway," Martina said. Harriet glanced over at the DC, but her expression was unreadable.

"Gus Barre, and David Wilkes," Stanley said, but Harriet could tell from the way he stared down at the carpet that there was something else.

"Who else?" She prompted him.

"Graham Taylor, the scouts leader," Stanley said.

"I thought the scout leader was a Graham Mayhew," Martina said. The surname rang a bell deep in Harriet's mind. It wasn't the first time she'd heard the surname. She just needed to remember where she knew it from.

Stanley shook his head. "No. Graham Taylor. He led the scouts. His daughter's name was Mayhew. She was born before he married her mother, Sylvia. He was with us that evening. He was the one who'd put the idea that Jack knew something into our heads to begin with."

"Why would he have done that?" Harriet asked, but the germ of an idea had already wormed its way into her mind.

"He knew him better than any of us ever could," Stanley said. "Why wouldn't we believe him..."

"What did he tell you, Stanley?" Harriet knew she was pressing him, but as far as she was concerned she didn't have a choice. They needed the truth.

"He said he'd caught him being in appropriate with the kids on more than one occasion."

"And if that were true, wouldn't he have asked Marjorie to keep Jack away?"

Stanley leaned forward and buried his face in his hands. "He knew things he shouldn't have known," he said. "When we were beating on that boy, Graham said things that--"

Harriet's stomach rolled, leaving her feeling nauseous. "He wanted you to hurt him, didn't he?"

Stanley lifted his face to meet her gaze. "Did I help the person responsible for hurting my Allison?" There was an unmistakable desperation to Stanley's voice that tore at Harriet's heart.

She opened her mouth, but the words wouldn't come. She nodded and watched as the desperation turned to anguish and then internalised rage. Stanley's shoulders began to shake first, and then his entire body started to tremble. "Those things he said Jack did, he was responsible for..." His voice broke and Harriet pushed onto her feet.

She made it as far as the front path and closed her eyes as she turned her face up towards the falling snow.

"I have to arrest him," Martina said from behind her.

"I know." It was all she could say. "We need to get back to the station. The team needs to know about the connection between John Taylor's father and the cold case."

"You think Taylor did this?"

Harriet shook her head. "No, I don't think it was John Taylor."

"Well, Graham Taylor is dead," Martina said. "Cancer remember?"

Harriet nodded. "I need to get to the station."

"The DS Scofield is five minutes out. We can

leave them with the FLO and I'll drive you back to the station."

"Thanks," Harriet said.

"I'm the one who should be thanking you," Martina said quietly. "I'm not sure who we would have put all of this together without you."

Harriet said nothing and went to wait in the car as Martina returned to the house.

THEY MADE it back to the station in record time, and Harriet made a beeline for Jodie and her group of analysts. She found the red-head in front of a screen. The blue glare gave her an unnatural colour, and the screen was partially reflected in her glasses.

"I need you to look into something for me," Harriet said without preamble.

"Is it pertaining to the case?" Jodie asked, without once lifting her gaze from the screen.

"Yes." It wasn't a lie. The cases were all connected, like an intricate spider's web of lies and deceit that had already seen five people lose their lives.

"Go for it," Jodie said, her fingers poised over the keys.

"I need everything you've got on Graham Taylor's daughter." Harriet could feel Martina's attention as she stood behind her.

"Matilda Mayhew," Jodie said. "Daughter of

Graham and Sylvia Taylor, formerly Mayhew. Half sister to John Taylor. You're not the first person to ask me to look into her."

"Who else?" Harriet asked.

"DC Green. They interviewed her yesterday. Although they had her listed as 'Tilly'. She volunteers with the scouts and Oliver was in her group for a short while."

"Wait, did you say John Taylor's half-sister?"

Jodie nodded. "John Taylor's mother was Gabriella Taylor. She died when John Taylor was five. He's Graham's son."

Harriet's heart flipped in her chest. "How old would Matilda have been twenty years ago?"

Jodie's fingers flew over the keyboard. "Eleven."

Harriet nodded and glanced back at Martina. "She would have known the children who disappeared. And she was friends with Jack."

"Matilda spent some time in a mental health facility some years ago," Jodie said, reading something off the screen.

"What for?"

"It doesn't say."

"We need to know what she was diagnosed with," Harriet said. "Can you find out?"

"If it's a matter of record, I can."

"I need to speak to Drew," Harriet said.

"There's something else you need to tell DI Haskell," Jodie said, her voice strained.

Harriet glanced down at the other woman, whose attention was fixed on the screen before her. "What is it?"

"Another boy has gone missing," she said. "An AJ Wilson was reported missing. He's from the same school as Oliver."

"That sounds familiar," Martina said. "I'm sure the boys mentioned the name AJ."

A sinking feeling hit Harriet in the stomach. "Is there any connection between him and the case involving the missing kids twenty-one years ago?"

Jodie gave her a withering look. "I need a little more information than that."

"Use their father's names; David Wilkes, Stanley Forder, Gus Barre?"

The clicking of keys was the only noise in the dark room. "AJ Wilson's mother was the daughter of a Gus Barre..." She paused and scrolled down the screen. "Sister to Gus Barre Jnr who went missing twenty-one years ago." She glanced up at Harriet. "Does that help?"

CHAPTER FORTY-FOUR

DREW SETTLED into the plastic chair opposite Taylor. The urge to reach across the narrow desk that lay between them just so he could wrap his hands around the other man's throat in order to choke the life out of him was overwhelming. Instead, he settled for folding his arms across his chest.

"Tell me about the shed," Drew said softly.

"Not until you lot tell me what happened before," Taylor said. His complexion had lost the pasty colour from before and now Taylor was ruddy-cheeked, his eyes fever bright and red-rimmed. If Drew didn't know any better, he might have thought Taylor had been crying, but then pieces of shit monsters like him didn't have emotions like that.

"I don't think--"

"We found Oliver Poole's body," Drew said, cutting Melissa off before she could finish. He caught her staring at him from the corner of his eye, but he didn't look in her direction. It was better to ask for forgiveness rather than permission, and this was the kind of situation where they couldn't afford to treat Taylor with kid-gloves. He'd been through all of this before, and he knew the dance only too well. If they gave him an inch, he would take a mile, and Drew wasn't about to let this bastard gain even a millimetre of ground. "You were right," Drew said.

"Right about what?" Taylor asked. Drew watched as the colour slowly drained from the other man's face, causing the red rimming around his eyes to stand out in stark relief.

"You said he was dead, you were right."

"I never said I knew for certain he was dead," Taylor said, and the hitch of emotion in his voice was unmistakable.

"Tell us about the shed."

Taylor shook his head. "No comment."

Drew flipped open the file on the desk in front of him and proceeded to pass the photographs of the evidence they'd found in the shed across the desk to Taylor. Drew didn't think it was possible for him to get any paler, but he was

A knock on the door brought a growl of frustration to Drew's lips, but he swallowed it down when he caught sight of Harriet on the other side of the glass. Pushing onto his feet, he tapped Melissa, and they exited the room together.

"You need to let me speak to him," Harriet said and her tone brooked no argument.

"I don't think you understand how this works," Melissa said sharply. "This is our interview."

"And I'm not trying to take it away from you," Harriet said. Drew could tell from her face that there was something she wasn't saying.

"What is it, what's happened?"

"Another boy has gone missing," Harriet said. Her gaze was unreadable as she met Drew's head on.

"Bollocks," Melissa swore emphatically, stealing the words right out of Drew's mouth.

"That's not all," Harriet said. She sounded so calm and Drew found himself wondering just how she could compartmentalise her feelings so cleanly. It was something he'd never been capable of, and he was almost certain he would never be capable of it, no matter how much he might want to.

"What else could there be?"

"Oliver Poole was the grandson of Stanley Forder." The name sounded oddly familiar, and it took Drew a moment to catch up with her. "The same Stanley Forder who was the father of Allison Forder, younger sister to Karen Poole."

"That's not all," DC Nicoll said, her voice taking Drew by surprise. He'd been so fixated on Harriet that he hadn't even noticed the other woman leaning against the wall. "AJ Wilson is the nephew of Gus

Barre Jnr, another of the children who went missing twenty years ago."

"Fuck." The word left Drew's mouth in a rush of breath. He dropped back against the wall, suddenly feeling as though someone had punched the air out of his lungs.

"So I'm not trying to steal the interview," Harriet said. "But I'm your best chance of figuring out what's going on here because I can guarantee you, John Taylor is wrapped up in all of this, we just don't know how yet."

"I don't think--"

"You're in," Drew said, cutting Melissa off.

"Drew?" Melissa sounded confused as she glanced over at him. "We make a good team, we don't need her to do the job you and I could do in our sleep."

"We can't risk this," Drew said. "We need to know what he knows." He turned his attention to Harriet before Melissa could tug on his guilty conscience anymore than she already had. "You sure you can do this?"

Harriet nodded and smoothed down the front of her shirt. "This is what I do," she said, a faint smile hovered on her lips. "I'm sure I can get him to tell us what we need."

"Then what are we waiting for."

CHAPTER FORTY-FIVE

TELLING DREW A LIE, even if it was a white one, didn't sit right with Harriet. But if she'd told him everything she knew regarding Matilda Mayhew, he probably wouldn't have let her through the door. What she did know was far too tenuous, and Drew wouldn't have allowed her to pursue that line of questioning.

"What's she doing here?" Taylor asked. Hostility dripped from his words. Not that Harriet could blame him. People like him, with the kinds of proclivities he had, would not like someone like her. People like Taylor relied on the general public's desire not to see the worst in humanity. It made it easier for them to lie and make it sound convincing. And in some cases they believed the lies themselves.

"I don't want to speak to her," Taylor said, leaning

back in his chair with his arms folded over his chest. "I won't speak with her here."

"Tell me about your father," Harriet said, levelling Taylor with her gaze.

"I'm not saying a thing to you." He spat the words at her.

"Your mother seems to think he acted inappropriately with you." Harriet made a show of glancing down at her notes. "Sorry, Sylvia. We both know she's not your biological mother."

Taylor looked away and shuffled uncomfortably in his seat. "She was as much a mother to me as Gabriella was; more so. I know Sylvia far better than I ever knew my real mother."

"So she's right then," Harriet said. "Your father was inappropriate with you?" Harriet could feel Drew's attention on her, but she ignored it and kept her gaze fixed on Taylor.

"He never touched me."

Harriet smiled grimly. "No, I don't suppose he did," she said softly. "Boys weren't his interest, were they?"

Taylor's gaze flickered up to meet hers, and she saw the truth reflected in his gaze. "No."

"He liked girls," Harriet continued. "Did he like Matilda?"

Taylor shuffled and coughed awkwardly. "No comment."

"Did he hurt her?"

"I said no fucking comment."

"You cared for Oliver, didn't you?"

Taylor started to pick at the edge of the desk. "He was a good lad."

"You wouldn't ever have hurt him," Harriet said gently. Her proximity to Drew made it easy for her to feel him as he stiffened in his chair. It was obvious he didn't like what she had to say, but that couldn't be helped. She would do whatever it took to get the truth from Taylor.

"Of course not." Taylor lifted his gaze to hers.

"Did you love him?"

"I--"

"Your father loved Matilda, didn't he?"

The colour drained from Taylor's face. "It's not the same."

"His love. It hurt her, didn't it? Did she tell you what he was doing..." Harriet trailed off as she saw the flicker of guilt in Taylor's eyes.

"Another boy is missing," Drew said.

Fear filled Taylor's eyes. "Who is it this time?"

"AJ Wilson," Harriet said. She pulled the school picture they had of the teenager from her file. Disgust rolled through her as she noted the way Taylor's eyes fixed on the boy. It only served to confirm her suspicion.

"Did you love AJ too?"

Taylor kept his eyes trained on the boy, but the nod of his head was unmistakable. "We cared about each other," he said, his voice hoarse with unspoken emotion.

"Why would Matilda do this?" The question didn't surprise Taylor. The resignation in his eyes as he sat back in his chair was unmistakable.

"She wants to hurt me," he said. "She can't hurt him, so she wants to hurt me instead."

"Instead, or as well?"

Taylor met Harriet's gaze, and this time the surprise in his face was unmistakable. "How do you--?"

"He made you help," Harriet said softly. "Didn't he?"

Taylor looked sick and stared down at his hands. "I never wanted to. I didn't like girls. I tried to tell him, I--"

"Did your father make you help when he killed Allison Stanley, Gus Barre Jnr, and Steven Wilkes, too?"

Taylor placed his arms on the table and buried his face in them. "He made me help get rid of the bodies."

"And what about Jack Campbell?"

Taylor nodded miserably. "He made us go back and finish the job... Had me dig the grave."

"And Matilda, how does she fit into all of this?"

"I think she suspected, but..." He trailed off.

"But what?" Drew asked, his voice low and controlled. "But he made sure she'd keep quiet.

When she lost the baby when she was fourteen she started having issues. She'd fly into these uncontrolled rages, lose time..." Taylor trailed off. "She went away for a while and when she came back, she was her old self. He'd moved on by then, left us all in the lurch and moved away to another area. Things were better."

Harriet sat and listened to everything he had to say and fought to keep her calm. After all, it was her job to listen without judgement. But hearing Taylor lay the whole sorry tale out for them tested even the limits of her empathy.

"The pictures. She left them for you," Drew said, sliding an image across the desk. Harriet caught a glimpse of Oliver Poole curled up on a cement floor, a teddy-bear clutched in his arms and felt her stomach lurch. He passed another one with a message scrawled across the back. "Our little secret," Drew said, tapping the image with his index finger. "That means something, doesn't it?"

"It's what he used to say to her," Taylor said. "What he said to us both. It was always our little secret."

"Where would she take AJ?" Harriet asked.

"To the same place it all began," Taylor said, staring down at the picture. "The old scouts den. It's where he used to take Matilda and the others. You'll find the other three there too, under the flagstones at the back. It was where he had me bury them."

Drew was out of the chair before Harriet could move. The door slammed after him as he went to prepare the team to go and search for AJ and Matilda.

"You think I'm a monster, don't you?" Taylor said.

"It's not my place," Harriet said. "But what you did to those children..."

"I never hurt them."

"You did the same thing to them that your father did to Matilda. You caused that same damage. There's no denying it."

He shook his head. "I loved them."

"They were children. Just like you were. Just like Matilda."

Taylor choked over a sob and buried his face in his hands as Harriet stood.

"I'm not the only one to blame. She's not innocent either," he said before Harriet had the chance to leave the room. "She knew."

Harriet stepped out into the hall and closed the door gently behind her.

CHAPTER FORTY-SIX

IT HAD BEEN difficult to give the order that they needed an Armed Response Team, but that didn't mean it wasn't the right one. His body thrummed with excitement as he waited. The entire place had been silent since they'd arrived, but anticipation laced the air. To Drew it almost felt as though the entire forest itself was holding its breath, just waiting or them to make their move. Uniformed police had been arriving in drips and drabs since they'd got into position, but there was still no sign of the cavalry and it was beginning to make Drew antsy.

Going in there without proper back-up could screw everything up.

The old scout's den's green paint had started to peel, revealing the rotted wood beneath. As Drew stared up at it, he couldn't help but think it was just more proof of how rotten the entire family had been.

"We should be out in front," Melissa said, her fury evident in her voice. "They should be here already."

Drew glanced down at his watch and nodded. She was right. They should have been here. But the snow had started to fall more heavily since they'd left the office, making the roads almost impossible to navigate. Pulling his phone from his pocket, he dialled the monk's number and waited for the call to connect.

"Sir, where are the ART? We're already here and the place is quiet." Drew didn't wait for his SIO to interrupt. "I'm worried that if we don't move soon, it might give her the opportunity she needs to kill another boy."

"They're stuck on the road out of York," Gregson said, sounding as sour as Drew felt. "RTA is holding the whole team up so you're going to have to sit still on this one."

"Sir, with all due respect, I'm not sure--"

"DI Haskell, there's protocol--"

The muffled sound of someone screaming broke Drew's concentration, and before Drew could say anything, the woman next to him had started through the woods.

"Shit," he swore.

"Sir, we don't have a choice, we can hear screaming." Drew ended the call before the monk could offer him further guidance. Whatever Matilda was doing in there was causing AJ Wilson to cry out, and he wasn't going to wait around in the woods and wait for her to kill him. Drew followed DI Appleton and motioned for Maz to keep a check on the perimeter.

Another scream ripped through the air, but this one was muffled in comparison to the last. A cold sweat broke out on Drew's brow. What if they were already too late? What if, by the time they made it inside, she'd already killed him? DI Appleton reached the building first and pressed her shoulder against the door. Like Drew, she was at least armed. They'd both passed their fire-arms training and were permitted to carry in certain situations. A potential hostage situation had warranted them both to check their guns out of lock-up and he was glad she'd suggested it.

A dull thud emanated from the building, and Melissa didn't wait for Drew's signal. She rammed open the door with her shoulder, causing the rotted wood to break up on impact. She disappeared inside, and Drew quickly followed her.

"Matilda Mayhew," Melissa's voice echoed in the deafening silence. "Police!"

A scuffling sound in the back of the building helped to fixate Drew's attention and flipped on his torch in order to illuminate the inside of the room they'd found themselves in. Drew's torch slid over something bulky on the ground. The sight of it was enough to make his blood go cold. He crossed the space, Melissa at his back, and he reached AJ in a couple of strides. The boy's movements were sluggish and jerky. He lay on his side, his hands and feet bound together. Beneath the clear plastic bag that covered his head, Drew could see the telltale blue colour on his lips that said he was suffocating.

Melissa crouched next to the boy and tore the bag off his head. He continued to twitch, but his eyes remained closed. "We need an ambulance," she called out as the sound of other officers arriving on the scene told Drew the back-up had finally arrived.

The slam of a door somewhere off to his right caused him to take off in that direction. He crossed the space and slipped out through another doorway. A small kitchenette that had seen better days greeted him, but it was the backdoor that caught his eye. "Shit," he swore.

Maz joined him in the kitchen as he tugged open the back door and stepped out onto the back porch in time to see a small dark shape disappear into the tree line. "She's in the woods." Drew threw the words back over his shoulder as he vaulted over the porch railing and landed on the ground.

Another officer shot off ahead of him and Drew had only a moment to realise it was DC Green before he disappeared into the woods.

Drew followed. Despite the uneven ground, he managed to keep his pace steady. But he was no match for the woman who'd spent most of her life heading up a scout troop and hanging out in the woods. Within a couple of minutes, the heavy snowfall and the darkening skies meant he'd grown completely disorientated.

Pausing, he strained for any sounds that might tell him he was at least on the right path. The only sound was that of the snow as it fell around him, muffling every noise in the forest. Lifting his torch, he swept it up and over the trees surrounding him and felt his stomach drop into his boots. Hundreds of pairs of eyes were reflected back at him. He turned and the hairs on the back of his neck rose as he realised the eyes were behind him, too.

He took a tentative step forward, putting him within touching distance of the nearest pair of eyes and was chagrined to find they weren't eyes at all, but bike reflectors.

"What the fuck," Drew whispered.

A muffled grunt, followed by a thud, sent him further into the forest. "Matilda, it's DI Haskell. There's no use--" Drew cut off, the words dying on his lips as he spotted the dark hunched shape of DC Green on the trail ahead of him.

"Tim?" Drew called out as he closed in on the young detective's position. He was rewarded with a low moan. Staying alert, Drew crouched next to the young man and reached out to him. He touched his shoulder and Drew's hand came away sticky and wet.

In the torch light DC Green's blood appeared black.

Taking a firmer grip on his shoulder, Drew rolled him onto his back and found that the snow beneath Green was stained red. Fumbling for his radio, Drew dropped the torch. He hit the big red emergency button, his sticky fingers sliding over the surface of it.

"Come on, Green." Drew's voice was ragged as he tried to put pressure on the multiple wounds that decorated Green's torso. Timothy coughed, foamy blood splattering onto his chin. His eyes were too wide. Drew knew shock when he saw it. "Shit, Timothy." The DC reached out, his hand grabbing blindly at Drew's arm as he tried to support the young officer. The radio in Drew's hand crackled. "You're safe," he said. "I've got you. You're safe."

CHAPTER FORTY-SEVEN

SITTING in the station later that night, Harriet stared down at the paperwork on the desk in front of her. The words were impossible to decipher, each one sliding into the next so that it was nothing more than a blur. Everyone in the room was still holding their breath, waiting for news on both AJ Wilson and DC Green.

"No news is good news," Olivia said as she set a cup of coffee next to Harriet's elbow and took a seat opposite her.

"Sorry?"

"The saying, no news is good news. Just because we haven't heard how they're doing doesn't mean it's bad news." There was a haunted look in Olivia's eyes as she glanced down at the file Harriet had been studying. "You don't need to go through that tonight. It can wait."

"I need to do something," Harriet said. "And trying to figure out where Matilda has gone seems like the best use of my time." It seemed like the only use of her time. Sitting waiting for the others to get back had been torture. And when she'd heard of what happened to DC Green, and the way they'd found AJ, well, it only served to make her feel even more useless than before.

"She'll have found somewhere she feels safe," Olivia said.

"I'm not so sure," Harriet said. "As far as she's concerned she has nothing left to lose."

"Well, Anna Wilkes is safe and accounted for, so it's not as though we have to worry about another kid disappearing."

From the corner of her eyes, Harriet spotted Jodie making her way through the desks toward them. "You wanted to know why she was in a mental health facility," Jodie said, speaking before she even made it to their side. "She was diagnosed at eighteen with DID, it's--"

"Dissociative Identity Disorder," Harriet finished for her. When Olivia's expression remained blank, Harriet continued. "Most people mistakenly know it as multiple personality disorder, but that's not exactly true. They aren't separate personalities, rather aspects of a personality that has become dissociated from the rest. It sometimes appears in those who have had to suffer through childhood trauma and from what I've learned from John Taylor and the photographs cataloguing the extensive abuse Drew's team brought back from the scout's den I'd say Matilda has definitely suffered extensive childhood trauma."

"Anything new?" Drew's question cut through the tension in the room.

"Matilda is suffering from multiple personalities," Olivia said quickly. She glanced over at Harriet and shrugged. "It's the fastest way to explain it without all the jargon."

Harriet sighed. "Dissociative Identity Disorder. She probably developed it as a type of coping mechanism. I've read case studies whereby the person with the disorder dissociated, creating a facet of themselves--" She cut off as the others' blank expressions told her they had no idea what she was talking about.

"Fine. The patient in question created a new personality, that of a man. One who was stronger and could endure the pain of the abuse they were suffering."

"Is that what Matilda has done?" Drew asked thoughtfully.

"It's possible," Harriet said. "But I couldn't say for certain without talking to her, or having a look at her case notes." She sighed and leaned back in the chair.

"Is there any news on AJ, or DC Green?"

Drew shook his head. "Tim is in surgery. So far all we've heard is that he has a collapsed lung. As for

AJ he's in critical condition. His parents are with him now and they're demanding answers."

Harriet nodded and glanced down at the files. Something that Drew had said tugged at a previous memory. AJ was with his parents, and they wanted to know the truth. Somebody else's parent had known the truth... As soon as the thought entered her head, she knew what memory was trying to surface. The comment Taylor had made as she left the interview room.

"She knew," Harriet said aloud.

"Excuse me?" Olivia said, raising an eyebrow.

"Who knew?" Drew met Harriet's gaze.

"Mrs Taylor. Sylvia Taylor. She knew what was happening."

"We can't say she knew everything," Drew said.

"No, Drew, she knew. And if she knew, and Matilda is trying to settle the score with everyone who wronged her..."

Drew nodded. "You think she's gone to her mother's house?"

Harriet pushed onto her feet. "I can't be certain, but it's the best we've got."

Drew snatched his coat off the back of a chair and started for the door. "Olivia, call DI Appleton," he said. "And tell them we need an armed response unit over at Sylvia Taylor's house."

"And what if I'm wrong?" Harriet said as she followed him to the door.

"We'll cross that bridge if we come to it," Drew said. "But for the record, I don't think you're wrong."

AN HOUR later Harriet stood with Drew and the ARU outside Sylvia Taylor's house. The place was in darkness, but there was an air of unnatural stillness about the place that didn't sit well with Harriet. The snow had stopped falling, and she was grateful for small mercies.

"You can follow us in..."

Harriet was only listening as the heavily armed men discussed their best move. From the corner of her eye, she could see Drew was practically vibrating with energy, but she couldn't say she felt the same.

The next few moments passed in a blur, and without waiting for Drew's permission, Harriet trailed him inside the house. The static of the radios as the team who had gone in ahead called for an ambulance barely registered in Harriet's mind as they moved down the same hall she been in just a few days prior. The carpet squished beneath her shoes, and she very nearly slipped as she stepped out onto the tiles in the kitchen.

Someone flipped on the light, illuminating the scene, and Harriet found herself wishing they had left it off.

Sylvia Taylor lay in the corner of the kitchen nearest her sink. She was little more than a bloodied lump of clothes and flesh, and Harriet's brain struggled to put the pieces of the puzzle together. What she did notice was Sylvia's walking stick, that lay in a puddle of dark blood in the middle of the floor.

Harriet turned and came face to face with a young, bloodstained woman at the table. She sat there, perfectly still, her bloodstained hands wrapped around a mug.

Matilda's expression was blank as she stared off into the middle distance, focused on something only she could see.

"Matilda Mayhew, you're under arrest--" Drew continued to speak but Harriet was no longer listening. Matilda turned to stare at them. There was blood streaked down her cheeks, and a smear of it sat beneath her eye.

"Why would you do this?" The question slipped out of Harriet unbidden.

"They didn't protect her, so I had to. And now I'm all she has left."

CHAPTER FORTY-EIGHT

ONE WEEK LATER, Harriet sat in the living room and stared down at the essay papers spread out around her. A low scratching at the front door caused the hairs on the back of her neck to stand to attention, but the fear quickly dissipated as Drew's key turned in the lock and he shoved the door open.

He stepped into the hall, carrying a blue carrier bag, and a large brown cardboard box still dusted in snow. "It's really coming down out there now," he said as he set the box on the floor.

"Maybe we'll have a white Christmas after all," Harriet said, as her heart slowly returned to a more normal pace. "What's that?"

"This?" Drew nudged the box with his foot as a smile crept over his lips. "This is the first box from my old place."

Harriet set the papers aside and climbed onto her

feet. "You went back there? You actually went inside?"

He nodded, his grin widening. "Don't look so surprised. At least now I won't have to keep buying new shirts every few days."

"Drew, this is wonderful news. I'm so pleased..."

"That's not all the news," he said. "AJ was released from hospital today. And Tim is out of critical care. They think another couple of weeks and he'll be able to go home."

Joy caused Harriet to beam from ear to ear. "The team must be thrilled," she said.

"You're a member of the team," he said, for a moment his expression darkened. "I know it wasn't exactly the outcome we wanted."

Harriet felt the joy she'd felt a moment ago slowly reduce. For too many families, Christmas would forever be a dark time.

"But we need to focus on the wins," Drew said. "Too often it doesn't feel like enough, but with AJ and Tim recovering I'm going to try to focus on the positives."

Harriet nodded, a smile still lingering on her lips. "I just can't believe you went back to your apartment yourself," she said.

"Well, I didn't really have a choice," Drew said. "That's the other bit of good news."

Harriet quirked an eyebrow in his direction. "So much good news in one night, I won't know how to contain myself." Her smile softened her words.

"I had to start emptying the place because I've found a new place to live."

"What?"

"I've found a house, on the outskirts of Whitby. The rent is maybe a little more than I was hoping for, but I can swing it. The beach is just a short walk from the place and..." He trailed off. "You're not pleased?"

"Of course I am," Harriet said, plastering a smile onto her face. "I just wasn't expecting it so soon, is all. You hadn't mentioned that you'd found somewhere suitable."

He shrugged and stepped over the box into the living room. "It was time," he said. "I couldn't keep living here, taking advantage of your kindness. And with that in mind!" He pulled a bottle of wine from the bag with a flourish. "I thought we could have a little celebration."

Despite the edge of sadness that threatened to settle over her, Harriet couldn't help but return Drew's grin. It hadn't dawned on her until then just how much she had enjoyed having him around. He wasn't always there. They both worked odd hours, but it was still nice in the evenings when she got in from the university and he was there on the couch. Soon it would be back to how it had been before, with nothing to greet her but the darkness of her house and her own loneliness for company.

"I'll get the glasses," she said. Pushing onto her feet, she busied herself with grabbing two wine-glasses from the kitchen; anything to get her mind off the sad turn her thoughts had taken.

She watched as Drew poured them two generous glasses and then took the one he offered her.

"I'm going to miss you, you know."

His smile was wide, causing the dimple in his cheek to appear. It was a rare occurrence, but Harriet had learned to savour the times when it did, and this was no exception.

"You'll be only too happy to have your quiet time back," he said. "Without me blundering in and out of here at all hours." Drew lifted his glass to meet hers, so that they clinked as they connected. "To new beginnings," he said.

"New beginnings," Harriet echoed. "And friendship," Harriet said with a smile as she took a sip of the wine. She had never liked change and if she was honest, she'd have much preferred if some things could have stayed the same.

GET THE NEXT BOOK!

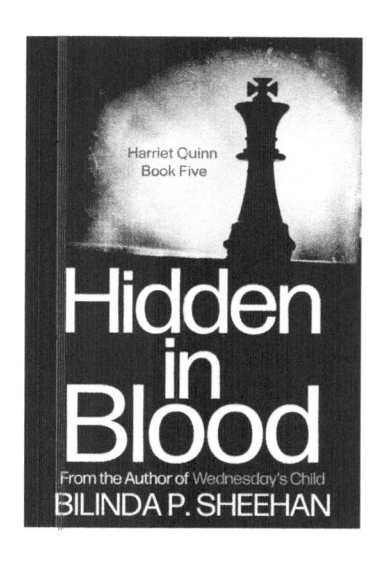

Harriet and DI Haskell return in the next book in the series.
Hidden in Blood

ALSO BY BILINDA P. SHEEHAN

Watch out for the next book coming soon from Bilinda P. Sheehan by joining her mailing list.

A Wicked Mercy: The Yorkshire Murders - DI Haskell & Quinn Crime Fiction Series

Death in Pieces: The Yorkshire Murders - DI Haskell & Quinn Crime Fiction Series

Splinter the Bone: The Yorkshire Murders - DI Haskell & Quinn Crime Fiction Series

Hunting the Silence: The Yorkshire Murders - DI Haskell & Quinn Crime Fiction Series

Hidden in Blood: The Yorkshire Murders - DI Haskell & Quinn Crime Fiction Series

All the Lost Girls-A Gripping Psychological Thriller

Wednesday's Child - A Gripping Psychological Thriller

Printed in Great Britain
by Amazon